"I'm not who you think I am, Creole," Grace whispered when he slid his hands possessively down her body.

"Who is?" he murmured.

"But you don't know anything about me. I'm not—"

"That's where you're wrong, *chérie.*" He caressed her waist, her hips. "I know you're sweet as honeysuckle and sexier than any woman's got a right to be."

She gazed up at him, her eyes pleading. For what, he wasn't sure, but suddenly he was determined to find out and give it to her. "I also know you're gonna let me kiss you again...."

He lowered his mouth to hers, slowly, so she could see him coming and tell him no. She didn't. Instead, she murmured a sweet surrender that nearly did him in.

He deepened the kiss. She tasted so good. Spicy like filé gumbo, mellow like wine. Erotic, like aroused woman. *So good...*

Dear Reader,

July is a sizzling month both outside *and* in, and once again we've rounded up six exciting titles to keep your temperature rising. It all starts with the latest addition to Marilyn Pappano's HEARTBREAK CANYON miniseries, *Lawman's Redemption,* in which a brooding man needs help connecting with the lonely young girl who just might be his daughter—and he finds it in the form of a woman with similar scars in her romantic past. Don't miss this emotional, suspenseful read.

Eileen Wilks provides the next installment in our twelve-book miniseries, ROMANCING THE CROWN, with *Her Lord Protector.* Fireworks ensue when a Montebellan lord has to investigate a beautiful commoner who may be a friend—or a foe!—of the royal family. This miniseries just gets more and more intriguing. And Kathleen Creighton finishes up her latest installment of her INTO THE HEARTLAND miniseries with *The Black Sheep's Baby.* A freewheeling photojournalist who left town years ago returns—with a little pink bundle strapped to his chest, and a beautiful attorney in hot pursuit. In Marilyn Tracy's *Cowboy Under Cover,* a grief-stricken widow who has set up a haven for children in need of rescue finds herself with that same need—and her rescuer is a handsome federal marshal posing as a cowboy. Nina Bruhns is back with *Sweet Revenge,* the story of a straitlaced woman posing as her wild identical twin—and now missing—sister to learn of her fate, who in the process hooks up with the seductive detective who is also searching for her. And in *Bachelor in Blue Jeans* by Lauren Nichols, during a bachelor auction, a woman inexplicably bids on the man who once spurned her, and wins—or does she? This reunion romance will break your heart.

So get a cold drink, sit down, put your feet up and enjoy them all—and don't forget to come back next month for more of the most exciting romance reading around…only in Silhouette Intimate Moments.

Yours,

Leslie J. Wainger
Executive Senior Editor

Please address questions and book requests to:
Silhouette Reader Service
U.S.: 3010 Walden Ave., P.O. Box 1325, Buffalo, NY 14269
Canadian: P.O. Box 609, Fort Erie, Ont. L2A 5X3

Sweet Revenge
NINA BRUHNS

Silhouette

I N T I M A T E   M O M E N T S™

Published by Silhouette Books

America's Publisher of Contemporary Romance

SILHOUETTE BOOKS

ISBN 0-373-27233-2

SWEET REVENGE

Copyright © 2002 by Nina Bruhns

Visit Silhouette at www.eHarlequin.com

Printed in U.S.A.

Books by Nina Bruhns

Silhouette Intimate Moments

Catch Me If You Can #990
Warrior's Bride #1080
Sweet Revenge #1163

NINA BRUHNS

credits her Gypsy great-grandfather for her great love of adventure. She has lived and traveled all over the world, including a six-year stint in Sweden. She has been on scientific expeditions from California to Spain to Egypt and the Sudan, and has two graduate degrees in archaeology (with a specialty in Egyptology). She speaks four languages and writes a mean hieroglyphics!

But Nina's first love has always been writing. For her, writing for Silhouette Books is the ultimate adventure. Drawing on her many experiences gives her stories a colorful dimension, and allows her to create settings and characters that are out of the ordinary. Two of her books, including this one, won the prestigious Romance Writers of America Golden Heart Award for writing excellence.

A native of Canada, Nina grew up in California and currently resides in Charleston, South Carolina, with her husband and three children.

She loves to hear from her readers, and can be reached at P.O. Box 746, Ladson, SC 29456-0746 or by e-mail via the Harlequin Web site at http://www.eHarlequin.com.

To all the children who have ever suffered abuse,
and to all the adults who really love them.

To my many Internet buddies
(and you know who you are!). You are a constant source
of fun, facts and cherished friendship. Viva technology!

Chapter 1

New Orleans Police Detective Auri "Creole" Levalois backed up deep into the sweltering shadows of his new French Quarter apartment's balcony. From his hiding place, he watched the woman in the apartment across the narrow courtyard slowly pull down the zipper of her dress. It was August, about 9:00 p.m. and still hot as a night in Hades.

It wasn't because she was undressing that Detective Levalois watched her, shrouded behind the hanging plants. Although that certainly added an interesting angle to the situation. Hell, if you were stuck doing surveillance for days on end, you might as well have something sweet to look at. But Creole was after something much more important than a nice view.

The woman lifted her thick blond hair off her neck, strolled to the fridge and reached into the freezer for a tray of ice. He silently studied her delicate chin, straight nose and long, elegant neck, all silhouetted by the refrigerator light. *Dieu,* she was a pretty thing.

He'd lucked out when he'd been able to flash his police

credentials and leap to the top of the waiting list for the vacant apartment directly across from the woman named Muse Summerville. The modest complex was typical French Quarter—ancient two-story brick buildings surrounding a postage stamp courtyard choked with flowers and greenery. Ribbon-narrow brick walkways used to lead to streets on either side, but years ago the gate to the street on this end had been bricked up. He and the Summerville woman now shared the deserted back side of the courtyard, their balconies forming a tight arch over the overgrown cobblestoned path, a scant four feet of air separating the black wrought iron railings. Very cozy.

From Creole's spot on his own balcony he could clearly observe her entire second-floor apartment. Like his, it was small, just a kitchen-dining-living-room combo and a bedroom with a bath attached. Tall, curtainless French doors led from both rooms out onto a balcony that ran the length of the apartment.

Just yesterday he had taken the plunge and moved his few belongings here. He didn't work out of the Quarter's Eighth District police station, but where he lived at this point in time was irrelevant. It was just a place to leave his stuff while he was out sifting through the dregs of New Orleans, pursuing his private revenge.

As long as he got what he was after, nothing else mattered. And Muse Summerville would give him what he wanted. One way or another, he'd make sure she did.

She moved from the kitchen into the bedroom, and he idly wondered what she'd done with the ice tray. With an irritated shrug he shifted his pinching shoulder holster to a more comfortable position. He'd really have to concentrate.

That evening he'd trailed her from her job at the law office of Leavy, Dell and Roland on Camp Street to a small restaurant in the Quarter, where she'd eaten alone, then home to Burgundy Street—also alone. It occurred to him a woman who looked as good as she did shouldn't be doing anything alone.

Where was her slimeball boyfriend? It definitely wasn't like him to leave his woman unattended. Not good. Not good at all.

Creole eased himself into a cramped iron bistro chair and wiped at a bead of sweat that trickled down his temple. The object of his surveillance turned her back on him, giving him an eyeful of slim waist and bare shoulders exposed by the wide-open zipper of her dress.

Nice. The male in him hummed appreciatively. *Si belle.*

Of course, looks were deceiving. Muse Summerville might have the body of an angel, but she was anything but nice. The woman was involved with some *bien mauvais drigaille,* some very nasty people.

He grabbed the tumbler of bourbon he'd set on the nearby table and closed his eyes, fighting the wave of rage that swamped over him at the thought of those people.

Unfortunately, during his quick search through her apartment yesterday he'd come up empty. The lock had been child's play. But he'd found neither hide nor hair of her small-time-hood boyfriend, Gary Fox. No address, no implicating letters or documents, not even a photograph. Either the scumbag was being very careful or he had cleared out. For Creole's own sake, he hoped it was the former. It was tough enough to stay sane in the broiling summer humidity of New Orleans under the best of circumstances, but if he'd lost the only lead on his brother's killer, he'd really go nuts.

He was counting on this unauthorized stakeout of the Summerville woman to lead him to Fox, and from him to Fox's boss—the man who had murdered his brother.

If Fox had soured on Muse, Creole could be in for a very long wait. Not to mention possibly getting thrown off the force if the captain found out he was still pursuing a case he'd been specifically barred from investigating. But he wasn't about to fail. He'd find out what he needed to know to bring Luke's killer to justice, even if it meant losing his career in the process.

He took a long, cooling sip of bourbon and opened his eyes again, calmer. The heat was still oppressive, but at least he'd beaten the rage back to where it belonged—in the blackest recesses of his heart.

Through the ornate curlicues of their two balconies and the open French doors of her bedroom, he watched the woman pause by the nightstand on her way toward the bathroom. There was a click and he recognized the tinny whine of KBON, a Cajun music station. His focus shifted to her pink satin-sheeted bed and to the purse and briefcase she'd tossed there upon arriving home a few minutes ago. His eyes narrowed consideringly. He'd give a lot for five minutes alone with that briefcase.

She kicked off her four-inch heels and grabbed a clip to pin up her long hair. But she didn't slip out of her dress until after she'd shut the bathroom door behind her. For the second day in a row, Creole was mildly surprised. Her skimpy file hadn't pegged Muse Summerville as the modest type. Not by a long shot.

Creole leaned back in his chair and tried to relax while he waited for her to emerge from the bathroom. Picking up his tobacco pouch, he rolled himself a cigarette.

He really should quit. It was a filthy habit, but one he and Luke had forced themselves to calmly master as adolescents, after going through hell together. Smoking had bonded the foster brothers during those grim times in a kind of wordless ritual of courage, and he hadn't quite been able to shake it since. Not that he'd really tried. He liked the coarse edge it added to his tough-guy image. It suited his purposes.

Shame he couldn't light the damn thing. If he did, he'd reveal his presence to the woman. *Bien.* He'd save his nightly smoke until after she went to bed. If yesterday was any indication, she'd hit the sack as soon as she finished her shower.

Right on cue she emerged, wrapped in a towel big enough to cover the essentials but small enough to give a man ideas. Her pale breasts spilled plump and round above the towel, begging for a man's touch; her bare, shapely legs went on for miles, hinting at other hidden delights. For a breathless moment he imagined those legs wrapped around his waist, her silky hair floating across his—

He frowned in annoyance. He shouldn't even be thinking such things. This woman was nothing but bad news. He had no business being attracted to her…even if it seemed half of New Orleans shared his opinion of her enticements.

And she didn't mind flaunting them, either. Her uncurtained bedroom was littered with heaps of cheap, gaudy, green, purple and gold Mardi Gras necklaces. Everyone knew what a woman had to do to earn those necklaces up on Bourbon Street.

Pulling open a dresser drawer, she leaned over and sifted through its contents, drawing out a sheer black baby-doll nightie.

Sacré.

Creole's mouth went dry, his mind dancing with unbidden visions of her sprawled across her queen-size, satin-sheeted bed wearing nothing but that nightie. Then she shook her head, replaced it and took out what looked to be a man's muscle-style undershirt and a pair of boxer shorts. Disappointment rolled through him, thick and powerful.

"Aw, honey," he muttered under his breath. "Don' do this to me, *chère.*"

He drilled a hand through his hair and slugged back a stiff belt of bourbon. *Le bon Dieu mait la main.* God help him. Where the hell was Fox? The man was either dead or a flaming idiot to leave a woman like this alone for two nights.

Surely he'd have heard on the streets if Fox was dead. He liked the other possibilities even less. Creole had spent the past two weeks pumping all his street contacts about Fox's whereabouts. Everyone had said the same thing—he was lying low for a while, reasons unknown. Where? No one knew. But Creole would bet good money Fox couldn't resist paying a visit to his fancy lady friend. After the show tonight, he'd double that bet.

So where was he?

Fox was the only one who could lead him to Luke's killer. The man had better show up. *And soon.* Creole had no desire to continue playing Peeping Tom to a woman who was already messing with his mind big-time.

He jerked up at the sound of footsteps on her balcony. She was coming out. *Damn.* Somehow he'd missed when she'd dressed in the man's underthings and fetched herself a cold drink.

Ice cubes tinkled merrily, and an old Cajun waltz wheezed softly from the radio as she walked to the balcony railing. To Creole's horror, she stared right at him. A cold sweat broke out on his forehead. He opened his mouth, about to give himself away and say something totally inappropriate, when she turned, set her glass down on a small table, and with a deep sigh lowered herself into the lounge chair next to it.

He almost keeled over in relief. She hadn't seen him. *Yet.*

Only a few feet of air space separated her balcony from his over the narrow path of the courtyard. She was practically close enough to touch. If he moved a muscle she'd spot him, despite the mass of hanging plants and shadows that concealed him in their dusky gloom.

She reached up and let her hair fall loose from the clip that held it. Backlit from the glow of the kitchen light, the golden waves surrounded her pretty face like a halo. She lifted it off her neck and sighed again, a sweet murmur that flavored the heavy air with poignant longing and frustration.

He could smell her soap. Jessamine. And caught himself just before he groaned out loud.

Instead he clamped his jaw tight. She shut her eyes, stretching back in her chaise, and he silently pushed out the breath that had backed up in his lungs. She dipped a finger into her tall glass, scooped out an ice cube and popped it into her mouth. Sweat crawled down the front of Creole's white T-shirt and pooled beneath the leather straps of his shoulder holster.

Pulling out another ice cube, she slowly trailed it over her neat chin, down her pale throat, and around her collarbone. Drops of melted ice gathered at the neck of her muscle shirt and purled downward. Even in the semidarkness, he saw the pucker of her nipples as they peaked in reaction to her chilly ministrations.

His breath caught in his lungs again.

Bon Dieu. This was not working. He would never make it until Fox showed up. He needed another plan—

She fished out another ice cube.

Fast. Fervently, he prayed she wouldn't—

She did.

Lord have mercy.

With a shaking hand, he struck a match and lit his cigarette.

Grace Summerville froze where she sat, mortified.

Jerked back to reality by a sudden flare of light on the opposite balcony, Grace let the ice cube slip from between her fingers. It had felt so good gliding over her heated skin, she hadn't even realized what she was doing.

A second streak of orange illuminated a dark male visage in its brief flash.

Where had he come from? Her face burned in embarrassment, adding to the already scorching temperature of the summer night. How long had he been sitting there watching her?

"Who's there?" she whispered, aghast that the man might actually answer.

"Don' stop now, *chère*," a sultry masculine voice rumbled from the dark shadows. "You're just gettin' to the good part."

The accent was unmistakable. Cajun French. She swallowed heavily. She'd heard about these hot-blooded Cajun men. They were intense. Passionate, like their music. Nothing like the calm, dignified South Carolina gentlemen she was used to.

Sweet heavens.

"I thought that apartment was empty," she said loudly, the last word cracking apart in her throat. She was certain she hadn't seen any furniture in the opposite apartment two days ago when the complex's super had let her into Muse's place—believing Grace to be her twin sister who'd misplaced her key—or this morning, when she'd left to go to Muse's workplace. Though she had to admit she hadn't paid too much attention after her initial check.

On the other balcony, a small point of light swooped up in a graceful arch and glowed bright red, followed by a thin stream of acrid-smelling smoke that floated out from the shadows.

"Moved in yesterday. I'm your new neighbor."

Despite the heat, his deep, sexy voice sent chills down Grace's spine. She jumped up, caught in a sudden glimmer of fear…and awareness. "Well, I'm sure your mama taught you better manners than to sit there in the dark and spy on people."

With lightning speed, she fled inside to the safety of Muse's bedroom, knocking over the lounge chair in her haste to get away from the man and his dangerously intriguing voice. Just before she slammed the French doors shut against the thundering of her heart, she heard him chuckle softly.

"*Mais, non, chérie.* Me, I don' have no mama."

Grace spent several pulse-stalled moments leaning with all her might against the locked bathroom door. She was positive the man would jump over onto her balcony and chase her inside. Lord only knew what he'd do to her then.

But after a few minutes it was obvious he had no intention of following her. Slowly she relaxed her death grip on the doorknob. "Grace Summerville, get ahold of yourself, girl," she muttered aloud in her best imitation of her own mama's honeyed South Carolina drawl. "This will never do."

Forcing herself to the sink, she bent and splashed her face with cool water. The idea was ridiculous, of course. No one in his right mind would leap across four feet of thin air, risking life and limb. Certainly not just to—

She gave herself a firm mental shake. She was being paranoid. It was getting to her, this whole situation with Muse. Not knowing where her sister was, or if something horrible had happened to her. The man on the balcony hadn't done a thing to threaten her. She just had a huge case of the nerves, that was all.

Grace ran a hand over her eyes, her turbulent thoughts fastening on her sister. She would find Muse. Somehow she would find her twin sister. She had gotten her out of trouble plenty of times before, and she'd do it again this time.

She'd be fine. They'd both be fine.

She and Muse normally called each other several times a week to chat. They lived in two different states but were still very close. Grace liked to think she provided a kind of balance and stability to Muse's whirlwind life, and to be honest, she loved listening to her sister talk about all her crazy adventures and romances. But the last few times they talked, Muse had been jumpy. Very jumpy. Her sister thought someone was following her. She'd caught quick glimpses of a thin, blond-haired man shadowing her to work, shopping, even when she went out in the evening. She'd tried to laugh it off as her imagination, but Grace could tell she was truly frightened. Muse had been more than nervous about an ex-boyfriend she'd recently split from. Gary Fox was thin and blond, a petty criminal, and he had not taken their breakup well.

When Muse stopped answering the phone last week, Grace had called the New Orleans Police Department. She hoped the events were not related to Muse's disappearance, but for every day that went by, she was more and more convinced it was no coincidence. And grew more and more worried.

The police had patiently taken down the information and said they'd look into it. She'd given them two days and called back. They fed her platitudes and reassurances, saying there was no sign of foul play and no evidence of a crime.

She hadn't been reassured. That same evening she'd boarded a plane heading south. She and Muse had a standing agreement, starting from when her sister had moved away from home at the tender age of seventeen. They'd solemnly promised always to tell each other about all of their plans. If either of them phoned the other with no reply for over two days, she was to come to the rescue, because she'd know something was very wrong. It was an agreement they'd kept religiously. At least she had. Muse had never had an opportunity, since Grace's life had always been depressingly predictable.

Grace flicked off the light, cracked open the bathroom door and peered out. Her heart sank. Eight-foot expanses of clear, mullioned glass stared back at her from the opposite wall. The white frames were depressingly uncluttered by curtains, the rods and rows of metal hooks hung shiny and empty. Muse had picked a heck of a time to take down her curtains. She'd searched everywhere for them that first day, but Muse must have taken them to be cleaned or repaired or something.

Grace studied the windows and French door, racking her brain for a way to cover the acres of glass. When she'd thought the other apartment was empty, the lack of covering hadn't bothered her so much. It definitely bothered her now.

She glanced out into the night. Her neighbor's balcony was engulfed in darkness, but she could feel his presence, potent and male, beckoning to her from the shadows, his black, glittering eyes on her, even now. At the thought of those eyes, a deep, primitive awareness stole through her limbs like a poison. She shook it off.

She hadn't needed more than the two seconds of match light to know exactly what kind of a man lurked there. The harsh angles of his cheekbones covered in a wash of mutinous black stubble, broad shoulders negligently slouched, the feral hunger in his black-browed eyes sending her their lustful invitation—all spoke more eloquently than words.

Lord above, she couldn't possibly stay here in the apartment this exposed, knowing those eyes would be moving over her at all hours. Watching her get dressed. Watching her eat breakfast. Watching her sleep.

With an uneasy knot in her stomach, Grace glanced down at the undershirt and boxers she'd put on in desperation after her shower. At least they covered her. More or less. Unlike the other things she'd found in that drawer. She'd packed a long cotton nightgown, of course. But in Charleston she had air-conditioning, something Muse's landlord apparently thought a luxury. She'd never be able to sleep in this heat wearing that heavy, voluminous garment.

But there was nothing to do about any of it tonight. Tomorrow she'd buy a lighter nightgown. And curtains, if she had to.

Taking a fortifying breath, she marched out of the bathroom, turned off the kitchen light, tossed her purse and Muse's briefcase off the bed and slipped between the pink satin sheets. The colorful glass beads draped throughout the room glittered and winked in the moonlight, and the several elaborate, feathered Mardi Gras masks Muse had hung on the wall above the bed stared down at her with laughing eyes, as if amused by her discomfort.

Determinedly she closed her eyes. She would ignore both those stupid masks and the man on the balcony and get a good night's sleep. She'd need it to continue her search for her sister tomorrow. She would forget all about him and the low thrum that had kicked up in her body the moment she'd spotted him watching her, and concentrate on finding her sister.

He was probably fat and ugly as a hound dog, anyway, the only thing sexy about him his soft Cajun accent. Well, and those dangerous eyes.

She set her jaw. *Sleep.* Muse needed her help, and no overweight, mannerless scoundrel of a neighbor was going to keep her from her task.

Not a single, solitary chance.

Chapter 2

Grace awoke with a start, bolting upright in damp, tangled sheets. The radio played softly on the nightstand, and a light breeze stirred from the old wooden paddle fan overhead. She glanced around the apartment in panic, sorting through the rosy morning light for a reason for her alarm.

Then she remembered: black eyes, a glimpse of broad shoulders, a gravelly patois of French and English.

With a groan she fell back onto the mattress. *The man on the balcony.* Had she really been *dreaming* about him?

Aside from his sultry eyes she hadn't even seen the man, let alone met him. Yet, already he was having an effect on her dreams. A very disturbing effect.

Covering her face with her hands, she moaned, "What does this mean?" Unfortunately, being a psychologist, she knew exactly what it meant.

She took a deep breath. She didn't need a stethoscope to figure out what the man's effect on her pulse was, either. Her heart still pounded like a jackhammer, and bitter experience told her it wasn't all from the dreams.

The Cajun on the balcony was a bad boy of the first order. Just the kind of man she desperately needed to avoid—not dream about. She should know better. She *did* know better. She knew all about men like him.

Oh, yes. She knew exactly what lay down that road. And she certainly didn't need her two psychology degrees to know she'd be a fool to consider going down it.

Ever.

Not with this man. Not with any man of his ilk.

No matter how alluring his bedroom eyes or softly persuasive his smooth bayou accent.

Clenching her fists, she sat up. Mama Summerville hadn't raised her baby girl to be a fool. No, sir. Not *this* one, anyway.

She had to get a serious grip. Better yet, she had to find Muse and then get out of town quickly, before she did something really, really stupid.

Springing out of bed, she went straight into the shower to scrub off the lingering feel of the dream on her skin. Mercy, she never had dreams like that. Sometimes the high school students she counseled would tell her about unusually intense dreams, but she'd always chalked it up to the influence of raging adolescent hormones. She had no such convenient excuse.

Maybe it had just been too long since a man had held her in his arms. What was it now? Two years? Three? Who knew. She'd been extra gun-shy since the last time. And she had no desire to repeat the experience.

A few disturbing dreams were a small price to pay for avoiding a big heartache. When it came to men, she was determined not to feel the bitter brunt of her bad taste in the creatures.

She prided herself on being a mature, reliable and responsible adult. Too bad those same qualities in a man had never once made her pulse quicken or her heart skip a beat. To her acute misery, she was always attracted to men who were reckless and handsome, charming and much too dangerous for a woman like her. Men who didn't stick around long enough to take the consequences of their numerous conquests. *Men like her father.*

She sighed, not about to ponder the deep significance of that particular neurosis. Her father was one subject that was closed forever, as far as she was concerned. She just wished Muse wasn't so darn much like him. It hurt to see her only sibling throw her life away in the shortsighted pursuit of mindless amusement, forsaking anything that smacked of commitment. Thank goodness Grace had the strength and good sense to avoid that variety of disaster, both in herself and in the men she dated.

Grace finished her shower, slipped on a silk robe hanging in the bathroom and detoured to the kitchen to start a quick pot of coffee brewing. She had a long day ahead of her if she was going to find Muse and bail her out of whatever trouble she was in, so she could get back to her responsibilities at home. And she'd have to hurry if she was going to get to Leavy, Dell and Roland by start of day.

Opening the closet, she flicked through the assortment of dresses there and let out an aggravated chuff. She glanced longingly at her own suitcase, brimming with sensible clothes, much more appropriate to working in a lawyers' office. There wasn't a single outfit in Muse's collection she would have bought for herself.

Silently she cursed being forced to impersonate her sister. It was the only way she could think of to gather information about her disappearance. With Grace's psychology background, it was a simple task to assume her sister's persona and say just the right things to make people believe she was Muse and to open up completely. But for two days now she'd been forced to choose from Muse's unbelievable wardrobe of short, slinky, tight or transparent garments, and don her strappy, spiky, neck-breaking collection of high-heeled shoes. The woman didn't believe in moderation of any kind.

Just one more thing the two of them didn't have in common. Anyone who thought identical twins were exactly alike hadn't met Grace and Muse Summerville. But for all that, Grace loved her sister dearly, and she knew Muse felt the same about her. She would do anything in the world to help her. Anything. Including wearing her outrageous clothes, if she had to.

Sweet heavens. What a choice. They were all too short, too tight, and way too...sexy.

She felt a prick of irritation. Everyone at school—including the male teachers—might think she was an old maid, but she preferred it that way. She liked to look professional. If a man couldn't see past a business suit to the woman beneath, he wasn't worth attracting in the first place.

Tight, sexy skirts caught the eye of the wrong kind of man. The kind of man who liked things short and sweet. The kind of man who wasn't looking for a lasting relationship. A man who took his fill and moved on, bored by the comfort of familiarity and threatened by the prospect of deep emotions. Regardless of the consequences for his young wife and children.

Definitely the wrong kind of man for her.

But today she didn't have any option. She'd have to wear short and sexy or risk missing a vital bit of information that could lead her to Muse.

Resigned, she snatched a turquoise sundress from its hanger, anxiety for her sister overriding all other concerns. Marching to her suitcase, she selected a set of matching lacy but comfortable underwear; she paused briefly at a pair of pantyhose, then dismissed the idea. It was hot enough to steam clams out there already. Better pale and comfortable than proper and roasting.

About to shed her robe, she suddenly halted and glanced over to the apartment across the courtyard. Not a good idea. Her new neighbor was nowhere to be seen this morning, but that didn't mean he wasn't lurking there somewhere, watching her.

After changing in the bathroom, she put on her makeup and assessed herself in the mirror. The turquoise dress was pretty, she had to admit, if too short. With cut-in sleeves, a round collar and a slim skirt with offset pockets, it showed off her figure and highlighted her golden hair.

She frowned. She looked exactly like her twin. *Bother.* All her life she'd worked hard to establish her own separate identity, apart from Muse. It was almost depressing to realize a mere dress could so easily obliterate her individuality.

Well, if that's what it took to find her sister, she could put up with a temporary loss of self-image. She was, after all, the same person inside, and that's what counted.

The aromatic smell of fresh coffee drew her to the kitchen, where she rummaged in a cupboard and found a large, lidded travel mug. She was late, so she'd have to get her caffeine fix on the twenty-minute walk to Muse's office.

Slinging the strap of her bag over her shoulder, she picked up Muse's briefcase, grabbed the coffee mug and went out the door. She locked it, sailed down the flight of steps, turned and carefully pulled the outer door closed.

Then from right behind her, she felt a rumbling masculine voice murmur, "Muse Summerville."

Creole grabbed the coffee mug that was about to fly out of Muse's hand as she spun to face him. Nervous little thing, wasn't she? She glanced anxiously around the small courtyard, almost as if she expected someone else besides him to be standing there.

"Wh-where…? H-how did you—" she stammered.

"Your name's on your doorbell." He nodded at the uppermost of two inconspicuously labeled buzzers next to the building's outer door.

She glanced at it uncertainly, then back at him, and swallowed. "Wh-what do you want from me?"

He'd been asking himself the same question since he'd watched her crawl into bed the night before—alone again.

"Just wanted to say good mornin' to my new neighbor."

Her tongue peeked out and swiped over her lips, diverting his attention up from the curves of her dress, where it had strayed after taking in the briefcase she clutched in her hand.

"That's, um—"

Dieu, she was even better looking close up. Not beautiful in the conventional sense, but she had a body that didn't quit, and her face was…intriguing. Surprisingly open and free of artifice. For a woman.

"—very nice of—"

Suddenly her whole face drained of color. She took a step back, bumping into the door. Okay, *bien*. She'd spotted the Glock, tucked neatly in its holster under his left arm. Hard to miss. His own personal American Express card, he never went anywhere without it. He probably should have put a shirt over the holster instead of wearing it openly over his T-shirt, but he'd wanted to see her response to a man with a weapon.

"You've got a—"

He hiked a brow.

"—a concealed weapon." She hugged her briefcase to her middle like a shield.

"Hardly concealed." He relaxed onto one hip and gestured vaguely with her coffee mug, which he still held. "Plain as day, I'd say." He sure would like to know what was in that briefcase.

"Are you some kind of police officer?"

He gazed at her consideringly. It surprised him that a cop would be her first guess, even if they were the only ones allowed by law to carry concealed. She peered back at him with nervous blue eyes. But, *non*, she didn't believe it for a minute. More likely she thought he was one of the thugs who hung around with her boyfriend, who didn't give a damn about gun laws.

Hell, who was he to disappoint her? He paused long

enough to make sure it sounded like a lie. "Me? *Mais,* yeah. I'm a cop."

"Then where's your badge?" she asked, surprising him again. The woman was just full of all kinds of surprises.

A slow grin crept onto his face. "Must have left it on the bed while I was getting dressed. Come on up an' I'll show it to you."

Shock chased the fear right out of those bright blue eyes. She stared at him for several seconds before replying, "I have to go now. Excuse me."

Her spine straightened, and she adjusted the strap of her shoulder bag neatly. With her pretty little nose in the air, she waited politely for him to back off so she could get by.

He didn't. He was too puzzled by her reaction—it was all wrong.

He hadn't really expected her to fall headlong for his not-so-subtle ploy to get up-close and personal—to her briefcase, of course—but it wouldn't have been too out of character if she had. After all, she'd been at least two nights without a man. According to the quick background check he'd done on her prior to moving in, she liked living on the edge, pushing the limits. She had a real reputation for liking men. Preferably wild, undisciplined men, the more dangerous the better. At the very least he'd expected a so-phisticated, flirtatious brush-off.

He must be losing his touch.

"Now, I know your mama taught you better manners than to walk away before I can introduce myself," he drawled, echoing her words from last night. "We are neighbors, *non?*"

A flicker of consternation passed through her expression. "I don't think—"

Her words halted abruptly when he casually raised her coffee mug and took a sip. She'd obviously forgotten all about it. Her eyes widened and her lips parted, and once again his gaze was drawn to those luscious lips. Shapely and plump, they were slicked with a wet shade of rose-colored lipstick. His tongue slid over the rim of the mug, instinctively seeking out a taste of them—of her. She watched his movements with a kind of scandalized fascination.

"Levalois," he said, growing more fascinated by the minute himself. "Call me Creole." He figured she wouldn't shake his hand if he offered it, so he passed the mug back to her instead. "Everyone does."

She looked at the mug as if he'd just handed her a squirming, mud-soaked kitten. Then her lips thinned and she brushed quickly past him, her knuckles white around the handle. He didn't even mind that her hand touched his arm going by.

"Good day, Mr. Levalois," she said in those sexy Carolina tones, smooth and cool as Southern ice. Like the ice she had erotically painted her bare skin with last night.

Her high heels clicked a sharp tattoo on the cobblestones as she hurried to the front gate and let herself out. His body was still shooting off sparks from the brief contact with hers—and from the sight of her shapely bottom swaying back and forth as she ran from him.

Lord have mercy.

"See you tonight, *chère*," he called after her, perversely amused when the gate smacked shut behind her with a clang that reverberated in the small courtyard like a gunshot.

He stood there for a full minute, gazing after her like seven kinds of idiot, before giving himself a swift inner kick in the head.

Dieu, the ringing in his ears must be seriously affecting his brain. Or maybe it was the lingering scent of that damned jessamine perfume paralyzing his ability to think rationally. He wiped the grin from his face.

What the hell had gotten into him? He couldn't afford to get distracted by a million-dollar set of legs, or lips that looked as if they could send him into orbit without half trying. He had work to do. And being attracted to this woman had no place in it.

He grabbed his notebook from where he'd stashed it in the stairwell along with his shirt, which he quickly slipped over his T-shirt and holster, and sprinted after her. The plan was to tail her to her office again, keeping a respectable distance between them. A professional distance. Making sure Fox didn't show up.

That is, hoping Fox *would* show up.

He caught up to her on Toulouse. Following as closely as he dared, he gave himself a silent chewing out. Sure, on paper she was exactly the kind of woman he usually went for—fast, easy and fun, with no strings attached. The kind with imagination enough not to mind his slight eccentricity about being touched and the…complications…it engendered. The kind of woman it didn't matter if you could trust because you never got involved deeply enough for trust to be an issue.

But Muse Summerville was strictly off-limits. She was a means to an end, period. Getting involved with her, hell, even flirting with her, would be a big mistake. It would jeopardize everything.

Wouldn't it?

Mesmerized, he watched the hem of that dress she was almost wearing skip back and forth along the tops of her dream-inspiring thighs as she hurried down the street.

But what if Fox never showed up? She might be able to tell him where the creep was hiding out. And questions about her boyfriend's whereabouts would seem more natural coming from a potential rival for her attentions.

Under the circumstances it made sense to try to get close to her. Moving in on Fox's territory might even make him turn up quicker, if the hood got wind of it. Suddenly getting to know her better struck him as a damned fine idea.

The fact that his body still hummed with electricity where it had brushed hers had absolutely nothing to do with it.

Pas rien. Nope, nothing at all.

* * *

Grace hurried down Toulouse Street, putting as much distance as possible between herself and Creole Levalois as quickly as possible. She didn't know what outraged her more, his transparent attempt to shock her by openly carrying a gun, or his audacity in drinking from her mug.

Goose bumps shivered down her spine as she recalled the way he'd drawn his tongue along the rim, licking up a last, glistening drop of liquid, gazing down at her with those glittering black eyes. She'd known exactly what he was thinking.

Because she was thinking it, too.

Lord, the man was an iron-clad menace.

The fine hairs on her arms stood on end, and she picked up her pace. *He was close.* His presence in the very air around her was almost tangible. Potent and male. Dangerous. Prowling up behind her like a wolf stalking its prey.

She fought a shiver. Now she knew how Muse must have felt. But unlike Muse, she had no intention of letting this man intimidate her. She walked faster.

In her haste, her high heel caught on a crack in the sidewalk, and she gave a yelp, about to go flying. A strong hand gripped her elbow, and she was pulled against a hard, masculine body.

"Careful there, *chère.*"

Him!

Instead of regaining her footing, she felt even more off balance. His chest was broad and his arms were strong as they banded around her, preventing her from falling. Her mind dizzied at how incredibly…good he felt.

This wasn't right. She should be terrified. The man was armed and following her.

And she *was* terrified.

Terrified by her traitorous body's willing response to him. Terrified by the knowledge that this was *not* the blond man who had stalked her sister—he was all her own. Terrified that all she wanted was to sink farther into his warm embrace and be held close until the silly trembling in her knees ceased.

She tore herself from his grasp and glared up at him. "Are you following me?" she demanded, brushing irritatedly at the spot where his fingers had circled her arm.

A grin sneaked across his mouth. The harsh hollows and angles of his face transformed into a landscape of mischievous valleys and crinkles. He shrugged. "Nice mornin' for a walk."

She blinked. Mercy, how could a man look so dangerous one minute and so innocent the next?

Innocent? Yeah, right. She took a step back, eyeing the conspicuous bulge below his left armpit.

Seeing the direction of her gaze, he leaned in and whispered, "Don' worry, I make it a habit not to shoot anyone before they've had their first cup of coffee. Doesn' seem polite, somehow."

She scowled. "Very funny."

He chuckled. "Hey, I'm a cop, remember?"

"Yeah, and I'm Little Miss Muffett."

A rowdy group of tourists jostled by on the sidewalk, heading for the twenty-four-hour bars on Bourbon Street. After they'd passed, his shoulders notched down almost imperceptibly, and she realized he'd probably been expecting her to stop them for help.

She probably should have. In fact, it was a fair mystery why the thought hadn't occurred to her.

"What do you want?" she demanded again. Just in case her judgment had gone out the window along with her good sense—after all, a box of black hair dye might cost all of two bucks—she added, "You've been following me for weeks. Why?"

His brows shot up. "Weeks?"

"That innocent routine doesn't fool me for a second. You've got one minute to explain or I start screaming." She looked at her watch to emphasize her point.

That ought to shake him out, one way or another. If by some miracle he *was* Muse's stalker and had information about her movements last week or her disappearance, Grace needed to know. Now.

His eyes narrowed. "Who's following you?"

She sent him a withering glare. "*You* are." And gave her watch another pointed look. "Forty-five seconds."

"Have you called the police?"

Now there was a trick question if ever she'd heard one. She chose to ignore it. "Thirty seconds."

"*Non?*" No?

"Twenty-five seconds."

"Now, why would someone like you be afraid of the cops?" He tilted his head, his piercing black eyes searched her face. "Unless you're hiding something? Or doin' something illegal."

"*You're* the one who's hiding something," she stated, and abruptly decided to start walking again.

"I've got a permit," he said, catching up to her. "Want to see it?"

That roguish grin was starting to annoy her. "You're completely obnoxious," she informed him.

He chuckled and gave her another one of those not-so-innocent looks. "I guess we can rule out hooker," he said. "Despite the dress."

She stopped dead and turned to glare at him, hands on her hips. "What's wrong with my dress?"

He looked her over leisurely, thoroughly, from the top of her head to the tips of her wobbling shoes. "Not a damn thing I can see."

Heat flooded from her cheeks clear down to her knees. It had inadvertently slipped her mind that she was wearing one of Muse's slinky outfits. Sputtering, she spun on a toe and resumed walking. "I'm being stalked by a Neanderthal," she muttered.

"Hey, I resent that," he protested with a hand over his heart. "I am no stalker."

She rolled her eyes. The man was truly impossible. And miles too impudent to actually be a stalker. Despite her irritation, she relaxed a trifle.

"Have lunch with me and I'll prove it."

"Sorry, I'm busy," she told him succinctly.

He gave her a Gallic shrug. It wasn't until after he'd walked her the rest of the way to Leavy, Dell and Roland, making seemingly innocent conversation the whole way, and she'd finally escaped into Muse's office and closed the door gratefully behind her, that she realized he'd never answered her question. If he wasn't the stalker, why *was* he following her?

She let out a groan. Just great.

He obviously thought she was her sister. She *had* to find out if he knew anything about Muse. Which meant that regardless of how much she wanted to avoid Creole Levalois and his dark, sultry eyes, she had no choice.

She had to talk to the man just one more time.

Chapter 3

Blowing out a breath, Grace set her purse and briefcase on the desk in Muse's office.

She really had to focus. She couldn't allow herself to be sidetracked by Creole Levalois's undeniable charm or his even more undeniably gorgeous body. Or the way he made her own body tingle with an awareness she hadn't felt in years…since the last time she'd fallen for the wrong man.

Not that she was falling for him. Not a chance on God's green earth. Heavens, the man was nothing but trouble. Trouble with a big, huge capital *T*.

A soft knock on the door brought her disagreeable thoughts to a halt. "Grace? Is that you?"

Grateful for the interruption, she greeted the man who poked his head through the door, "Robert, come in. Yes, it's me." It was Robert Dell, Muse's boss.

The first thing she'd done yesterday morning was to come to the midsize law firm of Leavy, Dell and Roland to alert Muse's employers to the situation. Muse worked as a paralegal, mainly hunting down legal citations and case law for the three senior partners. Everyone had been surprised when Grace appeared at the office asking questions. Apparently Muse had never mentioned a sister.

Robert Dell strolled into Muse's office, his gaze skimming over the desk and computer before settling on Grace. "I take it she hasn't shown up?" he said, not without sympathy.

"No. And I'm really getting worried."

He nodded, not one of his impeccably styled silver hairs out of place, and asked, "No luck when you looked through her files yesterday?"

"Nothing even remotely suspicious popped out. I had a feeling her disappearance wouldn't be work related. I'm pretty sure it's personal."

"I still think you're overreacting," Dell said, tapping a perfectly manicured finger on the top of a file cabinet. "Like I said yesterday, she's always coming in late and taking days off on a moment's notice. She's probably lying on a beach somewhere in the Caribbean at this very moment."

Grace leveled him a look. "Why did you keep her on if she's so irresponsible?" She never did trust a man who took such pains with his appearance.

He shrugged his thin but elegantly suited shoulders, avoiding her gaze. "Muse is terrific at research, and the clients like her a lot. That's why we're willing to put up with her somewhat unconventional work habits."

Research. Sure.

He gave her a thorough glancing over and added, "I don't suppose you're looking for a job?"

She politely declined. "But I would like to talk to your staff today. To get more information on Muse's friends, where she hangs out, her favorite shops and restaurants, that sort of thing. Would you mind?"

He looked reluctant, but after a moment's hesitation, relented. "Very well. But I'm sure she'll be back in a day or two, wondering what all the fuss was about."

"I hope you're right," she said as he took his leave.

Admittedly, this wasn't the first time Muse had simply vanished somewhere on a whim, pact or no. But the fact that her sister had been so frightened on the phone had Grace worried. She could still hear the fear in Muse's voice the last time they'd spoken. And she had been gone nearly a week now, a long time even for someone as impulsive as Muse.

Grace picked up her coffee mug to take a much-needed sip of the strong, steadying brew. Her lips had almost touched the rim of the mug when suddenly she remembered.

Darn! She yanked the mug away from her mouth. She was not about to put her lips where that man's tongue had lingered so suggestively.

Carefully setting down the cup, she stared at it. She could almost see Creole's heavy-lidded eyes taunting her, daring her to drink. To sample the essence that had been left there by his mouth and tongue. To taste him…savor the forbidden. *Go on,* chère, *try me.…*

Almost in a trance she reached for the mug and lifted it, bringing it slowly toward her lips. They parted of their own accord, eager to betray her with their wanton curiosity.

They wanted to taste the flavor of his tongue, to imagine the texture of his lips as they caressed her, the heat of his mouth covering her own and drinking from her until they both trembled with the thirst for more. Then her lips would whisper sweet encouragements as he slipped off her dress and tasted her body, licking and sipping as he drowned her in kisses, down her throat, over her breasts, around her belly, until he reached—

Sweet heavens.

She jerked the mug away and slammed it to the desk so hard it left a dent in the wood. She paced away, spun and regarded it with blossoming horror.

She was doing it. Letting a totally inappropriate man get

to her. Something she'd vowed never, ever to let herself do.

There was no doubt in her mind Creole Levalois was a rebel, a man who scorned society and convention. A confirmed loner. One who, to get what he wanted, would beg a woman to reform him, and then laugh at her naïveté when she tried and failed. Leaving her alone and crying her heart out for her efforts. But a man who was so tempting in his primitive allure that he never lacked for scores of women who were willing to take the chance.

She knew his type all too well. And she was not about to make the same mistake as her mother had. Not a chance.

Better by far to put her vivid imagination to use in finding her sister rather than spinning impossible fantasies about a man who would only burn her. Badly.

Grabbing a tissue, she scrubbed determinedly at the rim of the mug until it shone. Then for good measure she lifted the lid and poured the liquid into a colorful ceramic cup sitting on Muse's desk.

There. She'd circumvented that little temptation very nicely, thankyouverymuch. Immensely satisfied with her self-control, she took a deep swallow of warm coffee, savoring the rich, calming flavor. And firmly ignored the little voice inside her head.

The one telling her it might not be quite as easy to avoid the temptation of the man himself.

Creole hit the on button on his cell phone and speed-dialed the number for the Gumbo Shop as he sat on the corner of his bed and kicked off his shoes and socks. He'd been walking all afternoon and was hungry as a gator in the springtime. That woman had led him from one end of the Quarter to the other and back again, twice, before finally coming home tonight.

What the hell had she been up to? He still couldn't figure out what had possessed her to traipse from one store to the next, making seemingly harmless chitchat with the clerks, then moving on. She hadn't bought a blessed thing all afternoon. He just didn't get it. Women didn't go into stores and come out empty-handed. Especially women like Muse Summerville.

She had to be up to something, and he aimed to find out what.

When the Gumbo Shop answered, he ordered dinner for two to be delivered in an hour. Careful to stick to the shadows of his bedroom, he changed into a fresh T-shirt, replaced his shoulder holster over it and strolled into the kitchen for a drink. He'd already unscrewed the bulbs in the fridge the day he moved in, so he didn't have to worry about Muse spotting him until he wanted to be spotted. Digging into a huge bag of ice in the freezer, he filled his glass to the brim, poured a generous finger of bourbon over it and propped himself against the wall to watch and wait.

Muse was walking around her apartment doing just about the same things he was. Except when she went to put ice in her glass, she found the ice tray full of barely frosted water. He couldn't hear the exact words she uttered at that moment, but he had a pretty good idea what they were. The corner of his mouth curled up. Dumping her ice tray in the sink just before he'd sneaked out of her apartment that afternoon had been divine inspiration.

She poured herself a glass of soda—without ice—and picked up the portable phone, then opened both sets of French doors, flicked on the overhead fan in the bedroom, stretched out on her bed and dialed. As silently as he could, Creole opened his own French doors and slipped out onto his balcony, but she'd turned on that damned radio again, so he couldn't make out a word she was saying.

He settled into his spot behind the hanging plants and took up his surveillance. Too bad he couldn't keep his mind on the case. Seeing her lying there on those pink satin sheets talking on the phone was turning his thoughts in a whole other direction. A dangerous direction. One that involved a black nightie and the memory of what she'd done with that ice the night before.

Dieu.

She reached her hand up into the air and seemed to touch the breeze blowing from the paddle fan, then turned her face into it as if she was receiving caresses from a lover. Creole shifted in his seat, disturbed by her sensual movements.

Who the hell was she talking to? Fox?

He had the strangest urge to leap over there and hang up the damn phone, lower himself on top of her and take the wind's place, softly stroking her face so she'd look up at him with the same rapturous expression she bore now.

It was unnerving. Women didn't affect him like this. Creole wasn't into soft caresses. Sex was intense. Powerful. Sometimes even rough in its fierce quest for physical fulfillment. Anything but soft. If he caressed her, it damn sure wouldn't be on her face.

She hung up, and he let out a strangled sigh of relief, but it turned into a disappointed groan when she walked into the bathroom for her shower without unzipping her dress as usual.

Just as well. The last thing he needed was more fodder for his fertile imagination. As he waited for her to emerge and dinner to arrive, he tried to put together the pieces of the puzzle Muse was creating for him. He'd been so sure he would find something when he'd searched her briefcase that afternoon.

She'd stopped at a nearby restaurant for lunch and he'd slipped back to her apartment, where she'd dropped the briefcase off earlier, to take a peek at the contents. But it had contained only a few files and a dry-cleaning stub, nothing interesting or relevant to Gary Fox or Luke's murder, and nothing that shed any light on her odd behavior that afternoon.

If she'd been asking the store clerks about a specific person, or information, he could have understood it. But when he'd shown his badge to them and asked what she'd wanted, they'd all denied she'd asked about anything in particular, just talked in generalities about the last time she'd been in, who was with her, what she'd bought, who'd paid for it.

If he didn't know better, he'd think she was investigating herself.

He shook his head at the crazy idea and grabbed his phone when she came out of the bathroom wrapped in a shiny robe. She went to the dresser and poked through those tantalizing sheer and filmy night things. It was just too tempting to pass up.

"Red one's got my vote," he said when she picked up the phone. He could see her frown at the red scrap of lace dangling from her fingers, then she spun and searched his balcony, spearing him with a wicked glare when she spotted him sitting there. He lifted his glass and saluted her with a grin.

"In your dreams, Levalois," she muttered into the phone.

"*Ah, non,* that was the black one. I remember distinctly."

Her jaw dropped, then snapped shut. "I'm hanging up now."

"No, wait!" He got to his feet and leaned against the balcony railing. "You've got to be hungry."

Even from ten feet away he could see her eyes narrow. "What makes you say that?"

"You haven't eaten supper."

She hadn't stopped after her long walk through the Quarter, which had frustrated him to no end. This time he'd planned to crash her solitary meal and use the opportunity to pump her for information.

"Were you following me all day?" she demanded.

"*Mais, non.*" He took a sip of bourbon. He wasn't lying. Not technically. After he'd tailed her to work that morning, he'd gone by the Eighth District station to check in with a friend who was keeping an ear to the ground for him. And then there was that half hour in the afternoon when he'd broken into her apartment. "Now, why don' you put on that red thing and come on out and eat supper with me?"

"I am pushing the off button."

The line went dead. He chuckled and hit Redial.

"You may as well answer it," he called over to where she stood glowering just inside the French doors. *Dieu,* she was cute. "Or I'll just yell from here so the whole Quarter can listen to our conversation."

She put the phone back to her ear. *"What."* It was more of a demand than a question, gritted out from between clenched teeth.

He switched tactics. "It's by way of an apology," he soothed, "for my behavior this morning." He left any kind of adjective describing his behavior to her discretion. Best that way, he figured.

He could see he'd caught her by surprise. He pressed his advantage. "You sit and eat on your balcony, I'll stay on mine. We can talk on the phone. What could be safer?" Before she could respond, his door buzzed. "The delivery's here. What do you like, jambalaya or étouffée?"

"Creole—"

"I'm not on the menu for dinner, *jolie.* Though maybe you could talk me into bein' dessert... Hold on."

He put down the phone, paid the delivery boy and directed him as to which bags he should take across the courtyard. He risked a glance at Muse before picking up the phone again. She was still standing in the French doors, clutching her robe and looking mighty indecisive. Uh-oh. Time for a little smooth talkin'.

"You got the crawfish étouffée. And there's gumbo, of course. Plus I sent along a half bottle of wine, in case you don' have any handy. Answer the door, *chère,* he's knocking. Don' worry, I tipped him well."

For a moment he thought she might refuse, but then she turned and padded to her door, accepted the bags and returned to the French doors. "This is very nice of you," she said softly into the phone. "I have to admit I am starved."

"Come on out an' eat, then," he urged, before she could change her mind. "Talk to me."

Grace reached up and touched her hair self-consciously. It was still wet from being washed, creating spots of moisture on the silk of her robe where it cascaded over her shoulders. She must look like a drowned rat.

"I should change and dry my hair."

"*Non. Vien.* Come. Before the gumbo gets cold."

She couldn't believe she'd actually consented to this madness. At least, she thought she had. She couldn't exactly remember agreeing, but she must have done. Maybe while her stomach was doing flip-flops at the sight of his broad chest in that snug T-shirt, or while her brain was spinning from the sound of his gravelly voice telling her he'd been dreaming of her in Muse's scandalous lingerie.

She fetched silverware and a glass, then stretched out on her lounge chair on the balcony. She peeked into one of the bags. "I'm ashamed to admit this, but after two years in New Orleans I still get étouffée and jambalaya mixed up. Which one's the étouffée again?"

"Rice with crawfish and vegetables over it, and spices, of course."

"And jambalaya's kind of similar, but has red rice, right?"

"Right. Because it's Creole, and most anything Creole has a tomato base."

She looked up, a smile playing with the corners of her mouth. "Does that mean you have a tomato base, too?"

She could see that disreputable grin winking back at her. He was lounging on a metal bistro chair on his balcony, bare feet propped up on the railing, eating gumbo from a striped carton. "Guess you'll have to taste me to find out."

"You saucy thing." She laughed, able to relax since he was safely on the other side of two iron railings and a leg-breaking drop. "How did you get that name, anyway?"

There was a long pause as she watched him slowly put down the carton and take a long sip from his glass. One-handed, he refilled it before setting it aside and picking up the carton again. When he spoke, his voice sent an Arctic chill crackling across the distance. "Where I grew up, people didn' think much of Cajuns or of blacks. They thought they were insultin' me by calling me a Creole, which they took to mean a French-speaking black person."

The topic obviously brought up bad memories for him. But she'd never been too clear about the distinction between Cajun and Creole, which as an outsider seemed to have somewhat fluid definitions. So she risked continuing. "That's not what it means?"

His broad shoulder lifted in the shadows. "Depends."

"On what?"

He cradled the phone between his shoulder and his ear, tipping his head to hold it in place as he ate. "Look, are you really interested in this, or are you just tryin' to distract me from other subjects?"

"Such as?"

"Such as why you never wear any of those sheer sexy things you have in that drawer."

"Both," she answered, almost choking on a spoonful of gumbo. "But seriously, I'd like to learn the correct definition."

His low chuckle resonated through the small courtyard, dispelling the earlier chill. "Fair enough. Well, in English it can mean a black French-speaker. But the original meaning was a European person born in a European colony."

"Of which Louisiana was one." The confusion started making sense.

"Exactly. But today, a Cajun speakin' French, he say Creole, he means Cajun."

Maybe not. "You're saying it means different things if you're speaking French or English?"

"You got it. Now, about those sexy things—"

"Forget it, Creole," she interrupted before he could get

any further. She finished off the gumbo and picked up her wine. "Let's talk about you."

"Let's not."

"For instance, let's talk about why you've been watching me."

"Honey, a man don' need a reason to watch *une jolie femme*—a beautiful woman."

The way he said *jolie femme* in that smoky accent sent tremors fluttering down her insides. Oh, he was good. She took a gulp of wine and tightened the sash on her robe.

"You're evading the question. I want a straight answer, and it better be good, or I really will call the police."

The phone went quiet, and she could see him lean back in his chair and regard her, considering her ultimatum. That alone made her pulse kick up. He had to have something to do with Muse's disappearance. Otherwise what was there to think about? A man on the make wouldn't need to think about it, he would just spout some empty flattery and a pickup line.

"Well?" she demanded, impatient for the information he could give her.

"*Bien.* I'll tell you. I'm looking for your boyfriend."

"Boyfriend?" For a moment she was so confused she could only gape at his unsmiling visage, staring back at her from the darkness of his balcony. Whatever she had expected, this wasn't it. "What boyfriend?"

He picked up his glass and twirled it, the ice tinkling in incongruous merriment. "So many I need to be more specific, eh? Guess I should have known."

The venom in the unexpected insult—in his whole utterance really—made her breath catch. "Listen, you—"

"Gary Fox. That's who I'm after."

No way she was getting into a debate over Muse's love life. She pushed aside the insult and centered on the facts. "Gary Fox? Why?"

"Unfinished business."

Her chin notched up. "So it has nothing to do with me?"

"Non."

That knowledge stung. More than she cared to admit. "Why follow me? Why not him?"

"He's dropped out of sight. But I figure he'll come around to see his lady love sooner or later."

So, Creole wasn't attracted to her at all. He'd just been using his charms on her so she'd help him find Fox. Anger swamped over her, shoving aside the irrational hurt that had sneaked past her defenses. What had she expected? She knew well and good what kind of man he was.

"I'm sorry to disappoint you, but I am not Gary Fox's lady love. You can watch from here until doomsday but he won't come around."

Creole's feet came off the rail and slammed to the balcony floor. "What are you saying?"

"I'm saying you've wasted your time and this lovely supper. Now, if you'll excuse me…"

"I haven't— Don't be—"

"Good night." She hung up the phone with a satisfying click and swept up the dinner things from the table, thoroughly disgusted with herself and her weakness for handsome, silver-tongued men.

"Hey!"

Ignoring him, she turned to stalk through the French doors. Instantly the phone rang in her hand.

"Answer it, *chère*," he called from his balcony.

"I have nothing to say to you." She hurried inside.

He bellowed after her, "Answer the damn phone, Muse!"

At his use of her sister's name, Grace froze.

What in heaven's name was she doing? Creole was after the very man she suspected of causing Muse's disappearance, and here she was acting like a sulking teenager just because he'd admitted he wasn't interested in her. She closed her eyes and counted to ten.

It was *good* he wasn't interested in her, because under no circumstances was she interested in him. Hadn't she assured herself of that a dozen times since this morning? The only thing she was interested in was finding her sister. And as much as it rankled, Creole Levalois might be able to help her. She owed it to Muse to use him just as he was using her.

She swallowed her pride and put the phone back to her ear. "What do you want?"

Creole exhaled when Muse turned defiantly in the doorway and waited for his answer. He knew enough about women to know he'd said the wrong thing. Women never cared much for hearing the truth. But he'd heard too many lies to be able to tell them comfortably himself, so he avoided it whenever possible, even in his profession. His following her *didn't* have anything to do with her personally. It was all about finding Luke's killer. Nothing else.

Before he could ponder the hazards of lying to *oneself,* he decided to come completely clean. If she really had broken with Fox, he'd need her help more than ever to run the bastard down.

He tried for an authoritative tone. "I know you didn' believe me when I said I was a cop. But I am. I'm Detective Auri Levalois, out of the First District. Call and check if you want."

"Auri? I thought you said your name was Creole."

"They call me Creole, but it's really Auri. *A-U-R-I.*"

"So what does all this have to do with me, Detective *A-U-R-I* Levalois?"

"I need your help."

She took a step back onto the balcony, a frown of suspicion creasing her brow. "What kind of help?"

"It's imperative I locate Fox. I've looked everywhere I can think of. I'm betting you know other places he could be hiding. Would you be willing to help me find him?"

She took another step forward, and he moved to the rail of his own balcony, closing the distance between them as much as he could. She halted. "Are you going to arrest him?"

He planned to kill the bastard. Slow and painful, just like they'd made Luke suffer. But not before Fox had led him to his boss, James Davies. "No," he answered.

She seemed to consider this. "Are you sure you aren't going to arrest him?"

Something in the way she said it made him think she might welcome that outcome. Interesting. He'd have to probe that a little, at a more appropriate time.

"There might be an outstanding warrant buried somewhere in his file," he said noncommittally.

She approached the rail of her balcony and nodded. "All right. But I have to warn you, I doubt if I know anything that will help."

Since they stood close enough to hear unaided, he put his phone down on the small table next to him, and she did the same with hers.

Their eyes met. The night breeze twined around them, stirring the hanging plants and the long tendrils of her hair. A drop of sweat trickled down her chest, glistening in the lamplight, to disappear beneath the front of her robe. Her lips parted slightly. Even though they stood on unconnected balconies, only a few feet separated them from each other. If he reached out and she met him halfway, they could touch fingertips. He didn't move.

Instead, he watched her, momentarily captured in a surreal vignette of fascination and tantalizing unobtainability.

"I'll take what I can get," he finally murmured.

"I want something in exchange," she said, jarring him out of his trance.

"What's that?" he asked, wondering if she felt it, too. More fantasyland.

From the table she lifted her abandoned glass of soda. "Ice."

"Ice?"

She took a sip, grimaced and lifted the glass in his direction. "Got an extra ice tray?"

He blinked, suddenly remembering this afternoon's bit

of mischief. She'd played right into his hands. Except now he had no reason to go over there bearing a bucket of ice. He'd already searched her briefcase and had also revealed to her who he really was. Getting any closer to this woman was unnecessary. Unnecessary and foolish—considering how badly she'd already managed to distract him from his true purpose in watching her.

At this point the only motivation for going to her apartment would be purely personal.

To get his hands on her.

Bad idea.

Really bad idea.

"Hang on. I'll be over in a minute," he blurted out, and headed for the kitchen, his hands already itching.

Chapter 4

Panic zinged around Grace's body like a crazy pinball as she watched Creole stride across the courtyard carrying a bag filled with ice.

She hadn't meant for him to come over. She'd just wanted him to toss her an ice tray from the balcony. But when she'd called over to make it clear, he'd pretended not to hear. She wrung her hands, listening to his footsteps resolutely ascend the stairs.

The loud knock on the door made her jump. *Oh, dear.* Under no circumstances would she let him inside.

She opened the door, blocking it as best she could, and took the bag of ice he held out. "Creole—"

"Close the door," he interrupted before she could say another word. He was still standing outside.

"Wha—?"

"Close the door," he repeated. "And lock it."

Rather stunned by her good fortune but not willing to question it, she hastily complied. "Thanks for the ice," she shouted through the solid wood. There was a note of giddy reprieve in the giggle that escaped her as she turned to the fridge. "Saved," she murmured in a rushed breath of relief.

"From what, *chère?*" asked a gravelly voice directly behind her. "Or should I say, from whom?"

She squealed and spun. "You! How did you get—?"

"In?" Creole dangled a credit card between two fingers and leaned his hip against the door—which was now firmly shut behind him, she noted to her dismay.

"I want you to get a new lock installed tomorrow," he said, and slid the card into his jeans pocket. "A dead bolt. This so-called lock is a joke."

Grace swallowed, tearing her gaze from his well-fitting jeans and back up to his black eyes.

"It wouldn' stop a determined squirrel. Or a fox," he added silkily.

Her mouth opened, but no sound came out. Not past the tightness that suddenly gripped her throat at his overwhelming male presence filling her kitchen.

"Anything could happen," he said, pushing off the door.

Her eyes widened as he closed in on her, but she couldn't move to save her life, stuck in the silken mesh of his provocative, low-spoken words. "I could be anyone. Anyone at all." He reached out and touched her jaw. She quivered at his light touch on her skin. "Scared?"

"Of course not," she managed to squeak past her trembling lips. "You're a cop. You wouldn't—" She stopped abruptly when she couldn't decide what she dreaded most he'd do to her. All her fears from the previous night swamped over her. *And the excitement.* "You'd never—"

One perfect black brow rose. "Are you certain?"

No, she wasn't certain at all. *Never* wasn't in the vocabulary of a man like Creole Levalois. She backed up a step, gripping the bag of ice against her chest in an ineffectual attempt to cool her raging blood and still the tremors that shot clean through her body. She took another step back. And another.

"I never showed you my badge, did I?"

He pursued her, step for step, slowly closing the distance by virtue of his greater size. His long legs ate up the space effortlessly, bringing him to within a hairbreadth of her. "Did I?" he repeated, more insistently.

"No," she reluctantly agreed. Her backside hit the counter.

"Like I said, I could be anyone," he murmured, and eased the bag from her clutching fingers. He set it on the counter, crowding her against the hard tile. "A killer, a thief…a rapist," he suggested in a rough whisper.

"Don't be ridiculous." Her knees shook so much she had to clutch the front of his T-shirt for support. "You brought me ice. A rapist wouldn't have brought ice."

The statement was absurd but all she could think of to refute his deliberate provocation. He was no rapist, and they both knew it. He might take her body, steal her heart and kill her with misery when he left her, but it would not be because of a faulty lock or a criminal personality. It would be because she wanted him so badly she didn't have the good sense to say no to the man.

"Okay, then, a kinky rapist."

Her breath caught.

His eyes glittered as he broke the seal on the bag and grasped a large ice cube, never letting her move. He had her trapped between his tall, powerful body and the solid barrier of the kitchen counter. She could feel his muscles ripple as he pressed against her—the sculpted wall of his chest, the iron-hard thighs as they tangled with hers. Slowly the strength to resist drained from her limbs, leaving them weak and leaden against his boldness.

"K-kinky?" she stammered, dropping her gaze to his hand, too curious for her own good.

"Mmm-hmm." As she watched in shocked fascination, he touched the ice to the exposed valley between her breasts, right where the vee of her robe met. She shivered uncontrollably. He trailed the cube leisurely across her chest, up the column of her throat to her chin and skimmed it over her lips. Heavy-lidded, he met her gaze, brought the ice to his own mouth and slid it in.

A groan whispered from her throat. A low, needy answer to the primitive dance he was performing.

Creole needed no other invitation. He seized her face between his hands and crushed his lips down on hers. They felt like flames against his own ice-chilled mouth. His thumbs tugged down on her chin and she opened for him, hot and molten like a volcano offering its essence. He took it, thrusting his tongue and what was left of the ice cube into her mouth. Again she groaned.

"Ah, *chère.*"

He wanted her. *Mon Dieu,* he craved to sample her like some addictive drug he'd gotten a brief, tantalizing taste of. He needed more. Much more. To test the potency of the high she'd give him.

Mais, non. He didn't do drugs or addictions. He'd always been able to resist before.

But the pull of this woman was too great.

The ice evaporated in the conflagration of their tongues. He grappled for another cube and tore away long enough to feed it to the fire. He held her head, and they passed the ice between their mouths. Back and forth, in and out, until it, too, dissolved in the intense heat.

Her fingers clutched his shoulders. He swept his hands down her arms, her hips, tugged at the thin silk belt that was the only thing standing between him and paradise.

She stirred, and offered a soft protest, pushing weakly at his wrist. "Please, no."

He grasped her hand. "What's wrong, *chère?*"

She looked up at him, her eyes round and liquid, her face flushed with desire. "I can't. I'm sorry. I just—" she licked her lips, swollen and wet from his kisses "—can't."

"Why? I thought—" The plea came out more as a whine and he cut it off in annoyance. No matter what life had thrown at him, never once had he whined. He wasn't about to start now.

She slipped from his grasp and moved away from the counter, stopping just out of reach. Frustration had him jamming his hands in his pockets.

"It's my fault. I shouldn't have let it get this far," she said, crossing her arms over her breasts.

"It's Fox," he stated, more to himself than her. "You're still in love with him."

"No. God, no. I was never—"

"Then, what? *Mon Dieu,* woman, we practically ignite just looking at each other!"

She dropped her gaze to her bare toes, toying with the curled-up edge of a linoleum tile. "Yes, I know." She squeezed her eyes shut. "But, well, I should tell you…I'm not… That is, I'm involved with…"

"*Another* man?" he impatiently completed her sentence when it trailed off. Not that he believed it.

"No, it's—" She looked up and darted him a quick glance. "I mean, yes. It's another man." A shadow of guilt flitted through her eyes, which she tried to squelch, but it was his job to spot deception, and he was very good at his job.

"You're a lousy liar," he said, and let it sink in a few seconds before grasping her upper arms and pulling her close again. The scent of warm jessamine swirled through his senses, distracting him from wondering why she would need to lie.

She squirmed to the side, trying to ease away from him. "I'm not lying."

Catching her around the waist, he turned and brought her up against the refrigerator. "Sweetheart, there is no way you could kiss me like you just did if you were involved with another man. Not unless you're a—"

"Maybe I am," she said, meeting his gaze defiantly, challenge written in her whole expression. Daring him to believe she was something his gut told him she wasn't.

He didn't. She was definitely hiding something, but it wasn't another man. It was also his job to follow his gut instincts, and right now they were telling him that no matter what this woman's file said, she wouldn't be kissing him if there was another man in her life. For some reason he couldn't explain, he desperately needed that to be true.

"No. You're not." He moved his hand to her throat, caressing the pale, delicate skin with his thumb. He leaned in and kissed her there, in the soft hollow above her collarbone.

She shuddered and let out a long sigh. "I'm not who you think I am, Creole," she whispered, her only objection when he slid his hands possessively down her body.

"Who is?"

"You don't know anything about me. I'm not—"

"That's where you're wrong, *chérie.*" He caressed her waist, her hips. "I know you're sweet as honeysuckle and sexier than any woman's got a right to be."

She gazed up at him, her eyes pleading. For what, he wasn't sure, but suddenly he was determined to find out and give it to her. He captured her hands in his and held them so she couldn't touch him, threading their fingers together. "I also know you're gonna let me kiss you again."

He raised their laced fingers above her head and held her to the fridge, leaning his elbows and forearms against the cool metal. He lowered his mouth to hers, slowly, so she could see him coming and tell him no. She didn't. Instead her hips did a little involuntary grind between him and the fridge, and she murmured a sweet moan of surrender that nearly did him in.

Grabbing on to his control, he eased his body against hers and deepened the kiss. She tasted so good. Spicy like filé gumbo, mellow like wine. Erotic, like aroused woman. *So good.*

A hot breeze swirled around them, teasing him with the scent of her perfume and the musky tang of sweat and desire. The refrigerator's motor kicked in, enveloping them like the hum of a billion insects.

He kissed her long and hard, until the taste and the feel

and the smell of her wove around him, holding him prisoner of a raw need he'd never felt before.

Her lashes fluttered up and she stared at him, lost and foundering in the sensual storm they'd created together.

"Ah, Muse."

Her blue eyes slowly focused on him, the dark pupils growing smaller. She flexed the wrists he had pinned above her head and caught her red, kiss-swollen lip between her teeth. He saw it tremble, almost as if she were suddenly frightened.

Or maybe it was just the vibrations of the fridge. A woman like her wouldn't be afraid of what was happening here between them. The apprehension he saw skittering in her eyes as she awaited his next move had to be his imagination. Or a reflection of his own gnawing fear.

Yeah, he wanted her. With the desperation of a convict craving freedom, he wanted her. But suddenly he was very sure he shouldn't take her. That if he did, the orderly world he'd built for himself would be threatened, the values and lessons learned over a lifetime forgotten, all because of the breathtaking response of a woman every file he'd read claimed was man-eating bad news.

He let her wrists go and stepped back, away from the heat and temptation of her body. "Yes, I know you, *chère,*" he quietly said, proud of how calm and level his voice sounded, not at all ragged, exposed and irrational, as he felt. "I know you better than you know yourself."

She looked so confused he had to stop himself from taking her in his arms again and kissing away her bewilderment—and his own—one inch at a time. Suddenly he didn't know himself nearly as well as he had only minutes before.

With iron restraint he reached out and ran a finger down her cheek. "Do us both a favor, *jolie,* and get your lock changed. Tomorrow."

Grace stayed leaning against the fridge for a long time after Creole walked out the door. She heard him pause just outside, and for a moment she was petrified he would change his mind and come back in. She thought about the lock he'd so easily penetrated, and knew there was nothing she could do to stop him if he chose to come back. For her.

And realized with a muffled sob that he wouldn't need to break in. She'd open the door for him herself.

But before that unwelcome thought was complete, she heard his footsteps pound down the stairs and the outer door crash against the wall. She listened as he turned away from his apartment and headed for the front gate. There was a loud clang of metal, then all was silent. Except for the thundering of her heart.

What had just happened?

Grace groped at the slick surface of the fridge behind her with her fingertips, fighting for purchase on something solid, to which she could anchor herself against the chaos running riot in her heart.

Just a kiss.

Creole had kissed her.

But it had been so much more than mere lips touching. His kiss had enveloped her like…like a full-length sable coat. A thing too hot, too forbidden, and way too costly for a woman like her. Something she didn't want and wouldn't ever consider keeping even if the opportunity presented itself. But something so luxuriously sensual and wickedly desirable that she couldn't resist trying it on, just for a minute.

She had never experienced anything like it. His kiss had been so thorough, so filling, so surrounding, so…perfect…it was as if it had reached deep inside and touched her very soul. As if *he* had reached deep inside and touched her very soul.

This went beyond attraction. Beyond chemistry. To something primal, something that called to the woman in her as nothing and no one had ever done before.

She would never be the same. In the space of a few

moments of insanity, she knew Creole Levalois had ruined her for any other man ever again. For how could she ever hope to find *two* men on this earth who could affect her like that, with just a simple kiss?

What other wondrous things could this man show her, do to her, if given the chance?

Grace let out a long, shuddering sigh.

Unfortunately, she'd never know.

Creole Levalois was not the kind of man she could ever trust enough to find out. What good was mind-bending passion if it was all one sided, and with no chance for permanence?

It was just a kiss.

Far better not to know. Not ever to know.

The next morning Grace awoke determined to put the man from the balcony and his unwanted kisses out of her mind for good. Those kisses couldn't possibly have been as earth-shattering as she remembered. There was no way.

She didn't know what had come over her last night, succumbing to Creole's obvious moves so easily. That he'd left before any more damage had been done was an undeserved blessing for which she was devoutly grateful.

What had she been thinking?

Obviously, she hadn't been thinking at all.

Well, that was going to change starting right now.

After quickly dressing, she put on a pot of coffee and reached for the phone. She had to make her daily phone call. It might be summer vacation and she might be in New Orleans rather than home in South Carolina, but her job as a high school counselor didn't stop. The kids needed her just as much now in summertime as during the school year, if not more so.

She frowned when the receiver wasn't in its cradle. She must have left it out on the balcony after last night's escapades. Deliberately stifling the urge to glance over at Creole's apartment, she kept her gaze firmly on the phone as she retrieved it and marched back inside.

While the coffee brewed, she stretched out on her bed and dialed Frank Morina's number.

"Hello, Frank. It's—"

"Hey, Grace. How's it going down there?"

"Ms. Summerville, Frank."

Frank Morina was seventeen and brassy as a ship's compass. He was still in school thanks to the grace of God and a little nagging from her, but he would no doubt be on the fast track to jail as soon as he graduated—by the skin of his teeth—come next June. The inevitability of it broke her heart. He was smart enough to recognize the value of an education, but was up against tremendous odds. An alcoholic mother, a father who had beaten him with tedious regularity as a child, and already a reputation with the law as a troublemaker.

But under his hard, devil-may-care facade, he was really a good kid, and Grace loved him like the little brother she never had. She was doing her best to turn the tide of his fate, however much it reminded her of the little Dutch boy and the dike.

"Awright, *Miz Summerville,*" Frank mocked cheekily, letting her know he was just humoring her, as only a rebellious teenaged boy could. "You find your sister yet?"

Sobering, the grin slid from her face. "No, I haven't. It's been two days, and to tell the truth I'm terribly worried."

"You want me to come on down there and help you look?"

She smiled into the phone. "No, thanks, Frank. I'm sure I'll find her today. But I appreciate the offer."

She had deliberately shared her family troubles with him in an effort to build mutual trust. His response to her frustration was heartening. He'd come a long way from the stonewalling freshman she'd met three years ago. But there was still a long way to go.

"So, how's your summer job?" she pointedly asked, steering him to a different source of frustration for her.

Frank snorted. "A damn waste of time. I'm quitting Friday."

This was what she'd been afraid of. Keeping Frank off the streets and out of circulation was his only chance in the long run, but she'd probably known all along he wouldn't last the summer at the low-paying construction job she'd finagled for him. Boys like Frank were easily bored. When they got bored they moved on.

"I'm sorry to hear that. What do you plan to do instead?"

He was silent for a moment, and she knew he had been prepared for a lecture. But as disappointed as she was, she wouldn't go there. Scolding and laying guilt trips would only let him dismiss her as one more authority figure trying to run his life.

"You know me. Jus' lookin' for a good time," he finally said, his voice a flustered mix of apology and defiance.

"Hmm."

Defiance won. "Met a real sweet girl t'other night. Her name's Nikki. Think I might spend my time giving her a memorable summer."

Grace almost choked. "Don't you dare! How old is this girl?"

"She's a senior at that arts magnet high school. Pretty as a picture, too."

She heard his love-struck sigh and knew the poor girl was a goner. Once he got his mind set on something, Frank and his considerable charm were impossible to resist. She just hoped he let this girl down easy when he got bored and moved on.

"You be good, Frank. I mean it. Don't do anything I wouldn't do."

"Hell, Miz Summerville," he chuckled. "I don't aim on dyin' no old maid. A body's got to have a *little* fun once in a while."

"Ouch," she said, unreasonably stung by his thoughtless honesty. "Thanks a lot."

She held the phone from her ear at the cuss word he uttered. "Sorry, Miz Summerville. You know I didn't mean anything by that. You're—"

"I know you didn't." She cut him off before the conversation could go any further. She didn't need to discuss her love life—or lack of one—with a seventeen-year-old. Even if he was right.

"Hell, maybe you'll meet some hot Louisiana man who'll sweep you right off your feet."

"I don't think so, Frank," she choked out, dodging the memory of just how close to the mark he'd come. "Now, you treat that girl right, you hear? And do me a favor. Think twice before you quit your job. I know it's not exactly what you want, but at least it's a start."

"Yeah, okay, I'll think about it. Good luck findin' your sister. And Miz Summerville?"

"Yes, Frank?"

"Thanks for calling."

As she hung up, that last, hesitant, little-boy admission brought a misty smile to her face. Moments like this were what kept her going at her thankless job through all the many setbacks and disappointments. Coming from a tough teen like Frank, those three little words really meant something special. That he trusted her with his walled-in, boarded-up feelings. She had no doubt she was the only person in the world—adult, anyway—whom he did trust them with.

It was a huge responsibility, not to betray the fragile trust the troubled teens she counseled gave her, and an even more huge frustration to have her hopes for many of these kids crushed when they left school and ended up right where they were headed all along. But if she put even one lost child back on the path to a normal, responsible life, it would be worth all her years of hard work and disillusionment.

Glancing at the clock, Grace went back to the kitchen and ate a quick breakfast while trying to come up with a plan for another day of searching for her sister.

Somewhere, there had to be something she'd missed. A clue to Muse's whereabouts that lay hidden in her desk or files which Grace had somehow overlooked. Or someone she hadn't thought to talk to. Muse just could not have disappeared without a trace.

She resolved to make another visit to Leavy, Dell and Roland and go through everything once more. Maybe there would be a message or word from Muse waiting for her when she got there. Or one of her sister's co-workers might have remembered something. Hopefully, after that she'd have a direction to search in. Otherwise, she'd have no choice but to head for Bourbon Street.

According to practically everyone she'd spoken to, Bourbon Street was Muse's favorite place to hang out and have fun. Grace had hoped to avoid it—being no fan of drunken tourists herself—but unless she came up with something better, she'd have to set aside her distaste and investigate the many bars along the famous street.

If posing as her sister had been uncomfortable up until now, she positively dreaded having to act like Muse in a place like that. But if it was what she had to do, she would.

She hurriedly cleaned up her breakfast things, grabbed her lidded coffee mug and headed out the door. As she descended the stairs, she mumbled a little prayer that she wouldn't run into any Cajun cops on her way to the office. She didn't think she could face her neighbor after last night. Even though this morning she'd made up her mind that her reaction to him could not have been nearly as intense as she remembered, she didn't care to test her conclusions anytime soon.

She made it all the way to Camp Street before she sensed him behind her.

Chapter 5

Compared to Creole's mood, the blossoming heat of the summer morning was positively Arctic. He'd had to follow her for five blocks composing himself before he could even approach the little liar without risk of exploding into a raging inferno.

He'd spotted her on a cross street as he'd stalked back from the Eighth District station where he'd passed a sleepless, uneasy night brooding and trying to regain his focus on locating his brother's killer. He'd spent hours going back over all the information available on Gary Fox and his boss James Davies, hoping for a flash of inspiration as to where they might have gone to ground that he hadn't already looked. But try as he might, other than dumb luck, the only avenue he saw was to continue working with Muse Summerville. Every other possible lead Creole had already chased down with no results. As he'd known all along, the woman was his last, best chance.

Unfortunately, thinking about Muse Summerville only

made things worse. His usual rational, dead-calm detective's instincts were in a state of total chaos regarding her.

It had just been a kiss, for crissake. So why did he break out in a sweat every time he thought about it?

He'd finally given up any pretense of trying to research Davies and had thrown himself into digging up all the info he could find on Muse Summerville. Somehow he had to deal with this intense, uncharacteristic reaction to the woman. Regain control over the situation and over his gut-deep confusion about her. And figure out why she was nothing like the woman described in every interview contained in her short stack of background files.

He snorted in disgust. No freaking wonder.

It had taken him nearly two hours of chain-smoking concentration to spot the one word that had triggered his epiphany. *Sister.* It had then taken him exactly six minutes on the Internet to discover the existence of Muse's twin, and within another hour he'd tracked down everything there was to find on Grace Summerville.

Grace Summerville. The woman who had played him for a class-A fool.

He muttered a string of Cajun epithets, but it didn't help his mood. He couldn't believe he'd done it again.

He should know better than to trust his feelings when it concerned women. *Il se fie pas les femmes*—they always betrayed him. Always. He swallowed down a thick, black swirl of memories. Memories best forgotten, of a boy abandoned too many times ever to willingly trust tender emotions again. Emotions like those aroused in him last night.

But Grace Summerville had lied to him. Taken him for a sucker's ride. And he intended to find out why, even if he had to kiss a confession from her deceitful little mouth.

His blood jolted at the thought of their kiss last night. The one that had sent him running for the safe sterility and orderliness of the Eighth District station. The one that, even now, knowing what she'd done, left him gasping for breath and hungering for more of the taste of her.

His strides lengthened on the hot pavement with a desperate need to confront her. Or maybe to kiss her again.

Dieu, what a sap he was! A frustrated growl rose in his throat. By now he was right behind her, and she must have heard it, for she stopped and turned to him.

"We've got to stop meeting like this," she said, all calm and cool and composed. As if last night hadn't even been a blip on her radar.

He ground his jaw in an effort not to snap.

"I thought we had an understanding," she went on, "about you following me. I said I'd—"

He continued to glower, still not trusting himself to speak, or even to move. Her poise faltered as it began to dawn on her that he was furious. Furious? More like a powder keg about to go off.

She stepped back. "Is there, um…something wrong?"

Confrontation was safer, he figured. "You tell me, *chère.*" He banded his arms across his chest and glared at her belligerently.

She blinked and stared back at him, gnawing her lip. "Uh-oh."

"Yeah. Uh-oh."

"I guess we'd better talk."

With that she swung around and made for the entrance to Leavy, Dell and Roland, which was just a couple of doors down. She said a few words to the girl at the reception desk before leading him into a small office in the back. When she closed the door behind them, he couldn't bite back his anger any longer.

"I could arrest you for lying to a police officer. It's called obstruction of justice."

She swiped her tongue over her lips and suddenly found his shoes fascinating. "I didn't lie. Not really. I never said I was Muse. You just assumed. How did you find out?"

"Your behavior."

"Excuse me?"

"This." He reached out with two fingers and tugged

none too gently on the sleeve of her dress. It was another one of those come-get-me numbers. The color of a hot Caribbean sunset, it clung to her like a limpet and showed enough skin to make a man dearly wish for a bottle of suntan lotion.

"You look like Muse, you dress like Muse. You live in Muse's apartment, go to Muse's office and play Muse all over the Quarter. But you don't act like Muse."

He pulled his hand back and rammed it in a pocket. "Muse Summerville would have gone to bed with me the first time I offered. Instead, you get all prissy and offended," he said scornfully. He felt a moment of satisfaction when her mouth dropped open. "And when I kissed you, I wasn't kissing a calculating, experienced woman who goes through men like butter. The woman I kissed was shy and naive, full of sweetness and innocence, too curious to stop me, but too damn scared of what she was feeling to go on. A woman who almost made me believe—"

Le bon Dieu. Good Lord. He halted, mortified at what was about to come out of his mouth. Her eyes rounded, and he realized his sarcastic, acid tone had made his description of her sound like poison, rather than the compliment it would have been coming from any other man.

Her mouth snapped shut and her spine straightened to a steel rod, then she turned on a high heel to stride behind the desk. He was grateful for the distance.

"I tried to tell you last night," she said, the words clipped with an emotion he pegged as resentment. "But you interrupted me." She graced him with a curdling look. "Something about knowing me better than I knew myself."

"Yeah, well." He jammed his other hand in his pocket. "Maybe I should ask to see that badge after all."

He conceded the slam as deserved and in the simmering silence tossed his shield wallet onto the desk, accepting her unspoken challenge.

"I want to know what's going on, Grace. And don't jerk me around. I'm not in the mood."

"Very well."

She carefully set her purse on the desk and walked to the window, staring out through the sparkling glass to the busy street below. The sound of traffic drifted up, along with the distant clatter of a streetcar bringing another load of tourists back from their walking tour of the Garden District. He could almost feel the tension rolling off her in waves.

"I'm looking for my sister," she began, and proceeded in five short minutes of explanation to annihilate all the anger and bitterness he'd worked up against her through the long night.

He uttered a single oath that succinctly summed up the entire situation.

"I doubt that would help," she replied, and turned to face him.

He wasn't so sure.

But he had to give her credit. Most women would still be high on their horse of indignation, unable or unwilling to speak to the man who'd delivered her a cutting insult moments before. But in her obvious worry over her sister, Grace seemed to have forgotten all about it. More luck than he deserved.

"I'll help you," he said before he could think better of it.

"That's not necessary."

"I want to," he assured her, and found he meant it. "We can help each other. Look, we both want to find Fox. It only makes sense to work together."

He could see it in her eyes. She wanted to turn him down. Send him as far away from her worried sight as she could get him. And suspicion, plain as the water in Lake Ponchetrain. Again she surprised him.

"All right. I can't afford not to. Except for Bourbon Street, I'm fresh out of ideas."

"*Bien.*" He tentatively closed some of the space between them. "Good," he repeated. He was lousy at apologies.

But suddenly he needed to set the record straight. "Listen, about what I said earlier. About the way you kiss—"

"Forget it," she interrupted, a faint blush sweeping her cheeks. She straightened a couple of files sitting on the desk. "It doesn't matter."

"It does. The fact is, I meant every word. It just didn't come out the way...well, the way it should have."

She shook her head, intently avoiding his gaze. "Oh, I don't know. You're absolutely right. I'm *not* experienced...and I'm sure that's something men like you don't find particularly attractive in a woman they're trying to seduce."

"I wasn't—" He stopped in frustration. Oh, yes, he was. And under normal circumstances she would have been right. But not this time. "You're wrong, Grace. I do find it attractive. I find everything about you attractive. And that's what had me so angry when I realized you were deceiving me. 'Cause the one thing I *don't* find attractive in a woman is betrayal."

She squirmed a little. "I'm sorry. I just didn't know if..."

He took a few steps closer. "If what, *chère?*"

"If I could trust you."

She looked up at him, and his heart squeezed in a fist. Hell, no, she couldn't trust him. Not as far as she could run in those ridiculous spiky heels. He'd have her for breakfast, lunch and dinner before he let her fly off home to South Carolina when this was all over. *Well* before. But he was pretty sure that wasn't what she was talking about.

"*Mais,* yeah, you can trust me," he said, surprisingly easily for someone who didn't believe in deception of any kind. "You can trust me to do everything in my power to help you find your sister," he added, more to assuage his guilt than to give her an oblique warning.

"Thank you," she whispered, gratitude and relief shining in her beautiful blue eyes.

"Don' thank me yet," he said, moving in on her. She

started, and he quickly bracketed her with two hands on the windowpanes behind her. "I'll want somethin' in exchange," he said, continuing their echoing game.

Twin flags of red appeared on her cheekbones, and her eyes widened. "Like what?"

"A kiss."

"A kiss?" Alarm rocketed through her expression.

"Uh-huh. I wanna see if that kiss we shared last night was as incredible as I remember. I couldn' stop thinkin' about it all night. About you. About how good you tasted, how good you felt in my arms."

She swallowed heavily.

"Were you thinkin' about me all night, too, Grace? About my lips caressing you? About my tongue slidin' inside you? Tasting you? Wantin' me to do it again?"

"No," she whispered shakily.

But he knew better. "You're lyin' again, *chère*." He threaded a hand in her soft fall of hair, breathing in its distinctive scent. *Her* distinctive scent. The scent that had haunted him all blasted night. "Tell me you don' want me to kiss you and I'll leave you alone," he murmured, slanting his mouth over hers.

She trembled once, then seemed to gather herself. "I don't want you to kiss me," she said more steadily and before he knew what was happening she'd slipped out from between his arms.

For a second he was so stunned he couldn't move. He'd been so certain...*was* so certain that, despite everything, she wanted him as much as he wanted her.

What was going on? He pushed off the window and stared after her as she stepped behind the desk again, bracing her hands on the back of the padded chair.

"Grace?"

"No, I don't want you to kiss me again. I'm just not interested."

"That so?" He leaned his weight on one hip and folded his arms. "I could have sworn you liked it as much as I did. You gave every indication you were enjoyin' yourself last night. *I'm* the one who stopped. 'Cause I knew you were scared and I didn' want to push you into anything you'd regret.'' *Or he'd regret.* ''I'm talkin' about a kiss, here, nothin' more.''

''A kiss for now. But what about later? No, I never should have let you kiss me last night. It was a mistake. I'm not Muse, Creole. I knew all along I would never get involved with a man like you.'' She looked away abruptly, gripping the chair like a lifeline.

Male outrage reared up to block the hurt that skipped through his body. ''So, what you're sayin' is I'm good enough for Muse, but not for you.''

''Don't be ridiculous.''

His jaw tightened. She'd stopped before the kicker, but he wanted to hear it. Needed to hear it. The whole, unvarnished, insulting truth about what was wrong with him as a potential lover—other than the *real* truth, which she had no way of knowing about.

''A man like me,'' he said calmly, despite his rising anger. ''Tell me, *chère*. What exactly do you mean by 'a man like me'? A cop? A Cajun? A man a little too dark, a little too poor, a little too uncouth for comfort?''

She glanced at him in surprise. ''No. Of course not.''

''Then what? Tell me. I'm dyin' of curiosity, here.'' He'd named all the usual reasons. He couldn't wait to hear hers. His character must surely have hit an all-time low. He ground his teeth together to keep from lashing out.

She studied him for a moment, as if deciding how much to reveal. Finally she said, ''Dangerous. That's what kind of a man you are. Just plain dangerous.''

He jetted out the breath he'd been holding. ''Dangerous?'' Hell, that's what women usually *liked* about him. He lifted an incredulous brow and waited her out, interrogation-style.

''You want the whole picture? All right, fine,'' she said, caving in to his subtle pressure. Then commenced to pin him like a bug. "You are charming, cunning and handsome enough to have women throwing themselves at you right and left, competing with each other to please you. But you don't get involved. Ever. Oh, no doubt you give your body willingly, but never your heart. When you get bored, which is inevitable, you move on without a second thought. You are used to having your way in all things, at all times, and you'll use any means at your disposal to get what you want. Including walking all over the hearts of those women who only want to please you."

She looked him right in the eye and said, "I've had my heart walked all over enough to last a lifetime, and have no desire to repeat the experience."

For a moment he couldn't speak. She'd pegged him so accurately he could feel the boreholes. Well, except for the hearts part. He'd always made sure the women he'd been with knew exactly what the score was. No strings, no expectations, just a good time, if they were into it. Hearts had never been involved.

He took a breath to compose himself. "That was quite a little analysis there. You ought to do that for a livin'."

"I do."

"*Mais,* yeah, I almost forgot. You're a psychologist."

"Yes."

Her eyes watched him with increasing apprehension as he strolled over to where she was standing behind the tall, padded desk chair. Before she could turn around to face him, he moved in, stepping right up against her back.

He could taste her nervousness at his close proximity. Her breath came fast and shallow, her shoulders dipped forward, as if she could escape him if she leaned far enough away. Her white-knuckled fingers dug into the dark-gray fabric of the chair.

"There's just one li'l bitty thing wrong with your theory, *chère,*" he murmured, bringing his mouth close to the delicate shell of her ear.

"And what's that?" she answered in a ragged voice,

doing her level best to appear unaffected by his breath fanning over her cheek. But he could see the slight tremble in her chin when he deliberately exhaled.

"Everything you say is true." He paused for effect, then whispered low and rough, "But you want me anyway."

She shook her head and her hair tickled his cheek. "No."

"Sure you do." There was no doubt in his mind, and he aimed to show her the truth of it.

"No."

He slid his fingers up her arms, then ran them lightly over her shoulders. A shiver sifted through her.

He knew he was just proving her accusations, but he couldn't stop himself. He wanted her too much. "Feel how your body reacts to me, to my touch," he commanded softly. He leaned down and brushed his lips over her neck, just below her ear. Her breath sucked in. "To my kiss."

"No," she denied, but she wasn't leaning so far forward now.

"Yeah." He kissed her neck again, lingeringly. Her face tipped up. He couldn't decide if it was to give him access or to pray for strength. "Admit it, Grace. You want me just as much as I want you."

"You want me?" she whispered, almost wishfully, which made no sense at all.

"Like air to breathe," he truthfully answered. "You know I do."

She turned in his arms and splayed her hands on his chest, could be to keep him at bay. Whatever. His muscles jerked at the intrusion on his body.

"Do I? You thought I was Muse," she said, her eyes giving away a vulnerability that made his tongue thicken. "You said yourself you were completely fooled. How do you know which one of us you really want?"

"Darlin', how could I want a woman I've never met?" he reasoned logically, struggling not to react to her hands on him.

"This isn't me," she said, glancing down at her outfit. "I wouldn't— If I'd been wearing a conservative business suit with my hair up, and little or no makeup on, the way I normally dress... If you'd known I was a high school counselor and not a party girl, would you have looked twice at me ? Would you have kissed me like you did?"

"Probably not," he admitted. He'd have known better. A woman like that would expect way too much from him. More than he was capable of giving. Women like that didn't want someone who—

"You see?" she said quietly, interrupting his much too clear assessment of their differences. He dismissed them.

"*Non,* no, you're wrong. Honey, if a man can't see past a business suit to the woman beneath, he's not much of a man. I might not have done anything about it, but believe me, it wouldn' have been because I didn' notice you."

She stared up at him, her face a study in astonishment. Something he'd said seemed to have rattled her perception of him. Or perhaps of herself.

He wanted to press his advantage, but just then the office door opened and the receptionist peeked in, looking almost as confused as Grace. He stepped back.

"Miss Summerville..." Grace whirled around, and the receptionist hesitated, glancing unseeingly between the two of them, as if it was commonplace for her to walk in on two people practically embracing in Muse's office. "I don't like to interrupt," she said. "But I thought you'd want to know right away. There's a call for you, on line two."

Chapter 6

Grace blinked uncomprehendingly at the receptionist, try-ing to pry her mind off Creole's bombshell and focus on what the girl was saying. It wasn't easy, for he had just said something so unlike her own perception of bad-boy Creole Levalois that it had rocked her to the core.

But she had to pay attention, because she suddenly re-alized this phone call could be the break she so desperately needed to find her sister.

She took a step back. "There's a call? For me?"

"Well, for Muse, really," the receptionist said, visibly flustered. "He won't say who he is, but he insists on speak-ing with you...that is, with Muse. I said she wasn't in, but he claims he knows that you're...that is, she, is here in the office." The young woman looked at her appealingly. "I didn't know what else to do."

"You did fine. Line two?"

The receptionist nodded, and swiftly retreated, closing the door behind her.

Grace glanced at Creole before nervously reaching for

the phone. "I hope this isn't someone selling life insurance."

"Wait." He swiftly put his hand over hers, preventing her from answering. "Sure you don't know who it is?"

She shook her head. "Not a clue."

"I wonder why is he so convinced Muse is here in the office."

With a skitter of apprehension, Grace lifted a shoulder. "Does it matter?"

"There's only one way he could know," Creole stated with a frown. "He's watching you and saw you come in."

She gasped as the implications sank in. "My God! It could be Muse's stalker!"

She eyed the phone warily, the blinking light seeming to taunt her. Just minutes before, as part of the explanation of why she'd deceived him about her identity, she'd told Creole about the blond man Muse had thought was following her. Grace had never spotted the guy, but that might have been because she'd been so caught up in Creole trailing her.

Had the other man been following her all along?

"I was sure he was involved in her disappearance," she said, trying desperately to think. "But if that were so, he would know where she is and wouldn't be calling here, would he?"

"Unless something went wrong," Creole said ominously.

"Oh, God."

He grabbed a pad of paper from the desktop and reached for a pen. "Whatever you do, get his name. Try to find out what he knows. If you think he has anything at all to do with either your sister's disappearance or Gary Fox, find some excuse to get him to meet you. Can you do that?"

"I'll try."

"Good girl. Now, answer before he hangs up and we lose him."

She picked up the phone. For the first time, she was

actually grateful when Creole stepped in close and slid his arm around her shoulders. Guiding the receiver between them, he put his ear next to hers so they could both listen.

She closed her eyes and said, "Hello?"

"Just what the hell do you think you're playing at?"

The violence in the tone of the man on the other end almost knocked the phone from her sweat-damp hand. "Wh-who is this?"

"Don't play games with me, woman. What in blazes are you doing? Have you told him anything?"

"Who?"

"Who the hell do you think?"

"I'm afraid I don't—" She darted a look at Creole.

"Listen, sweetcakes, if you've talked and screwed this deal up, I swear to God if he doesn't kill you first, I will."

Shock widened her eyes. The man couldn't possibly mean Creole—

"Name," Creole mouthed intently, a scowl plastered on his face.

She drew herself up and clamped down on the tremor in her voice. "Who is this?" she demanded. "If you have something to discuss with me, we can meet face-to-face."

A momentary silence cut through the phone line, sudden and complete. Then there was a soft click, and she knew the man had hung up.

"Damn," she muttered, the first time in memory she actually felt like using a much stronger word than the one she allowed herself. This trip was becoming veritably riddled with firsts. Not a good thing, considering how she valued an ordered and predictable life. The realization helped marshal her wits, and she looked at Creole. "Sorry I messed up. Now what?"

He used exactly the word she'd had in mind a moment ago, then took the phone from her hand. "Hell if I know. But you can be sure we haven't heard the last of this guy. Not if he's been watching you. We'll just have to wait him out to see what he wants."

She shivered. "I can't say I like that idea."

"*Non.* Me, neither."

The intent grimness that swept over his features surprised her. He was looking at her as if he wanted to strangle something—or someone. She just hoped it wasn't her.

"Who do you suppose he was talking about, um, killing me?"

"Good question. Sounds to me like your sister is involved in something she didn't tell you about, and got in over her head. Which, unfortunately, sounds like just the sort of thing Gary Fox could have had a hand in."

"And you think this stalker guy is somehow connected to Gary Fox?"

"If the stalker's the one who called, it's more than possible. What I'd like to know is what he didn't want Muse to tell me. That could be the key to this whole thing."

Grace rubbed her temples, which had begun to throb. "Oh, Muse, what have you done this time?"

Creole perched on the corner of the desk and contemplated her. "You rescue your wayward sister often?"

She nodded miserably, too woe struck to deny it. "She's always been a bit wild and reckless. Just like our—" She stopped and dragged a lock of hair behind her ear.

He waited a moment for her to go on, but when she didn't, he said, "It's hell being the responsible one, *non?*"

As if he'd know anything about being responsible.

"I love my sister," she replied, feeling an absurd need to defend her actions to a man who undoubtedly claimed more kinship with her sister's carefree lifestyle than with her own innate sense of duty. "I don't consider it a chore," she added for good measure. *Usually.*

He just smiled that infuriatingly knowing smile of his.

"Anyway, what do you think we should do now?" she asked, dumping the responsibility squarely back on him.

The corner of his lip curled up infinitesimally—an oh-so-subtle, instinctive male gesture that left little doubt in her mind what he'd prefer to do at any given moment. Just like that, a rush of heady awareness avalanched through her and brought her thoughts screeching back to their previous topic of discussion—before the phone call.

You want me anyway.

Sweet heaven, she really had to start thinking before she spoke around this man.

She braced herself for another round of deflecting his sensual assaults, and was strangely disappointed when he merely said, "What were you planning to do this morning?"

Regrouping, she sighed. "Go over everything here in the office one more time. Hope I missed something the last ten times."

"Bien," he said. "I'll take the computer. You take the file drawers."

"You won't be able to access client files. Just her personal ones."

"Those are the ones I assume we need."

All business, he slid into the desk chair and punched the computer's on button, shifting before her eyes into detective mode. The transformation was amazing. Gone was the sexy, laid-back Cajun rogue, in his place a no-nonsense professional whose fingers whipped over the computer's keyboard with laser efficiency. Totally in control, intent on his task, he seemed to have forgotten she was there.

Somehow the picture struck her as very wrong.

The indolent, swarthy angles of his face had coalesced and sharpened into knife edges of concentration. Even in his casual short sleeves and jeans, he looked steady as a rock. Yet, she knew very well he was as unreliable as a man could be. Sitting there, his gaze fixed on the computer screen, he appeared dedicated and even dependable. When in reality, as he had just admitted not fifteen minutes ago, he was completely uninterested in commitment of any kind.

With a shake of her head, she dismissed the strange dichotomy of his appearance as wishful thinking. Talk about delusional.

She had to assume his lack of commitment included his job. He showed no signs of being concerned over not reporting in. "Don't you ever go to work?" she muttered, a bit testily.

"I am at work," he reminded her without looking up.

Walking to the file cabinet, she clamped her teeth. "You're looking for Gary Fox officially?"

"Yeah."

"I thought you said it was 'unfinished business.'"

"It is."

"Unfinished police business?"

A muscle ticked under his eye. "I can't say."

"But you're not going to arrest him," she recalled.

"Nope."

He held his face impassive and continued searching through the computer files as if their conversation weren't agitating him in the least. But she was a trained psychologist and knew all the signs. He was hiding something from her. Something big.

"So, what do you need him for?" she persisted.

Creole's fingers ground to a halt on the keys, and he looked positively murderous for a second, then the professional mien was back. "I'm investigating a homicide."

She saw a drop of sweat bead up on his temple, despite the air-conditioned temperature in the room. "Whose?" she pressed.

"Sorry. Can't discuss the case."

Just as she feared, he'd clammed up on her. "Can't or won't?" she snapped, unable to remain objective any longer, and yanked open a file drawer. "If he killed somebody, I have a right to know."

"And why's that?" His calm was infuriating.

"He may have kidnapped my sister!"

That brought him up short. *"Bien. C'est vrai."* He folded his arms across his chest and regarded her. "Okay. Fair enough."

Thank God.

His mouth went thin and menacing. "Gary Fox is small-time, nickel-bag scum who thinks he's a big shot because one of New Orleans' biggest crime lords, James Davies, lets him hang around with his gang. The Feds have been after Davies for years, for drug running and distribution, plus he's a suspect in a half dozen unsolved murders. Fox is strictly a gofer in the organization. Davies uses him to deliver messages and what have you. His most consistent job seems to be fetching Davies's café au lait and beignets every morning, no matter where he is. At least it was until two weeks ago."

She stared at Creole, incredulous. "Café au lait and beignets?"

"From Café du Monde." He shrugged. "Not a felony at this point, so we couldn't arrest him."

"But he stopped."

"Two weeks ago."

And Muse had vanished just a week later. A bit too much of a coincidence for Grace's comfort. "So why are you looking for Fox and not this Davies guy?"

"We are looking for Davies. Fox always knows where he is, in case there is a message from the trenches or beignets to deliver. I'm counting on Fox to lead me to him."

"But I don't see why—"

"Davies has gone underground. And he's very smart. Once he disappeared for two whole years. The Feds, the DEA, hell, every law enforcement agency in the country was looking for him, but they didn't find him until he was good and ready. After the only witness against him had suffered a mysterious accident. A fatal one."

Grace had a really bad feeling. "So what's changed? Has he done something else? Have you gotten new evidence against him?"

Creole turned back to the computer, and she could practically hear the doors slamming between them. "Can't talk about it," he said, his tone icy and final.

A visceral chill snaked down Grace's spine. Judging by

Creole's expression, James Davies had done something truly awful this time.

Her heart sank. Could Muse be mixed up with this horrible criminal? She'd only mentioned Gary Fox in passing in their phone conversations, until that last time, anyway, but there was no telling what Fox had been able to talk her into doing. Muse wasn't known for thinking things through. If it sounded exciting, she went for it.

But Muse had broken up with Gary Fox weeks ago.

Hadn't she?

Grace spent the whole morning and half the afternoon with Creole, poring over every computer file and bit of paper they could unearth in Muse's office. Creole found out some fairly interesting things about her sister hidden in the records of her Internet and e-mail archives, everything from online access for her bank account to correspondence with several persons of dubious backgrounds. Unfortunately, none of it shed any light on her disappearance. At least, that's what Grace hoped.

While it was possible Muse had set up a date with an Internet acquaintance, which had then ended badly, Grace doubted it. That would be just the sort of thing Muse would chatter on endlessly about over the phone, if she had been considering it. Muse enjoyed shocking her conservative sister. Besides, Creole appeared to know his way around computers pretty well, and he'd found no sign of any really suspicious e-mail exchanges.

Outrageous, yes. But not suspicious. Still, he'd jotted down the various repeat e-mail addresses and was going to give them to a friend of his who was good at finding out things on the Internet that no one else could. Just in case.

Over the past six hours of fruitless searching and waiting for a phone call that never came, Grace's creeping despair had been kept at bay only because of a growing confidence in the man working by her side.

After shutting down the computer, Creole rubbed the

palms of his hands over his eyes, which were rimmed with fatigue. A wisp of guilt floated through Grace before she batted it away. She couldn't help that he'd stayed up all night trying to figure out who she was. He should just have asked.

"Why don't you go home and take a nap?" she suggested softly. "You look ready to drop."

She went over to where he was leaning back in Muse's chair and without thinking scooted onto the desktop next to him. Her miniskirted dress rode way up her thighs, and she hopped off like a spark from a log, just before he wrenched his hands away from his face.

"I'm fine," he insisted.

Instinctively she reached over and brushed a short, black lock off his forehead, not taking it too personally when he turned away. He must still be furious with her.

"No, you're not." She smiled. "You haven't even glanced at my legs since I walked over here."

He returned her wry smile with just a touch of hesitation, and said, "*Dieu*, I must really be tired."

She chuckled and ran her fingertips down the side of his face, enjoying the feel of his warm skin under them, the hardness and hollows of his cheekbones, the soft creviced lines next to his eyes and mouth. He jerked back, leaving her hand suspended in the air.

From the depth of his eyes a strange hybrid of apology and alarm stared back at her. He seemed almost fearful of her touch. Strange. She curled her fingers into her palms and filed away his unusual reaction to analyze later. "We're done here. Go."

He dropped his lids, the thick lashes almost disappearing in the black smudges under his eyes. "What will you do?"

She moved away and started straightening the piles of files they'd left in disarray on the desk, to give herself something to do besides take him in her arms and let him rest his weary head on her shoulder. Even for someone who nurtured and healed people for a living, the need was so strong it scared her.

"There are a few stores I didn't get to yesterday," she answered him, carefully guiding her thoughts away from dangerous territory. "I'll go talk to the sales clerks and see if they remember anything."

"I should go with you."

"Not necessary."

"But—"

"I was by myself yesterday and did okay." She turned and found his gaze following her movements like a shadow. "Besides, I'll feel a lot safer if you are awake and alert tonight for Bourbon Street."

He sighed deeply and swiped his hand over his eyes again. She could tell he wanted to argue but couldn't find the flaw in her logic.

"*Bien*. But just for a couple of hours." He sighed again, aggravation at himself evident. "I can sit stakeouts for days with no sleep. I don't know what's with me today."

She chose not to think about the possibility that he'd been plagued with difficulty sleeping since the night they'd met, as she'd been. She'd found rest impossible, knowing he was just across the courtyard. Probably lurking on his balcony watching her.

As he was watching her now.

He always seemed to be watching her. She didn't mind admitting she found the sensation frightening. What she *did* mind admitting was that she also found it exciting. Unbelievably exciting.

"I have an idea," she blurted out, before she could heed the warning bells going off like crazy in her head. "About tonight. A way to get Fox's attention."

He raised a brow and laced his fingers over his stomach. "Yeah?"

"You know how I told you he didn't take it well when Muse broke up with him? And that she thought the blond guy might be him? Or someone working for him?"

"Uh-huh."

"I'll be pretending I'm Muse tonight on Bourbon Street, right?" He nodded patiently. "Well, I thought if you pretended to be my...that is, *Muse's* new boyfriend, and we really played it up, it might get back to Fox and he'd come after you."

Creole shot out of the chair, setting it spinning backward on its casters. "No!"

Shocked at the vehemence of his reaction, she gasped and tried to back away. "But—"

He grasped her arms. "No!" he repeated, and she was sure he would shake her to emphasize his point, but he just held her fast. "It's too dangerous," he said.

But there was something in the way he said it—too quickly, almost like an afterthought—that made her think it was just an excuse. That there was really some other reason he didn't want to pose as Muse's boyfriend. But what could it possibly be?

"Be practical," she urged. "You said yourself he's the only way you'll find this Davies character. Why not try my plan? Sure, it might not work, but it could. What do you have to lose?"

He stared at her as if she'd already lost her mind and was in danger of infecting him with her madness. "That's not the point."

"Then what is?"

His fingers tightened on her arms, then he dropped them. "It's just not a good idea. I won't do it. End of discussion."

"But—"

He closed his eyes, opened them and gave her a level look. "We'll do it the same way you handle the stores. You act like you're Muse and try to learn whatever you can from the people who recognize you in the bars. I'll be close by, in case you need me, watching."

Watching, always watching.

"I saw how everyone was taken in yesterday. You're

good at this impersonation stuff,'' he insisted. ''There's no need to do anything differently.''

She had major doubts about that, but it was obvious he'd dug in and was immovable on the subject.

All right, fine. If that's the way he wanted to play it, no problem. Her psychology skills had helped with her ruse, in getting people to trust her without even knowing she was putting them at ease. As well, it aided in filling in certain bits of her sister's personality with which Grace had little acquaintance. Creole wasn't necessary, anyway. He didn't seem to understand what it meant to be Muse. Grace did. And she planned to play Muse to the hilt, with or without his help. It was the only option.

If she didn't do something radical, and soon, she feared she'd be sitting in an empty apartment forever, waiting in vain for her sister to reappear. For, despite Creole's reassurances to the contrary, after the phone call that morning, Grace was more convinced than ever that something bad had happened to her twin. And in order to lure the responsible party out into the open, she'd have to make a huge splash.

Tonight, one way or another, she intended to do just that. And just pray whoever it was noticed.

A few minutes after nine o'clock, Grace glanced across the courtyard to Creole's apartment for the hundredth time in the past hour. He was still asleep.

He'd asked her to call and wake him at eight, but she hadn't had the heart. He'd looked so incredibly tired when they'd parted at Muse's office around four that afternoon.

She could see him through the window, sprawled across his unmade bed, lying on his stomach, presumably in the same position as when he'd hit the mattress after getting home. He hadn't even bothered to take off his shoulder holster, which was clearly visible against the stark white of his T-shirt, even from this distance. She didn't guess he'd moved so much as an eyebrow since she'd gotten back from her useless snooping at the stores. Poor baby.

Oh, well. He hadn't wanted any part of her plan, anyway. She could do this by herself. In fact, it would probably be easier without him watching her every move. Making her self-conscious.

Wondering what it would be like to go out on the town with a man like him. Uncivilized. Untamed. Able, with one glance from those meltingly sexy eyes, to make a woman feel like dancing till dawn and then making love until noon.

Wishing he wanted to be her boyfriend, even just pretending for one night.

Her eyes popped. *Where had that come from?*

The very last thing she needed was Creole getting ideas about being her boyfriend. It was bad enough he'd kissed her senseless and held her and tried to make her admit she wanted him.

Which she didn't. Truly.

She snapped herself out of her inappropriate thoughts and marched to the closet. She'd already showered and done her hair and put on more makeup than she'd used since the Halloween she was fourteen and had dressed up as Frankenstein's monster. With any luck she looked a little better tonight.

She flipped through the closet and settled for a short denim miniskirt and a bright-pink crop top. Very Muse, she decided after slipping on matching strappy shoes and examining herself in the mirror. With one last look at Creole's sleeping form across the courtyard, she grabbed a small, flamingo-shaped shoulder bag from the dresser and headed out the door.

Next stop, Bourbon Street.

Chapter 7

Creole woke slowly and stretched his stiff limbs till they cracked in the soft, silent darkness. He lifted a heavy eyelid, mildly amazed. It seemed he'd finally managed to get some much-needed rest.

For a second he couldn't figure out what could have made him relax enough to fall into a dead sleep after so many months of tossing and turning. But then he remembered.

Grace.

He rose groggily and peered across the courtyard at her apartment, a reluctant smile coming to his lips. *Jolie* Grace Summerville. Pretty as a sunrise and smart as a swamp cat. And just as determined as a hungry gator to find that sister of hers—if she had to set the whole Quarter on its ear to do it. And she just might, at that.

He didn't spot her right away, and figured she was in the bathroom getting ready for their expedition tonight. Best he see to getting ready himself—it was already dark out so she must have let him sleep a bit longer than they'd planned.

He jumped in the shower and afterward tugged on jeans, replaced his holster over his still-damp skin, and covered up with a loose, Miami-style pineapple shirt. When he was tying his shoes he suddenly realized he still hadn't seen Grace.

He froze in midloop, a multitude of unpleasant possibilities rocketing through his mind, until it fastened on the one that was the most plausible.

She'd gone without him. *Quelle bêtise!* The little fool.

He ground out a string of epithets, stuffed his tobacco pouch in his shirt pocket and jammed his cuffs and wallet into a pocket. Then, since he'd be drinking tonight, he slid the Glock's clip into his other pocket. And sent up a quick prayer that she was unharmed.

Incroyable. He couldn't believe it. He just couldn't believe it. He'd given her strict instructions to wake him. Not to leave without him.

They were working together. They had a plan.

A plan....

"Ah, *non.*" Groaning, he shot out the door and headed for Bourbon Street. He should have known. He'd nixed her little boyfriend scheme and she'd decided to work solo instead.

Or maybe this was her way of getting even with him for saying no to her idea. Women didn't like it when a man said no.

As he hurried down the narrow streets, hoping against hope he'd run into her before she got lost in the tangle of bars and tourists that packed the main strip, he silently berated himself. He saw all too clearly what had happened, as evidenced by the way he'd been able to sleep the sleep of an innocent babe relying on his mother's presence to keep him safe.

In a moment of weakness he'd actually trusted Grace.

But he knew firsthand that mothers weren't always there

when a baby woke up crying. And he hadn't yet met a woman who could be trusted. Not completely. Not with your life. Or your heart. Certainly, Miz Summerville had proven she couldn't be trusted with either.

How had it happened that he'd let down his guard so easily, in spite of everything she'd done?

Because he wasn't thinking, that's how.

At least not with his brain.

He groaned again and whipped around the corner onto Bourbon Street, expecting the worst.

He was not disappointed.

The raucous old street teemed with people. Like a herd of brightly dotted locusts, they swarmed along the narrow thoroughfare carrying a wild assortment of plastic and foam go-cups. The night was sweltering. Tourists and natives alike were clad in as little as they could get away with. Creole was glad he'd forsaken the usual T-shirt under his looser shirt, which allowed air to waft up beneath it providing an occasional puff of relief from the heat. He could use some cooling down.

A heady scent of sweet daiquiris and sweaty, perfumed bodies permeated the air, along with the usual Friday-night Quarter smells of frying seafood, rotting garbage and a trace of Mississippi River mud. Music blasted from every bar and restaurant lining the street, a cacophonous mix of zydeco, rock, blues and God knew what that other stuff was supposed to be, all at a volume that required people to shout to be heard over it, just adding to the general din.

But Creole wouldn't change any of it. Not for the world. He loved the Quarter and all its eccentricities and sinful excess. It was a place a man could surround himself with the crush of humanity in all its forms and yet be untouched and alone if he chose, simply melting into the crowd and enjoying the ever-changing scene. It was one of the few places he felt at home. Relaxed. Unthreatened.

Normally.

But the sight that greeted him as he skirted a big knot of people clustered under the balcony of a popular dance bar sent his blood pressure straight into orbit.

The crowd outside swayed and pulsed to the beat of a rock band playing inside the bar. Several women danced with each other in the center of the group, to the appreciation of male onlookers. Grace was right there in the middle of it. Naturally.

Creole stepped back to the opposite side of the street, away from the throng, and climbed the shallow steps of a restaurant for a better view. Immediately he knew just what was going on.

His hackles rose at the sound of enthusiastic masculine clapping and hungry wolf calls, and even more at the clickety-clack of Mardi Gras necklaces being rattled, dangling from eager male fingers over the rail of the packed balcony. He knew very well what the men wanted. The show they expected to see. One that Muse had obviously given them many times before.

But would Grace?

He rolled a cigarette and told himself to calm down. She had no choice but to play along. He himself had forced her into this role by rejecting her other plan. But that knowledge didn't calm him. For some reason it only made him angrier.

He'd told her no because he'd thought it would be too hard to masquerade as her boyfriend. To dance with her, flirt with her, put his arms around her, kiss her like he meant it—all for the sake of the investigation—and then have to take her to her door and leave her there, knowing she'd never let things go any further than that. Knowing she'd never allow him to follow her in and back her slowly onto that big, satin-sheeted bed, cover her with his body, taste her desire. And make love to her all night long.

But this was worse. Much worse. Dammit, he didn't

want those other men leering at her. Pawing her. Offering their cheap bounty for a glimpse of her sweet flesh.

Funny, he'd never realized before what a stupid, barbaric custom it was, bribing women to bare their breasts in exchange for a handful of gaudy glass beads.

He took a deep drag of harsh tobacco smoke. *Dieu.* He had to get ahold of himself. Grace didn't look as if she objected to the prospect of showing her charms to all and sundry. Maybe the innocence he'd sensed in her was all an act. It wouldn't be the first time he'd been fooled by a woman.

She was moving her whole body to the music, laughing and throwing coquettish glances at the men along with the other women, and lapping up the undivided attention they were getting from all sides. She squealed in delight when her companion lifted her T-shirt to reveal her bare midriff and was rewarded with a small shower of necklaces and encouraging whistles.

Creole clenched his fists, his cigarette snapping in two. He felt an all-too-familiar sting of pain and flicked it to the pavement. As if caught in a nightmare, he watched a second woman tear off her top and twirl around in a full circle to give everyone an eyeful before slipping it back on over her naked breasts. The crowd went crazy. Creole saw Grace falter in her dance and stare at the woman wide-eyed. But then she was back in the rhythm, and he figured he must have misinterpreted the momentary shock in her expression.

"Muse! Muse! Muse!" the crowd chanted expectantly, all eyes riveted on Grace. Creole's mouth suddenly tasted of bile, but he couldn't force himself to look away.

Then she saw him. Her gaze fastened on his and for a split second he swore he saw a look of fear and dismay in her eyes. That she would break free of the mass of grasping male hands and run to him.

It was only then it dawned on him. She had *no idea* about this quaint little custom of *au sauvage. Damn.*

But before he could move, something stopped her where she stood. Her eyes went blank and her chin lifted. She grasped the hem of her too-short, neon-pink top and jerked it up, revealing a lacy black bra and its contents to everyone looking. Her gaze never left his as necklaces were flung at her from all directions.

He felt a drop of something warm and wet on his fingers and realized he'd dug them into the rough brick of the wall behind him. Pain stabbed through his fingertips but they wouldn't release.

"Hey, Muse!" a long-haired man yelled, and grabbed drunkenly at Grace's shirt, which she finally pulled down. "Since when do you wear a bra?"

The other men surrounding her took up the chant, shouting for her to take it off, obviously fully expecting her to do so.

This time he could plainly see panic flood Grace's face.

He wasn't even aware he'd moved. Suddenly he was at her side, pulling her against him, a possessive arm snaking around her body.

"She wears a bra since I told her to," he snarled at the man, ready to do battle for his woman. "You got a problem with that?"

Grace melted into Creole's arms, never more glad to be rescued in her entire life.

Not that she'd ever actually *been* rescued before in her entire life.

It felt good. Unbelievably good. She'd thought she could pull off tonight's investigation alone, but she sure hadn't counted on this last bit of nonsense. Good grief. To think they'd actually expected her to—

"Hell, no," the pest who'd been hanging on to her shirt assured Creole, backing off at his aggressive posture. "I don't have a problem with that."

"But the lady's boyfriend might have a thing or two to

say about it,'' a greasy-looking punk called from behind the pest.

The punk's threatening smirk yanked her back to reality.

''*This is* the lady's boyfriend,'' she corrected him, and plastered herself to Creole's chest.

Heck, she had no problem changing horses in midstream if it got her out of taking off her shirt in front of a horde of drooling morons. And especially if it enticed Gary Fox out of hiding, which it looked like it just might do.

''I missed you, baby,'' she cooed up at Creole, winding her arms around his neck. She gave him a big, wet kiss— to make it clear what she was doing. And also to knock him off stride. In case he was still miffed. She hadn't forgotten that murderous look he'd given her from across the street. ''Where've you been, sugar?''

''Right where you left me, darlin'. Asleep in bed,'' he returned. ''You shouldn' have done that, *chère*. I didn' like waking up without you.''

Then he kissed her back. For the benefit of the witnesses, of course. But real enough to curl her toes. He speared his fingers through her hair, holding her head immobile, and covered her mouth with his. She could feel the suppressed anger in the spring-loaded muscles of his hands, his body, his probing tongue. Anger…and something more.

Jealousy?

An unexpected thrill chased up her spine. She parted her lips and let him claim and plunder, soothing his male pride with the only balm she knew would help—surrender.

''Think we convinced him?'' he murmured when he finally lifted his mouth from hers.

''Convinced *me*,'' she answered shakily, clinging to him for fear she'd slide to the pavement if he let her go. *Sweet heavens.* They watched the punk shake his head, muttering something about somebody not liking it, and lumber away. ''I think I need a drink. A big one.''

''Don' ever do that again,'' Creole said, and let her go. She assumed he didn't mean the kiss. It was all he needed to say. The look on his face told her he'd make sure she didn't, even if she had other ideas.

"I won't." Surprisingly, she meant it. "I've learned my lesson."

"Bien." He gave her another quick, intense kiss. *"Vien.* Let's go get that drink."

When they turned to go into the bar, one of the onlookers lurched toward them. "Hey, buddy, you're bleedin'!" he exclaimed, sloshing his beer at Creole's hand. He peered at his cup, then deliberately sloshed some more, rinsing the blood from Creole's fingertips. "There, thatottadoowit," he slurred with a satisfied nod, and tottered away.

Creole shook the remaining drops off his fingers. "Thanks. I think."

Grace frowned and reached for his hand. "How did that happen?"

"Doesn' matter," he said, wiping it on his jeans. He slung his arm around her, and she felt the hard, distinctive shape of his gun prod her shoulder.

She jumped away. "Do you always carry that thing?" she protested, glaring at the subtle bulge below his armpit.

"Always."

She let him pull her back under his arm and lead her into the bar, but tried to avoid contact with the warm metal, which, of course, turned out to be impossible. It rubbed up against her, almost as if he was teasing her with it.

"Even to bed?" she asked without thinking, mortified as soon as the words had left her lips.

"Yep."

She remembered him sprawled across his bed, the holster hugging his side like a lover. "Doesn't it get in the way?"

"Mais, non. Women, they think it's exciting."

Heat rose in her cheeks. "That's not what I meant."

He grinned at her discomfort. "I take it off in the shower." He gave an unrepentant shrug. "Since you're so interested in my personal habits."

They'd shouldered their way to the bar by now, and Creole ordered without consulting her. She scowled at his back, resenting the annoying chauvinist habit. But he ignored her censure when he swung back to her, waiting for the barkeep's return.

He leaned his butt against the bar and crossed his arms over his chest. "You don't find the idea exciting?"

"Huh?"

"My gun," he prompted.

"Oh." She wasn't sure to which idea he was referring— him in the shower without his gun or him in bed with it. "Actually, I find the idea kind of strange. Why would anyone want to wear a gun to bed?" she asked, choosing the less graphic visual.

The corner of his lip curled in a disreputable half smile. But before he could answer, the drinks arrived, two large white foam cups with straws sticking out. One concoction was brown and one was pink.

"Milk shakes?"

He handed her the brown one and pulled her to the back of the room, where the music wasn't blasting quite so loudly. "Not milk shakes. Daiquiris."

"If you say so." She couldn't recall ever seeing a brown daiquiri that she could remember. She took an experimental sip. It was delicious. All chocolate and creamy but with a little kick. She took another sip.

"Look out, here we go," he whispered in her ear.

"Muse!" A voluptuous woman in hot pants approached them and hugged her enthusiastically. "Where have you been, girl? Haven't seen you in weeks!" She looked Creole up and down with obvious approval. "Never mind, hon, I can guess." She winked, gave her a kiss on the cheek, rubbed the glossy lipstick print off, said, "See y'all 'round," and sashayed away into the crowd, gone before Grace could get a word in edgewise.

"Handled that well, I thought," she said wryly, to Creole's amused chuckle.

"Don' worry. I doubt she could have told us anythin', anyway."

It turned out all they had to do was stand there sipping their drinks on the fringe of the dance floor, and people of all ages, sizes, sexes and descriptions stopped to say hi to "Muse" and exchange a few words with Grace's apparently very popular sister.

After a half dozen or so had come by, she felt considerably more relaxed in her role of impostor. Her psychologist expertise wasn't even needed to pull it off. She greeted strangers like old friends, flirting with the men, who took one look at Creole and rethought whatever they'd had in mind, and hugging and exchanging conspiratorial winks and giggles with the women, who gazed at him with open envy.

She found she was enjoying being the center of attention for once. Especially Creole's. He never let her forget he was there, keeping an arm around her waist or his hands on her shoulders as she leaned back against his chest. Occasionally he bent down and nibbled on her neck or her earlobe as she spoke to some other man. She especially liked that. She played it up, encouraging him with her appreciative responses to linger at his task. To make their involvement together…that is, their *pretended* involvement together, unmistakable.

For the benefit of the witnesses.

"I wanna dance," he murmured after a particularly obnoxious man had been persuaded to leave her alone. Creole took her cup—which to her surprise was empty—and tossed it along with his own onto the tray of a passing waitress. *"Vien."*

She raised her brows when he bypassed the dance floor and led her out into the street. "Um…"

He was holding her hand so she had no choice but to follow him into a smaller establishment a few doors down, where a different kind of music was playing. Not that she would have objected to moving on. She didn't particularly care for the loud, belligerent rock of the previous place.

"Let's get another one of those milk shake things," she suggested as they passed the service bar. It seemed everyone always had a cup in their hand in the Quarter, and she felt underdressed without one.

He grinned. "All right. What's your favorite fruit?"

"Bananas," she answered promptly, then smiled suggestively.

The look on his face was priceless. Well worth the blush that ripped across her cheeks at her uncharacteristic boldness. Being Muse for a day must have affected her brain.

When their drinks came, he handed one to her without comment and pulled her onto the tiny dance floor where couples drifted to the sounds of a soft, bluesy combo.

Sipping her drink, she nestled into his arms. "This is nice," she said, meaning the romantic music.

But the milk shake, er, daiquiri, was nice, too.

And his arms.

"Mmm-hmm."

They tightened around her. She could feel every contour of his muscled body as he held her close. His chest, his legs, his thighs, his— Oh, dear, there was that gun again.

With her free hand, she circled his neck, toying absently with his hair. She smiled. He smelled so-o-o good. And dancing was so-o-o relaxing.

"Very nice."

Gently he grasped her straying hand and pulled it down behind her. Braiding his fingers with hers, he held it between his palm and her bottom. Kind of an unusual dance position, but she didn't object.

She didn't object, either, when his lips sought hers. Soft, warm, sweet, they caressed her slowly, the taste of him spinning like cotton candy through her giddy senses.

As he held her hand, his fingers started roaming, playing over the contours of her panties outlined under her skirt.

That was kind of nice, too.

It was all kind of nice.

Everything about him was kind of nice.

In fact, much *too* nice.

"I'm not going to sleep with you, you know," she said, more to remind herself than him, and therefore was vaguely startled that she'd actually spoken the words out loud.

His fingers paused, then resumed their wandering. "*Mais,* yeah. I remember. You don' want your heart walked all over, and you think I will."

"Right," she affirmed, nodding gravely for emphasis. She licked her lips, wishing he'd kiss her again.

"You're only letting me kiss you and hold you because it's in the plan. Part of our investigation strategy," he murmured into her ear.

"That's exactly right." She exhaled with relief, glad he understood so perfectly. She snuggled a bit closer to his chest. "Strategy."

"But I wouldn', you know."

"Wouldn't what?"

"Walk all over your heart."

She thought about that as they swayed together, trying to decide why he'd say such a ridiculous thing. To trick her into sleeping with him, no doubt. Well, she wasn't that dumb. Despite what his mind-numbing kisses were doing to her ability to think rationally.

"Right," she repeated with a roll of her eyes, and laid her head on his shoulder. She sighed. He had such a nice, comfy shoulder.

A strange female voice intruded on her dreamy contemplation of his anatomy. "Jell-O shooter?" it asked.

"Excuse me?" Grace disentangled herself from Creole and blinked at the waitress who carried a huge, simply huge, tray of plastic shot glasses filled with suspiciously jiggly red stuff.

"Um, okay," she said, and peered at her milk shake, which strangely enough was empty again. Huh. She handed it to Creole and accepted a small glass from the waitress.

While she was trying to figure out how to drink the silly thing, he dropped their empty cups into a nearby trash can and took two of the shooters from the smiling waitress. Grace scowled at her, and she went away. Ha.

"Bottoms up," Creole said, and she watched, fascinated, as he dipped his tongue into the shallow glass and scooped up the contents with it. The red globule slid languidly down the length of his talented tongue, disappearing into the depths of his deliciously sinful mouth. A queer feeling heated the pit of her stomach at the sight. Like she wished she could follow it in there and explore the pleasures it was experiencing, melting in the moist, cavernous heat of his body.

No, this would not do at all.

She shook off the wicked impulse and mimicked his motions. She giggled, squishing the gelatin between her teeth before swallowing it. This was rather fun. But it hit her like a locomotive. "Lord have mercy, that stuff's strong!"

He waggled his eyebrows and downed his second.

She giggled again and admonished him, "We'd better get back to work. Maybe we should try another place."

"All right," he agreed, and they threaded their way out onto the street again.

Outside, it was still sultry, but not as close as it had been in the bar. She took in a deep breath, smelling the damp, musky fecundity of the night air. She'd always loved the summer heat. Folks in Charleston left the city in droves during the hot season, but Grace thrived in the warmth and humidity. At school they made jokes about her hot-blooded nature, but that's just what they were—jokes.

They had no idea.

And she had no intention of telling them.

Hand in hand she strolled with Creole along Bourbon Street, stopping every few yards when one of Muse's scores of acquaintances hailed them to exchange greetings and check out Creole. Unfortunately, they all wondered what she'd been up to for the past week, which was no help at all. Grace would have been disappointed, if not for the fact that she could plainly see that she and her "new boyfriend" were creating quite a sensation tonight. If this plan to lure Muse's jealous ex out of hiding didn't work, nothing would.

In between conversations they sampled several more of those milk shake things and listened to band after band playing a wonderful variety of music. When the mood struck, they danced.

And kissed.

Grace told herself she shouldn't be so eager to feel his mouth on hers. She really shouldn't encourage him.

Because it was only part of The Plan.

For the benefit of the witnesses, she reminded herself for the hundredth time.

Not because she loved Creole's kisses.

Even though she did. A lot.

She loved the way his lips moved sensually from one corner of her mouth to the other, painting the seam with his tongue, gently seeking entry, then arousing her to the point of dizziness with the erotic, velvet way he tasted every inch and corner of her all-too-willing mouth.

But it had nothing to do with that.

Nope. Nothing at all.

Swallowing, she jerked to a halt in front of a narrow shop filled with T-shirts, Mardi Gras masks and voodoo dolls. Creole glanced at her questioningly.

"It's not that I wouldn't *like* to sleep with you," she clarified, as if an hour or two hadn't passed since her first declaration on the subject.

He looked surprised for a second, then his face went carefully serious. "I know. But I'm not the type of man you want."

"Well, not exactly," she hedged, swinging Muse's flamingo purse back and forth like a pendulum. Maybe she could hypnotize herself and really *become* Muse. That might solve a few insurmountable problems.

He was looking at her expectantly, so she added, "It's more like you're *precisely* the kind of man I want."

His brows disappeared into his scalp. She smiled, tasting him on her lips.

"No, you don't understand," she continued. "I'm hopeless. I always fall for men like you. The *wrong* kind. Handsome bad boys who'll only leave me and break my heart into little pieces. Just like my father. You see? I have to avoid them, er, you."

His jaw dropped, and he gazed at her, as if deciding which bizarre statement to respond to first.

Oh, brother. She held up a hand before he could decide. She couldn't believe she'd said that stuff about bad boys and her father. He probably thought she was a prissy little prune with an Oedipus complex.

"Anyway," she said, turning determinedly to continue marching down the street. Except she was having a hard time marching at the moment. Her feet seemed to have acquired minds of their own and refused to do more than amble alongside Creole's dependable guiding footsteps. "Anyway... Darn, what was I saying?"

"That you'd like to sleep with me."

She darted him a glance, certain he was laughing at her, but his face was perrrfectly sober...er, somber. "Yes," she said, striving to retrieve the lost threads of her original point. "But you'd only get bored and leave me, and I'd get hurt, so it's just not a good idea to sleep with you. Even if I'd like to."

"I see." He steadied her when the sidewalk inexplicably altered positions under her feet, and said, "I don't suppose it would do me any good to point out that it'll actually be *you* who will leave *me* when we find your sister and you decide to go home?"

That stumped her for a moment. The argument was just a li-i-ttle too logical. It had to be another one of his tricks.

"No," she said, as her fuzzy mind scrambled to find the flaw. "No," she repeated firmly when she couldn't find any. But she knew it had to be there somewhere. How could *she* ever leave someone as delectable as Creole Levalois? It was unthinkable.

"My drink is empty again," she announced, waving it like a banner of distraction. It was those darn small cups he'd been insisting on since they'd finished the first two big ones. He *said* it was so she could try different flavors, but she suspected he was afraid she might become inebriated.

She snorted derisively. As if.

He obliged her with another thimbleful of icy concoction from a take-out bar—purple this time. She'd given up a while back trying to guess the flavors, just enjoying the way the slippery liquid cooled her parched throat going down. And the mellow way they made her feel.

She thanked him politely and watched him toss back a whole bottle of plain water without taking a breath. His square jaw tilted up, drops of sparkling silver spilling over his lips and chin and running over his Adam's apple. She had the strangest urge to lean over and lick them off.

She swiped her tongue over her parched lips.

Mercy, he was handsome.

"I suppose I could sleep with you."

Immediately, she slapped her hand over her mouth. She had definitely not planned to say *that* aloud. She just couldn't understand what had gotten into her tonight.

He pinned her with a searching look and slowly wiped his chin with the back of his hand. She was powerless to move a muscle, unless it was to dissolve a little when he said, "I'd like that."

She felt herself in danger of melting all over the sidewalk. She reached out and pulled herself over to a nearby wrought iron gate, leaning against it for support.

"That is…" she backpedaled, suddenly scared to death. "That is, if you really promise I can be the one who walks all over *your* heart and leaves *you.*"

"That's a virtual certainty," he said dryly. But she didn't

get a chance to ponder the sardonic bite to his tone. Because just then two men walked up and stopped right behind them.

One of them was holding a gun.

Chapter 8

At the sudden shock that leapt into Grace's eyes, Creole spun around. And came face-to-face with a 9mm Beretta semiautomatic.

He slowly raised his hands so the two men behind the gun could see them, and eased himself in front of Grace. He didn't reach for his Glock, because he knew the weapon wouldn't do him any good. The clip was in his pocket, which was his rule anytime he was drinking.

Besides, one look at these two guys told him they weren't your average druggies out to cover the day's expenses courtesy of a couple of unsuspecting tourists.

He kept his mouth shut, waiting for them to make the first move.

"So," said the first guy—the one not holding the Beretta. He wore a blazer, despite the stifling heat, so Creole figured Mr. Cool just hadn't bothered to draw whatever weapon was hidden under it. That could be a good sign. That plus the fact that Creole wasn't already splattered all over the sidewalk.

"So," Mr. Cool repeated casually. Too casually for a guy toting a gun. Damn, this was serious. "What exactly are you two playing at?"

Grace took a wobbly step to come out from behind him, and he moved with her, blocking her path.

"Hey!" she groused.

"Just out having a good time with my woman," Creole answered Mr. Cool equally casually, ignoring Grace's irritated shove at his back. "What are *you* playing at?" He glanced pointedly at the Beretta, which was quickly lowered and stowed in a holster under the second guy's jacket.

Just as he thought.

"If you know what's good for you, you'll take *your woman* right back where she came from, and stay there until you're sure nobody comes after her. And if I have a mess to clean up after this little stunt tonight, I'll be the first person you'd better watch out for, *Detective Levalois.*"

Behind him he heard Grace gasp, echoing his own surprise at hearing his name come out of the man's mouth. He took a step forward. "Just who the hell are you?"

"Doesn't matter. What matters is that we know who *she* is, and she *ain't* Muse Summerville." The man's expression went all triumphant, as if that bit of news would come as some kind of shock to Creole.

"Where is she?" Grace yelled, bursting out from behind him before he could stop her.

"Grace, take it easy," he ordered, grabbing her as she was about to launch herself at Mr. Cool.

"What have you done with my sister?"

The man's eyes narrowed as he looked back and forth between them. Grace's struggles were surprisingly forceful, but he hung on, all the while watching the two strangers for a sign of trouble from that end.

None came. Instead, he detected a flash of sympathy as Mr. Cool said, "She's safe and unharmed. For now. But what you did tonight may have put her—and yourself—in some serious jeopardy, Miss Summerville. My advice would be to get out of town. Fast.'' He turned to Creole. ''As for you, Detective, I'll be speaking with your captain. I imagine he'll be real interested in what you've been doing on your so-called 'leave of absence.'''

With that the two men turned and vanished into the crowd faster than he could blink.

''Damn,'' he muttered.

Grace had stopped wriggling and now turned to stare at him with wide eyes. ''Creole? What does it all mean?''

He hugged her to his chest, only now noticing the way his hands shook. ''It means you can stop worrying about your sister. Muse is safe.''

''How do you know for sure? Who were they? Do you trust them?'' Her words all ran together in her eagerness to be reassured.

''FBI, I expect,'' he said in answer to all three questions.

''FBI?'' she echoed, pulling away with a stunned expression. She gave a nervous hiccup. ''I don't understand. What makes you think they're FBI?''

Biting back the reasons he really wanted to name, he said, ''The haircuts, jackets and weapons are always a dead giveaway.''

Not to mention the threat to turn him in to the captain. He jetted out a breath, worried. He'd gladly sacrifice his job to find Luke's killer, but he wasn't even close yet. He needed more time—time with a badge in his pocket.

''After a while as a cop, you learn to recognize the signs,'' he added, when she didn't look completely convinced. ''They're Feds. Trust me.''

Her arms came around him again and she whispered, ''I do trust you.''

She sighed against his chest, and something twanged in the vicinity of his heart. Like a steel wire snapping. His heart stretched and swelled a little where one of the many tight bands surrounding it had been broken by this extraordinary, unlikely woman.

''I can trust the FBI, right?'' She looked up at him, hope

shining from deep within. "I can't imagine what Muse has gotten herself into, but... Oh, Creole, she's alive and safe! If the FBI says she's okay, it has to be true!"

He smiled at her beaming face, hiding the confusion creeping into his soul. "*Mais,* yeah, *chérie.* I'm sure you can trust what they say. Every word."

"Thank God." He caught her when she stumbled a little. "I think I need to sit down." Laughing, she fanned her face with a hand. "All this excitement, or something."

"Or somethin'." He chuckled and glanced around, then fiddled with a lock on the wrought iron gate behind her for a second and pushed it open. The brick path it revealed disappeared into a dark, ribbon-thin courtyard between two ancient buildings. "There's a bench in here. But just for a minute. It's late and I really should be gettin' you into bed."

A sudden crackle of electricity charged the air as his words echoed softly around the tiny private garden they'd entered. It was only a few square feet of lush foliage surrounded by mossy brick buildings on three sides, so he couldn't miss the way she paused on her way to the bench, and turned her limpid blue eyes on him.

He hadn't meant it the way it had come out. Not that he didn't also mean it the way she'd taken it. But he hadn't dared hope she was serious when she'd said all that earlier, about sleeping with him. He knew only too well her feelings on the subject. And on him.

At least he thought he did....

"Come over here, baby," she said in that honey-sweet South Carolina accent of hers that always sent his body into slow spirals of yearning. She held out her hands to him. Smiling. Beckoning.

Suddenly he was scared witless. And he knew with dead certainty he shouldn't get even an inch closer to her.

He shook his head and backed himself up against the brick wall behind him. "No, Grace. Now that you've found out Muse is safe, you'll be leaving. This can only end badly. For both of us."

Dropping her hands, she gazed at him for a few, endless seconds, and his heart sank, knowing she could only come to the same conclusion. She tipped her head and walked toward him, coming to a stop an arm's length away.

Might as well be a million miles.

"There's just one li'l bitty thing wrong with your theory, sugar," she drawled, bringing her finger to the top button of his shirt.

"What's that?" he answered in a voice that had gone stranglingly hoarse. This was the second time she'd repeated his own words back at him. Damn, did the woman remember everything he'd ever said to her? She moved to the second button. "What you say is true. We both know it is. This can only end badly for us."

Close enough. He licked his lips, terrified to hear what he knew was coming next.

"But—" she touched the third "—I want you anyway."

Oh, God. *"Chère—"*

"Hush."

She pressed up against his body, and kissed him. Put her lush mouth on his and begged for entrance with her supplicant tongue. He could no more deny her than he could stop the tidal wave of desire that flooded over him at her actions.

He let her kiss him, moaning her name over and over as he gave himself up to the exquisite, dizzying sensation of being wanted beyond reason.

She wanted him. He wanted her. What else was there to say?

It was just sex, he told himself.

Just sex.

She tasted of a dozen flavors of daiquiri and a tang of Jell-O. But under the fruit and the cream and the liquor, he found the taste he wanted to lose himself in—Grace's own heady essence of woman, desire, longing…trust. All rolled into one intoxicating nectar.

A rough, impatient male sound fought free of his throat,

and she caught his hands in hers just as he meant to grasp her, claim her, take her.

His pulse raced, but he knew without being told she didn't want him to move.

Her fingers trailed to his wrists and drifted slowly up his forearms. Instinctively he stiffened, his own fingers curling to tight fists. His lips stalled on hers, hot and moist, and his breath came in a deep gasp. *She was touching him.*

He looked at her, teetering right on the edge of panic, but her lashes rested on her cheeks, an expression of profound enjoyment on her face. Her hands continued to glide up his arms, raising a rash of gooseflesh.

Heaven help him.

He squeezed his eyes shut and let her continue, his already abused fingernails jamming into his fisted palms.

He could bear it. He could. Just for a few seconds.

For her.

Her touch was soft and delicate, worshiping. Sliding over his tough hide like cool silk. Massaging a profound need into every pore as she went. He fought back the insistent urge to stop her any way he could.

Up, up, with questing fingers she weighed and measured every cord and muscle of his arms, lingering on the contours of the rock-hard biceps he'd built up over years of punching sandbags and rookies at the gym. No one had ever touched him so tenderly, so…lovingly.

He swallowed hard. He'd never felt anything so torturous in all his born days. Her hands on him felt so good. So good he almost forgot he couldn't bear being touched. Almost.

To cover his confusion, he dove back into the kiss. He jerked his hands to her hips and pulled her tight into him. Into his aching need. Angling his mouth over hers completely, he sucked at her succulent lips, tangled her tongue with his, desperately wooing her attention back to their mouths. Anything to make her stop.

It seemed to work. Her hands abandoned his arms and grasped at his shoulders. As they did, one bumped against the Glock. A small sound of protest escaped into his mouth. His heart skipped a beat thinking she might remember who he was, what he was, and pull away. But her hands settled lightly on his chest and he silently thanked every saint he could remember from the few times he'd been dragged to church as a child.

Then her fingers started working their voodoo down the front of his torso. Desperately he thrust his tongue even deeper into her mouth. She whimpered. He wanted to whimper, too. This was too much! More than he'd bargained for. He couldn't—

Suddenly he felt his shirt lift, and her fingers curled onto his bare flesh. He froze, wrenching his eyes open.

The innocent eroticism of her movements paralyzed him before he could even think to pull away. Her fingers inched up his chest, accompanied by a hard wave of gooseflesh from the tips of his toes to the top of his scalp.

Her shy exploration stunned him, caught him by complete surprise. The undemanding gentleness of her movements soothed and appeased the burning coil in his stomach, the acid aversion to being touched, which threatened to erupt and consume him. Her lips brushed against his. The goodness, the rightness of her, took his breath away.

Unaware of his inner chaos, she continued to kiss him and hesitantly slide her fingers along his waistband. He forced himself to stand still for her, lulled into a sense of trust he'd never before experienced with any woman. With anyone at all, except Luke. His heart pounded like he was running a high-speed pursuit.

But suddenly he didn't know who was the pursuer and who was being chased.

She didn't feel like a woman who would betray him.

He could be wrong. Hell, he'd been wrong often enough for two lifetimes. But she'd made it clear she didn't want to be doing this any more than he did, and yet here she was, doing it anyway.

Just like him.

He swallowed the thick lump of panic that crouched in his throat and tried to relax. But he couldn't. The feel of her warm, smooth hands sliding up and down his chest was setting him on fire. Filling him with a crazy desire to rip off his shirt and his holster and let her touch him wherever she wanted, for as long as she got pleasure from it. To let her strip him naked and trail those satin hands and velvet lips and clever tongue all over his body, making slow, sinuous love to him right here in this small patch of paradise, for hours and hours, day after day, until all his doubts and suspicions and the hurts of a lifetime melted away like ice in her hot little mouth.

His body shuddered, and he realized she had her hands far up his chest. Her nails scraped softly against male nipples that had never known such scorching pleasure before this very moment.

He groaned and grabbed her wrists.

Non! He had to stop this. Get control of her. Of the situation. *Of himself.* Before she crept under his skin, into his heart, and was able to betray him, like they always did.

"Stop!"

And he had to tell her about…everything.

"Stop," he repeated, slowly letting out the breath that had backed up in his lungs.

Her lashes fluttered open, and she stared at him with sensual, heavy-lidded eyes. He pulled her wrists behind her and pinned them there, leaning back against the brick wall for support, pulling her between his legs. He swallowed again, sorting through the anarchy that ran rampant in his mind and his body.

She tipped her face up to his, and he rested his cheek against her forehead.

"Before this goes any further, I need to explain. There are a few things you've got to know about me."

"I already do," she softly replied. "You don't like being touched."

Shock rippled through him. "How did you…?"

She smiled tenderly. "Wild guess." A mischievous twinkle crept into her eyes and she wiggled her fingers, still caught in his grip. "You aren't going to make it easy on me, are you, *A-U-R-I* Levalois?"

He knew he shouldn't allow this to happen. For her sake. For his own. But he wanted her so damned badly. Ah, hell, what could one night hurt? If she was okay with...everything. He let her wrists go.

He shook his head and gave her a wry grin. "Nothin' about Creole Levalois is easy, *chère,* especially this part of him. Best resign yourself to that if you intend to go through with this."

"Then, I suppose *I'll* just have to be easy instead, for tonight." She winked at him and his soul leapt.

"I can live with that."

"So, is it just hands?" Her pert brow raised, and for a second he couldn't think what she meant. "Or do you dislike any body part touching you?" She traced her finger nonchalantly between her breasts.

For another second he couldn't think at all, then choked out, "Hands. Just hands. Fingers are the worst. Other parts are...f-fine. I usually use handcuffs when I—"

She looked momentarily shocked, but then a coquettish smile spread over her lush mouth. "That should be interesting."

She backed away from him, moving toward the gate, encouraging him with her eyes to follow.

"And don't pull my hair. It makes me nuts."

She pursed her full lips. "Okay. I'll remember that."

There was something different about her. Something he couldn't put a name to. Something...incredibly provocative. She watched him stand there uncertainly, seducing him with those slumberously sexy doe eyes.

He knew just which part of his body was leading him on, but there was no way he could resist her siren call, even if he'd wanted to. And he didn't want to.

Just sex.

"No strings?"

"No strings."

He took a step toward her, and she took one backward. Another. And another. Until she tumbled out the gate, giggling and squealing in mock terror, with him hot on her heels.

He chased her the whole way to Burgundy Street, catching her, kissing her, losing her again. They ran laughing through their courtyard and stumbled up her stairway, until the door of her apartment presented a momentary blockade to their impatient hunger. Breathless, she fumbled for her key, but before she could even unzip her purse he had the lock jimmied and the door open, and was backing her toward the bedroom, kissing her madly, tossing her purse into one corner and her pink top into the other. He kissed her long and hard, drawing out her sighs and moans with his teeth and tongue. Her body ground against his, reminding him of the pleasures he had in store.

"Ah, *chère*," he whispered. "I've wanted you from the first moment I laid eyes on you." He was so hot he ached with it.

"I know." She slid from his embrace and slanted him a half-lidded glance. "Why don't you make yourself at home on the bed, while I slip into something more comfortable?"

If she insisted. Rational thought had long since flown, replaced by a craving that started in the soles of his feet and permeated every inch of him, clear to the ends of his hair. He had no idea if this was a good thing or a huge mistake. He just knew she'd changed her mind and now she wanted him, and he wasn't about to give her a chance to change it back again. He had to have her, or die of pure need.

He popped off his shoes and stretched out on the bed with a ravenous growl, placing his wallet and clip on the nightstand, and his handcuffs within reach.

When she emerged from the bathroom, she was wearing the black nightie and nothing else. He let out a long hum of bone-deep anticipation. *Black lace on pink satin sheets.* This was the vision that had haunted his fantasies for endless days and sleepless nights. He closed his eyes and sent up a brief prayer of thanks. "Whatever I did to deserve this, remind me to keep doin' it."

She leaned against the doorjamb in a flamboyantly sexy pose. Her luscious nude body shimmered beneath the sheer fabric of the nightie like a glimpse of Shangri-la.

He had died and gone to heaven. No doubt about it.

He stretched out his hand toward her. "*Vien ici.* Come to me, *jolie.*"

She strolled slowly to the bed and lowered herself onto him where he lay, placing her hands to either side of his head.

"You're different tonight," he murmured as her lips met his. His innocent angel had become a temptress.

And he had become her slave.

"Yes," she affirmed throatily.

Her breasts hung full and ripe above him, her sumptuous thighs straddled his. He grasped her hips and pulled her closer.

She rubbed against him, slow and tantalizing. "I can feel your gun," she purred.

He choked back a wicked chuckle, knowing she wasn't even in the vicinity. "So you like it after all."

Her smile was catlike. "Could be."

"Shall I tell you what *I* like?"

"What's that?"

"I like you in this nightie." He slid his hands up her sides, relishing the feel of her hot skin, the sight of his hands on her body through the transparent lace. "I like it a lot."

"You mentioned that once."

"In fact, I like you in it so much I think I'll take it off." He lifted the hem and pulled it over her head, flinging it to the floor.

His pulse thrummed at the incredible sight of her naked body straddling his. Any second he'd explode with want. He had to slow down. They had all night.

She tongued his jaw. "Is this how it happened in your dream?"

Better. *So much better.* "Fulfilling my fantasies, *chère?*"

"*Our* fantasies," she murmured. "I've always wondered what it would be like to be Muse."

"You don't need to be Muse," he assured her. "You're doing just fine as Grace."

She gave him an oddly knowing look, and for a second he wondered if he'd missed something.

"Do you have any idea how hard it is for me not to touch you?" She sighed, lifted a hand and traced it through the air, hovering just above his nose and cheek and down his chest.

"*Mais,* yeah." He took the opportunity to flip her onto her back and ease between her legs. She looked up at him, all bare and hot and bedroom-eyed, and he nearly lost it for good. "Guess I'll just have to distract you." *And himself.*

She giggled and relaxed into the pillow, raising her arms in an erotic pose. "You're a bad boy, Creole Levalois."

It was the second time that night she'd called him a bad boy. Both times with the smile of a woman about to taste the fruit of the forbidden.

He reached for the handcuffs. "I try my best."

He dismissed a niggling warning buzz in his mind, and slid his free hand onto her breast. She moaned and the tip peaked to a hard point under his palm. He bent down and took it in his mouth. *Dieu,* she was sweet! He hated to restrain her. But he had no choice.

"A *very* bad boy." She moaned in pleasure. "But that's okay." He squirmed as she reached between them and slowly started unzipping his jeans. "Muse is a very, very bad girl."

He frowned, torn between ecstasy and alarm. "What?"

"It's all right," she leaned up and whispered in his ear, "Tonight I'm being Muse for you."

She touched him and his head spun like a cross-eyed whirlpool. "*Non, chère.* I've got exactly the woman I want, right under me. You, Grace.'' He grabbed her wrist, readying the cuffs.

Her head wagged from side to side. ''Muse.''

''*Non.* I don' want Muse,'' he insisted. ''It's Grace I want to make love to.''

''Impossible,'' she whispered, and giggled softly. ''Grace would never let a man like you make love to her.''

So she kept saying.

Yet here she was in bed, naked, panting for him.

He tried to wrap his brain around that paradox, but all those daiquiris and the three shooters he'd drunk earlier didn't make the job easy.

It's just sex.

He glanced down at her bare breasts, plump and exquisite. He wanted to ravish her until they were both a heap of trembling, sated flesh, unable to distinguish where she ended and he began.

Just sex.

But dammit, he wanted *Grace* beneath him, not Muse.

Suddenly his mind did a screeching U-turn and came to a crashing halt. Back at all those daiquiris and shooters.

Ah, hell.

With a blinding clarity he finally understood.

She was right. *Sober,* Grace would never allow herself to be in this position.

And to his everlasting dismay, something else hit him with equal clarity.

It *wasn't* just sex. Not by a long shot.

Chapter 9

"What's wrong, baby? Creole?"

Grace looked up at him, her eyes heavy with the heat of desire, and, he knew now, one too many daiquiris.

Creole sank his face into the pillow next to her, tossed the handcuffs aside, and groaned in sublime frustration. Damn, damn, *damn.*

He might be a bit far gone himself, but not *that* far gone. The colorful Mardi Gras masks on the wall above the bed seemed to laugh mockingly at him.

He had to be crazy. Completely nuts. Out of his pathetically misled skull.

But there it was. Staring him in the face. When he made love, he wanted it to be with Grace—100 percent Grace. No hesitations, no pretenses, no masks, no false courage. No daiquiris. And no Muse.

He couldn't go through with it tonight.

Not like this.

So he blurted out the only reasonable justification he could think of that would not land him in a heap of immediate grief. ''Sorry, honey, but I just realized…I didn' bring along any protection.''

Grace nuzzled his neck, pulling him back down when he would have risen. ''Don't worry, sugar. Muse is nothing if not prepared.'' She opened the top drawer of the nightstand. It was filled to overflowing with small, square packets.

He stared at the drawer, his shaky excuse self-destructing before his eyes. His gut twisted. There was no other way out of this. He'd have to tell her the truth.

When he still didn't say anything, she looked up at him worriedly. ''Did I do something? Accidentally touch you, or—''

''*Non, chérie.* Nothing like that.'' He ground out a curse. ''I'm sorry. I just…can't.''

''Oh.'' Her eyes didn't meet his, and her voice held the slightest quaver when she said, ''Can't, or won't?''

''Won't,'' he said resignedly, already bitterly regretting his decision. *Dieu,* this was the hardest thing he'd ever done in his life, bar none.

He wanted her. But he wanted *her.*

''What made you change your mind?'' The words were nonchalant, but she still wouldn't look at him, and now he could see a sheen of tears in her eyes.

''Oh, darlin','' he said, and pulled her unyielding body close. She didn't move a muscle. ''I haven' changed my mind. Can't you feel how much I want you? How incredibly much I still want you?''

She swallowed when he lowered his body completely onto her, fitting perfectly into her pliant curves. She couldn't possibly miss how aroused he continued to be, even as he declined to fulfill that desire.

''Then why?''

He took a deep breath and tried to put it tactfully. ''You said it yourself just now. If you were sober, you'd never be in this bed with me. I guess I'd be a total jerk if I ignored that kind of statement, no matter how much I'd like to pretend I hadn't heard it. But you're right, *chère.* We've both had a lot to drink tonight. Too much to make this kind of decision.''

She was silent for a moment, then said, ''Oh,'' again. Slowly her eyes filled with something else… Oh, no. It was embarrassment.

She gave an uneven laugh and covered her face with her hands. ''I should have known I'd blow it,'' she whispered. ''I've never been any good at this seduction stuff.''

He bent to kiss her fingers, one by one. ''Darlin', if you were any better at it, you'd be dangerous.''

''Sure.'' Her laugh turned into a self-deprecating groan. ''Oh, why me? This kind of thing would never happen to Muse.''

Easing her hands away from her face, he laced his fingers with hers on the pillow. ''You're right, it'd never happen to Muse. Because a night like this would mean little to her, and any man would know that. But with you, it's different. Darlin', I'd give anything to be able to go through with what we started. But I know good an' well that eventually you'll wake up sober, an'—''

''And you're afraid I'll hate myself in the morning,'' she completed.

He gave her a lopsided smile, knowing she'd already forgiven him. His heart eased in profound relief. ''Naw, I could live with that.''

She choked out a surprised chuckle. ''What, then?''

He brushed his lips over her cheek, savoring the closeness, the nearness, the completeness he felt, cradled in her body's embrace. ''What I'm so afraid of is that you'll wake up and hate *me* in the morning. I couldn't stand that.''

He held his breath as she looked up at him, lips trembling, eyes pooling with liquid. ''Oh, Auri,'' she whispered, surprising him again by using his real name. ''I could never hate you.''

He laid his cheek on hers, praying it was true. But it was early days yet. He sighed. ''Nobody's called me Auri in a long, long time.''

Not since Luke. His foster brother had always called him by his real name, ignoring his youthful macho defiance when he'd started answering solely to the insult the others called him by.

"Do you mind?"

"No." And strangely, he didn't. No one else had been permitted to breach that particular protective wall, ever. But with Grace, it somehow felt…safe. "No, I don' mind."

He sought her lips and gently plied them with his. It was a kiss of understanding, of accord, of promise.

And of contained heat and need.

She made a little noise, and he deepened the kiss. Just a bit more. He could stop. He could. He would. But right now he needed to feel her, taste her, enjoy her bare body beneath him, because this might well be the last time he'd ever get the chance.

"I do love how you taste," he murmured, and delved deeper still.

"And I love how you kiss," she said on a sigh when he let her up for air.

What man could resist an invitation like that? He kissed her long and wet and unhurried, until his mind numbed and his body burned for release.

Her hips did a slow undulation against him, and her foot scraped up his jeans, looped over his leg and rubbed the back of his knee.

He groaned, tore his lips from hers, and rolled off her in a single motion. Definitely time to stop.

"Ah, *chère,* you aren't goin' to make it easy on *me,* are you?" He laughed, because if he didn't, he'd fling himself back on top of her and make love to her until dawn— sometime next week.

She canted onto her side, leaning on her elbow to peer down at him, and smiled. A very feminine, tantalizing smile. "Revenge is so sweet."

He groaned again. "*Donc, pitié!* Have pity, *jolie,* on a man in pain."

She leaned forward and ~~kissed~~ his jaw. When she lifted, the vixen was gone. In her place was a guileless little girl. "I guess you were telling the truth about wanting me." Her mouth curved up, and he thanked God he'd passed her test, whatever it was.

"I should go," he said, loathing the thought more than he could ever have imagined.

"No, wait!" In a flash she was on top of him, her hands grasping the pillow on either side of his head to prevent his escape. "Please don't go," she said anxiously. "We don't have to—" her head tick-tocked back and forth "—you know. We can just hold each other. That is—you could hold me…or not, if you don't want to. Just…don't go."

"Darlin'—"

"Please? Didn't those men say I might be in danger?"

She had a point. In his greed for her, he'd almost forgotten their warning. Lord, he had no choice. It was his job to protect her.

Besides, he wouldn't be getting any sleep, anyway—regardless of where he made his bed. That was a damned certainty. So why not pass the night with his arms wrapped around her warm body? If his hands strayed a bit in the darkness, well, what harm would it do at this point? As long as he didn't take advantage of her, tomorrow morning he'd be able to look himself in the mirror with his self-respect intact. More or less.

And he'd know she was safe.

On the other hand, who would protect her from *him?*

"Honey, the way I'm wantin' you, that probably wouldn' be the best idea."

He could watch her from the balcony. That would work.

Her eyes beseeched. "Please? I don't want to be alone."

Aw, hell. She looked so desperately vulnerable at that moment, he couldn't have made himself leave if Luke's killer was waiting for him right outside the door.

Sometimes doing the right thing was hell. But he'd long

since found he couldn't live with the alternative. This was one of those times. As amazing as it seemed, this strong, compassionate woman needed *his* strength and compassion right now, and whatever the cost, he'd be damned if he'd let her down.

"All right, *chère*. I'll stay. But only if you'll let me keep my promise."

Even in the moonlit bedroom, her smile was blinding. "Thank you."

She melted over him like French vanilla icing on spice cake, filling every nook and cranny of his anatomy with her luscious sweetness, draping over his chest, adding light and a piquant normalcy to the dark, seasoned, sharpness of his existence.

She kissed him once, then settled against his side, one hand tucked under the pillow at his shoulder, her other grasping the corner of the pillowcase on the other side. His heart was touched more than he could say by her instinctive protectiveness toward him, her unconscious awareness of his difficulty with hands on him.

"I've got a wicked crush on you, you know," she murmured, nibbling suggestively down his throat.

There was a definite impish note in her voice.

He pursed his lips against a grin and said, "Flattery will get you nowhere, *chère*. I'm not makin' love to you tonight, no matter how much you beg."

Although the idea did have an incredible appeal.

Especially when she moved like she was doing, rubbing the entire length of her hot, silky body against his. He caught himself purring. Actually purring.

"*Non.* This isn't working." He tried to dump her off, but she ignored his efforts.

"I thought it was working pretty well, myself." She batted her eyelashes.

"You are a very naughty girl, Grace Summerville," he admonished sternly, fighting the amusement bubbling up in him from under his flagrantly painful arousal. "You promised."

She grinned up at him and he lost the battle. He let out
a belly laugh and she joined in, and they laughed together
until tears ran down her face and his sides ached nearly as
much as his—

Dieu, he couldn't believe he was laughing in bed. And
with a woman, no less.

He couldn't remember that happening since...since he
didn't know when. Hell, since forever. The only time he
could ever remember laughing in bed was on the rare occasion when Luke had told some raunchy joke he'd overheard somewhere. As kids they'd always shared a bed, even
when it wasn't necessitated by the cramped, dirty conditions of the various foster homes they were shuffled between. It had been safer that way, sleeping spine to spine,
each guarding the other's backside, sharing what little
warmth there was to be found between their tough, skinny
bodies. Soaking up the few, precious hours of gentle human
contact.

He hugged Grace tight, wiped the mirthful tears from her
cheeks and thought he'd never been so happy with another
human being in his whole life. She was everything he'd
ever fantasized in a real family—loving, affectionate, gentle, intelligent, loyal. And she made him laugh. He could
get used to that—spending a whole lifetime with a loopy
grin stuck permanently on his face, just watching her make
him laugh.

It was a damn, crying shame it was all just a fantasy.

Tomorrow morning she'd wake up and remember she
didn't like men like him, and then she'd be gone. Back to
Carolina.

They settled down to sleep, him clinging to her, she nestled into him, her head tucked into the crook of his neck.

After a moment she asked in an overly innocent voice,
"Wouldn't you be more comfortable if you took off your
shirt?"

He had to give her credit for persistence. He couldn't keep that loopy grin from breaking out. "Not a chance," he assured her.

"Spoilsport." He could feel her pout even through the fabric of the offending garment. But it was followed by an unmistakable smile.

"Nice try though."

"Harrumph."

They lay together in companionable silence waiting for sleep to come. The big old paddle fan above them whirred softly, and the sounds of the city filtered faintly through the French doors. Out the windows Creole could see a sliver of moon gleaming over the roof of his own apartment. The smells of the Quarter clung to his clothes, and the seductive fragrance of Grace's jessamine perfume wafted from her hair. He stroked the soft skin of her back, slowly caressing her sensual curves, running his fingers through the long, silky tresses draped over his chest and shoulder. Every so often she'd touch her lips to his throat, giving him a tiny butterfly kiss.

"Chère?"

"Mmm-hmm?" she answered drowsily.

"If you still want me tomorrow mornin', just say the word. I'll be happy to oblige."

A sleepy chuckle vibrated against his chest. "I'll bet you would."

"Just wanted you to know that."

Her cheek rubbed against him and he lifted his chin so she could caress his whole throat with her satin skin. He gave a sigh of pleasure when she licked at his rough beard.

"You're goin' to kill me if you don' stop, honey," he reluctantly said. He'd be hard till Christmas as it was.

"Serve you right," she mumbled, and yawned. In a voice barely awake, she added, "Think I changed my mind."

His heart sank, but hadn't he known all along she would? "Yeah?"

"Yeah. I think you *do* like being touched, after all."

It took a second for the change of topic to sink in and register. By the time he'd thought about it enough to respond, she'd fallen asleep in his arms. Her breath came deep and regular, and she unconsciously cuddled closer, sliding her leg between his thighs when she couldn't get close enough.

He smiled, not caring about the frustration that still pulsed through his veins. He'd trade a hundred, a thousand, nights of meaningless sex for this one night holding Grace. He loved the taste of her lips on his tongue, the sound of her laughter in his ears, the scent of her desire in every pore. And yes, the feel of her body's touch on his.

"*C'est vrai, mon coeur.* I guess I do, my love. I guess I do, at that."

Grace awoke gradually, one body part at a time, to the sensation of a warm, muzzy cocoon enveloping her. Her lips woke first, curving up in instinctive pleasure. But no, she must still be asleep, for in her dream she was surrounded by the scent of him. Creole. Detective Levalois. Auri.

She hummed a note of drowsy contentment. In her dream she could also feel his hard, muscular body at her back, molded to her like a custom-made glove. One powerful masculine arm was banded across her chest, his hand fastened on her breast; the other was belted over her hip, cupping her intimately. A spurt of dizzy excitement shot through her at the possessiveness of the gesture. Especially when she realized she was naked.

Mercy. Her dreams just kept getting better and better.

Now if she could just get *him* naked, she'd never want to wake up.

Unfortunately, her past experiences didn't run to being able to fill in the necessary details on a body like Creole's, even in her dreams. The few men she'd seen naked hadn't come close. Not even the star of her first love affair, Luther

Giancanno and his varsity jacket, was in the same league. When it had come right down to it, Luther's physique had turned out to be more padding than reality. Just like his love.

Of course, she *had* seen that Mickey Rourke movie where there was a brief scene with him naked—

Suddenly she was startled by a noise behind her. Something that sounded remarkably like a soft snore.

Her eyes popped wide open and a quick glance downward confirmed the naked truth—she really *was* in bed with Creole Levalois, and it *wasn't* a dream, either. She jerked her eyes up to scan the nightstand for further evidence. The abrupt movement sent a thunderbolt of agony shooting through her head. At the sight of his belongings scattered there above the open nightstand drawer, appalling memories of last night's behavior exploded through her mind in Technicolor detail.

Every single, solitary, humiliating one.

OhGodohGodohGod. That couldn't have been her. She simply could not have done all those embarrassing things.

Mortified to the core, Grace tried to ease herself from Creole's grip. But instead of letting her go, his arms increased their hold on her.

She swallowed heavily, wincing at the headache that began to pound like a kettledrum in her head. Under other circumstances, she might have taken a minute to explore the feeling of his hands on her body. It was something she'd wondered about, fantasized over, but had known would never actually happen. Yet here she was, in exactly the position she'd been dreaming of for days. She should enjoy the moment—briefly—before he woke and she'd have to scramble away lest he think she really wanted to be there.

Which she didn't.

Honestly.

Yes, okay, okay, she'd tried to seduce him last night, but that had been the alcohol speaking, not her own wishes.

Truly. She knew better than to get involved with a man like him. Knew it to the marrow.

But right now she couldn't even think for the hammering in her head, let alone appreciate Creole's considerable male assets.

She let out a low moan and lifted her fingertips to her temples, rubbing circles to try to ease the pain.

"I suppose this means you've got a headache," Creole's voice rumbled wryly from behind her.

She caught herself just in time. "Don't make me laugh, you stinker. This is all your fault."

She absently noted he didn't move his hands, but didn't have the energy to protest his scandalous familiarity.

He chuckled softly. "How do you figure?"

In truth, the very least of the acute embarrassment she felt was over her nudity. Which might have surprised her had she actually been capable of thinking about it.

"I'll let you know when my brain's back in one piece." She groaned in torment, not completely sure whether from the discomfort of the hangover or from the memory of her outrageous actions of last night. What a fool she'd made of herself!

She groaned again.

"Can I do anything? Hold your head? Massage your feet?"

Feet? "No. Thanks. I don't even want to think about moving for a few minutes."

"Okay."

His arms shifted, and he removed his hands from their intimate positions, folding them loosely over her waist instead. She wanted to groan again, at the loss of the intensely personal connection to him. Now she really did feel naked. Naked, cold and miserable.

"Creole," she whispered. "I'm so sorry for…for everything."

"I'm not."

God, he was sweet. "I don't like to admit it, but you were right," she sighed.

"I know. You would have woken up hating me."

She wished. "No. It might have been awkward, but I wouldn't have hated you."

"Damn. I knew I should have given in and let you have your wicked way with me."

She chuckled, then moaned at the resulting fire in her head. "God, you're obnoxious."

"So you keep telling me."

"I'm trying to apologize, here."

"Sorry." She felt a light kiss in her hair. "You don't have to apologize. It was as much my fault as yours. I should have seen what was happening. I was blinded by my lust."

She couldn't help but smile and was relieved when it didn't hurt. Much. "Yes, well, you weren't the only one."

This time the kiss came on her shoulder and lingered. "I, uh, I don't suppose…"

She shook her head before thinking. "Ow! As I said, you were right. Not a good idea."

His breath jetted onto her neck. "No. Guess not." Suddenly his warm body was gone from behind her, and he gently rolled her onto her back. He touched the tip of her nose lightly before pulling the sheet up around her and sliding off the bed. "I'll look for some aspirin."

"Creole?"

He paused and turned, raising a brow.

"You are truly a gentleman, Creole Levalois."

For a second he looked taken aback, then he grinned and gave her a wink. "Don' spread that around, *chère*. I've got a reputation to maintain."

He came back with a couple of pills he'd scrounged from Muse's medicine cabinet and helped her sit up, sheet tucked under her arms, and swallow them down with a glass of water he'd fetched from the kitchen.

She'd never felt so pampered. He fussed over her as if

she was dying of some exotic disease, rather than just suffering the effects of too much to drink. It made her go all warm and mushy inside, and if it weren't for her grinding headache, she'd be on top of the world.

In fact, Creole was being so nice, if she wasn't careful, she'd be in danger of starting to believe he really cared.

But before that thought could really sink in, the phone rang. They looked at each other in surprise.

"Expecting any calls this morning?"

"No," she said, wondering nervously if last night's masquerade was already producing results. The FBI agent's words drifted through her achy head, making her even more anxious. She'd used the warning to sway Creole to spend the night with her, but she was ashamed to say it had only been a last-ditch ruse to get him to stay. In her mixed-up state, she simply hadn't wanted him to go, and she'd known the cop in him wouldn't leave her unprotected if he thought she was in danger.

She squeezed her eyes shut, cheeks flaming, remembering the wanton behavior she'd exhibited last night and wondering what on earth had gotten into her. In her wildest imagination she'd never have believed herself capable of such things! Sweet heavens, what he must think of her!

"It's for you." Creole's harsh statement sliced through her unsettling thoughts. She started at the sharp, icy edge to his voice.

Opening her eyes, she took him in at a glance. His face had changed completely from a moment ago. Instead of her tender, sympathetic caregiver, she saw a shuttered, almost angry man staring back.

He held out the portable phone. "It's Frank."

"Huh?" For the life of her she couldn't think who Frank was.

"I'm goin' across to take a shower. Meet me in the courtyard in an hour. There are a couple things we need to discuss before you leave town. We can grab some coffee and talk." With that he turned on a heel and stalked out.

Leave town?

What the heck had just happened? She wanted to call out to him, to run after him and demand to know what had changed so suddenly. She made to follow him, then noticed the phone in her hand.

Annoyed, she raised the receiver. "Hello?"

"Tsk, tsk, tsk. Miz Summerville, I am mighty shocked," a familiarly cocky teenaged voice drawled into her ear.

Oh, *that* Frank. This was one phone call she couldn't blow off. She eased back onto the pillow. "It's not what you think, Frank Morina."

Her student chuckled knowingly. "Sure it isn't, Miz Summerville. Now, what was I saying last time we talked, about findin' yourself a handsome Louisiana man to—"

"*Frank,* what exactly is it you're calling about?"

"I need a reason?"

She sighed and smiled into the phone, resigned to talking to her student rather than chasing after Creole. And to being teased for the rest of her natural life about her "handsome Louisiana man." Word would no doubt spread through school like lovebugs in September.

"No, of course you don't need a reason. I just hadn't expected it. I'm glad you called, though." And she was. This was surely the breakthrough she'd worked so hard for, for three long years. *He'd* actually reached out to *her.* "I'm really glad."

"Yeah?"

"Yeah. You know I always enjoy talking to you. Now, what's up?"

"I just wanted to tell you I quit that job yesterday, like I said I was." He waited silently for her reaction.

Under no circumstances would she give him the one he'd come to expect from every other adult in his world. "Well, I'd be lying if I said I wasn't disappointed. What are your plans for the rest of the summer?"

"Remember I told you about Nikki? That girl I met?"

"The one from the arts magnet school?"

"Yep. She's promised to teach me how to throw a pot."

Grace chuckled at the image *that* conjured up. "I assume you mean on the pottery wheel, and not at someone's head."

He guffawed. "Now you know I'd never hurt nobody." This coming from a boy who regularly earned detentions for fighting in the halls. "We sorta started the other night. It was so cool."

He went on to tell her about the makeshift studio she had built in her folks' garage and the different clays she used and the electric pottery wheel and the things she made on it and the colorful glazes she brewed up herself. His enthusiasm brimmed over, and joy at his obvious happiness filled her heart.

"And last night she let me help her mix up a new batch of clay. We ended up rollin' on the floor, soakin' wet 'n' drippin' mud, and I tell ya, Miz Summerville, I think I've decided to become a sculptor." His playful confession made her laugh out loud, forgetting all about her headache. She could just imagine what had happened on that floor between the two hormonal teenagers covered in slippery clay. But after the night she'd just spent, she was the last one to scold.

"Oh, lordy, Frank, I just hope you two are being careful."

"Almost every time."

"Almost?"

"So tell me true, Miz Summerville. Who was that guy who answered the phone? He seemed a bit uptight, if you know what I mean."

She decided yet another lecture on the wisdom of abstinence would fall on deaf ears, so she let the change of subject pass. "That was Detective Levalois. He's been helping me find Muse. Oh! Speaking of whom, we found out she's safe!"

"That's great! I know how worried you were." Frank seemed genuinely gladdened by her good news, and again she was heartened by the way he'd opened up to her. Maybe this time she wouldn't fail. Maybe this time she'd be able to steer a good kid back onto the right path.

"Now, about this detective guy. He hasn't tried any funny business, has he? 'Cause if he has, I'll be on the next plane down there and—"

"Thanks, Frank, but that won't be necessary. He's been a perfect gentleman." *Unfortunately.* She shooed away *that* traitorous thought. "I should be coming home soon. I can't wait to meet Nikki."

"Yeah, you'll love her as much as I do."

She smiled wistfully as she said her goodbyes and hung up. Young love was so special. So hurtful and agonizing, but so very special. She'd paid a high price for Luther, her own first love. But even knowing how it turned out, she wouldn't have missed it for the world. Changed it, yes. Skipped it, no.

She just prayed it would go better for Frank and Nikki. Especially Nikki. She sounded like a sweet girl. And Grace knew a boy like Frank could break her heart into a million pieces without even trying. Nikki didn't have the bad example of Grace's father to show her the inappropriateness of her choice in boyfriends. Grace was certain that while the naive, romantic girl dreamed of cottages and picket fences, as Grace's mother had done, Frank was dreaming of something quite different. As much as she loved the boy, she couldn't delude herself about his sense of responsibility. Or lack thereof. He was too much like her father had been at that age. Poor Nikki.

Dragging herself out of the bed, Grace went into the bathroom to get ready. She'd been on the phone a long time, and only had twenty minutes before meeting Creole.

Creole. Now, there was another inappropriate boyfriend if ever she'd seen one. And although she wished she could deny it, she'd allowed more than one naive thought of picket fences to sneak through her own mind since meeting him.

Creole was an emotional disaster just waiting to happen. A catastrophe she'd narrowly escaped twice now.

Or had she?

Just the thought of seeing him again, brushing up against him, kissing him, set her skin to tingling and her pulse to tripping. And caused those old yearnings for something more in her ordered but lonely life to surface at the worst possible time.

Sweet mercy.

No, she thought with a plummeting heart. Disaster had definitely already struck. Last night, she'd told him she had a crush on him. But the truth was far, far worse.

Somehow, somewhere, between the first daiquiri on Bourbon Street and the last aspirin this morning, she'd fallen hard for this sexy, complex, wounded man who called himself Creole.

She picked up her purse, carefully locked the door behind her and walked down the stairs to meet him in the courtyard.

And wondered what in the world she was going to do about it.

Chapter 10

Grace followed Creole as he nabbed a prime table right next to the sidewalk at the Café du Monde, the French Quarter's favorite coffee stop, according to him. Table karma, bull. She'd seen that five he'd slipped Pierre, their waiter.

She adjusted her dark glasses and took a seat across from him at a postage-stamp-size metal bistro table.

"So," she said, proud of how she didn't even scowl after he went ahead and ordered for both of them without consulting her. Yet again. "What's eating you? I thought *I* was the one with the hangover."

He, on the other hand, *was* scowling.

"Who's Frank?"

She peered at him over her sunglasses for a second, annoyed at the evasion. "Not that it's any of your business—"

"As the man you did your damnedest to seduce last night, I think it *is* my goddamn business!" he shot back.

Her jaw dropped. He couldn't think— He couldn't possibly be...*jealous?* She leaned back in her chair, removed her glasses, and regarded him. He looked distinctly uncomfortable with his outburst but didn't appear ready to back down. She gave him an amused smile.

"He's one of my high school students. One of the high-risk kids I counsel."

His eyes narrowed. "High school?"

"Don't even think it, Levalois," she warned levelly.

"Then why's he calling you in New Orleans?"

"Because he's intelligent and sensitive and his parents are abusive and he needs a steady, supportive adult influence in his life even during the summer, so I talk to him every few days to try to keep him from self-destructing." She gazed at him mutinously. "Besides, I like him. Like a little brother," she added, for some obscure reason she couldn't fathom.

"A little brother, eh?" he said, and she reluctantly admitted to herself that she could fathom it very well, and was glad when she could see he believed her and that he felt a little foolish about the whole thing and wasn't even ashamed to admit it.

That's when she knew she was *really* in trouble.

"Tell me about your work," he said.

So she did, as they sat there sipping café au laits—which she grudgingly conceded was exactly what she needed to scatter the last remnants of her headache—munching on the weird but delicious fritter-like things he called beignets, and watching the world stroll by the crowded, cozy outdoor terrace.

The more she talked, the more thoughtful he grew, and when she eventually lifted a shoulder and concluded, "So, that's what I do for a living. Not nearly as exciting as being a cop, no doubt. But I love it," he just stared at her, an indecipherable look on his face.

"You're one awesome lady," he finally said.

She blushed at his praise, both pleased and puzzled by

his reaction. "Most people think I'm crazy to waste my time on kids who are doomed for failure anyway."

"Then they're fools. Nobody's 'doomed for failure.'"

She smiled. "I agree. As long as those kids keep listening, there's hope. I won't give up on a single one until they tell me to go to hell. And probably not even then."

The admiration in his eyes was unmistakable. And there was something else lurking in them, too, which she couldn't quite figure out.

"Stubbornness can be a good thing," he quietly allowed.

They shared a smile, and suddenly she thought perhaps they weren't so different as she'd always assumed.

Which was very dangerous thinking. Because he was hard enough to resist when she was convinced he was all wrong for her. What chance did she have if she thought he even remotely understood the important things in her life?

"You'll be leaving soon," he said, almost as if reminding her—and maybe himself—that any relationship between them was doomed for failure, too.

"Yes," she agreed, sweeping aside the stab of regret that acknowledgment engendered. "What will you do now? About finding Gary Fox, I mean?"

"Ah." His expression clouded, and his mouth turned downward. "I honestly don't know. You—that is, Muse was my last real lead."

She suspected, and the look in his eyes confirmed, that there was much more going on in this case than he'd been telling her. "Why is it so important to you to catch him?"

"James Davies, Fox's boss, murdered my brother."

Shock knocked the breath from her lungs. "Your brother?"

"Yeah."

Instinct had her reaching for his hand on the table, but at the last second she pulled up. Instead, she leaned forward and brushed a kiss over his cheek. "I'm so sorry."

A muscle twitched in his jaw, but otherwise he betrayed nothing of what he might have been feeling. "Luke was my foster brother. We weren't blood. But we grew up together, and he was all I had. He was my brother in every way that mattered.''

She digested the wealth of information about Creole contained in those few simple sentences. No wonder the man was so wounded. The foster care system was a bitch at the best of times. And for a kid like Creole…she shuddered to imagine.

''What happened to him?''

He gazed off in the distance, reliving God-only-knew what horrors from the past. ''We had a rough childhood,'' he said at last. ''Luke…Luke didn't come through it so well. He ended up— Actually, he was a drug addict, and a small-time dealer, in and out of jail. Me being on the job could only help him so much.''

She kept silent, her heart breaking for the anguish this strong, proud man had endured, was still enduring, because of the random destiny of birth.

''As far as I could tell, there was a drug deal that went wrong. The drugs were recovered, but Davies thought Luke had double-crossed him, and took him out. But not before he'd tortured him for a few days.''

She was horrified. ''But why torture him?''

He lifted a hand and dropped it. ''Who knows? For kicks, probably. The man's a sadistic bastard. What was left of Luke's body turned up in the Intracoastal Waterway, near a town called Louisa. By the time I got there, they'd found most of him. Except his fingers.'' Creole looked up, raw pain in his eyes. ''I guess they didn't think he could be identified without them.''

Her vision blurred, her heart aching. ''But you recognized him.''

He turned his head and lifted his cup to his mouth. But she noticed he didn't drink. ''He had a tattoo.''

She blinked back the sympathetic tears that wanted to fall. He wouldn't want her pity. ''The police. Couldn't they—''

"I am the police," he reminded her. "To be fair, they're doing what they can. Which isn't much, as long as Davies stays invisible. I've been ordered off the case. Too personal." He gave her a sardonic smile, which didn't have a hint of humor in it. "But when I saw Luke in that body bag, I made him a solemn promise." His shoulders squared. "I don't give a damn about orders. I'm going to see that bastard Davies fry, if it's the last thing I do."

"Oh, baby," she said softly, "I'm so very sorry."

He set down his cup and after a brief second glanced over at her. "Thanks," he said, his face calm and composed, as if they hadn't just talked about him losing the only person in the world who had ever meant a thing to him, once again a man in control of his universe.

He leaned forward and motioned for her to do the same. She met him halfway, but he didn't give her a kiss, as she'd somehow expected, even hoped.

"I like how you call me baby," he murmured, disarming her completely.

"It's a South Carolina thing," she returned, marginally flustered at the abrupt change of mood. "Don't take it personally. We call everybody baby. Infants to grandpas."

"Sure, *chère*." He grinned, effectively slamming the door on the previous subject. "Still, I like hearing it."

"I'll be sure to say it more often."

With a slight jerk of his chin, he motioned her closer still, until their lips were a fraction of an inch apart. "Mmm. Sugar," he said softly.

"Uh…" Now she was definitely flustered. What the heck was he—

"You've got powdered sugar on your nose."

She blinked. "Oh." Those darn beignets were covered in the stuff. Pounds of it. She probably had powdered sugar all over her face. Her cheeks heated.

"Want me to lick it off?"

Lord have mercy. "Creole—" She tried to retreat, but his hand shot out and grasped her behind the neck so she couldn't budge. "This is crazy," she sighed, just before her eyes closed and his tongue trailed slowly up the ridge of her nose.

He kissed first one eye, then the other, and then he whispered, "I wish you weren't leavin'."

"Me, too," she murmured, and realized what he was really saying, and asking, but didn't see any way around the cold, hard facts that his life was here and hers was in Carolina, and even if that could change, the kind of people they were wouldn't.

Her heart went out to him for all that he'd been through—and for the man he'd become because of it. But the truth remained, his troubled life had molded him into a man who was afraid of love and commitment and would never settle down to one woman. She saw that plain as the rough shadow of his beard on his face. She worked with boys who would become Creole. Hell, her own father *was* Creole—though he had never been able to pull himself out of the morass to the extent Creole had succeeded in doing.

She drew in a deep breath and let it out on another sigh. And then she kissed him. A tender, poignant kiss, that conveyed her own wishes, and her sadness that they couldn't ever come true. Not with him, anyway.

"Well, isn't this cozy." A nastily familiar voice cut short their kiss—luckily, because it was threatening to become much more than she'd intended.

Saved by the FBI.

"Get lost," Creole growled.

"Now, I wish I could do that. Really I do. But unfortunately, I've gotta deal with this loco cop who thinks he's Dirty Harry, and his misguided girlfriend, who are well on their way to screwing up almost two years of work for me."

Creole let her go and turned to the man she recognized as the agent with the aviator shades from the alley last night. "Give me one reason I should give a damn," he said.

"Your job."

"I don't think so," he retorted, filling her with alarm. Hadn't the man said something last night about going to Creole's captain?

Creole reached into his shirt pocket and pulled out his tobacco pouch, proceeding to leisurely roll himself a cigarette. Grace could practically smell the testosterone flood the air.

"If this were an official visit," he continued, "you'd be identifying yourself and showing me your ID, not making idle threats."

"Well, well." The FBI agent pulled a chair from a nearby table and straddled it between them. "I may have underestimated you."

After lighting his smoke, Creole gazed assessingly at the agent. "And you might be smarter than you look."

The man gave a forced laugh. "Cute. Look, sorry about last night…"

Grace lost the thread of the conversation when her awareness was snared by a ribbon-thin finger of smoke curling about Creole's ear. It slid along the sturdy masculine whorls, twined around the modest lobe, flirted with the collar of his Miami shirt and the neat, black hair above it.

She watched the wispy smoke with a twinge of envy as it prowled over his shoulder and down his shirtsleeve, wishing he'd allow her own fingers to caress him so lovingly. A tiny cluster of blue lines peeked out from under the sleeve, barely visible. A tattoo?

"So I guess what I'm asking is, will you help us?"

Creole's eyes sought hers, and her attention snapped back to the present. To her dismay she realized she'd missed something important. He was silently asking her opinion.

"Of course, it would mean that Miss Summerville would have to stick around New Orleans for a few more days," the agent said, looking at her hopefully.

"I could stay," she blurted out, belatedly realizing she was speaking to a completely different question than the one the FBI man was posing. "I mean, what do you think?" she asked Creole, to cover her slip.

"I think…" he said, then halted. He slanted her a glance that might have been amused if it weren't so searingly sexual. "I think we'd be pleased to help you, Agent Morris," he said, directing his comments to the man who'd apparently introduced himself while she was off in her smoke-induced hallucinations, "but only on the condition that you fill us in on everything. And I do mean *everything*."

Sweet heaven, what had she gone and done? Had she really promised to delay leaving, when every instinct screamed at her to get away from this place, from this man, as quickly as possible?

"Very well. Agreed."

She fought a queasy feeling in her stomach while Agent Morris flagged down Pierre and placed an order for more coffee and beignets. She risked a glance at Creole, who sealed her vexation with an impudent wink.

There was no doubt in her mind what was on *his* mind, nor the motive to which he attributed her sudden change of plans.

The question was whether she was willing to admit it to herself.

"Believe it or not, Miss Summerville, the other Miss Summerville—"

"Muse?"

"Yes, Muse is working with us."

Again, shock ripped through Grace. "You're kidding, right?"

"Wrong. We recruited her over six months ago. She was helping us get information on James Davies, through her boyfriend Gary Fox. She had just met Fox a few weeks earlier, and they seemed taken with each other. We did a background check, and she seemed pretty straight and honest, if a bit misguided in her taste in men. So we approached her."

"You approached her." Grace's head was spinning so fast her headache was beginning to come back.

"Yes."

"To work undercover for you."

"Well, sort of." Morris squirmed around a bit in his chair. "More of a snitch than an operative. She said she liked Fox but didn't care for the stuff he was into. She thought Davies was an animal, selling drugs to kids, and was glad to help us put him away. Strictly voluntarily. She wouldn't accept money from us." He had the grace to look slightly embarrassed by the admission.

Too stunned to speak, Grace was grateful when Creole asked, "Where is Muse now?"

The agent squirmed again and pulled at the collar of his button-down shirt. "I'm not totally, exactly sure."

"What?" Grace burst out. "I thought you said she was safe!"

"She is, she is," Morris rushed to assure. "She's being protected by one of our best agents, Remi Beaulieux. But he's a bit unpredictable—comes from the years he spent undercover as a jewel thief—and, well, they seem to have…disappeared together."

"Disappeared." Her vocabulary had degenerated to that of a feebleminded parrot, but for the life of her she couldn't gather her wits enough to sound coherent. Again Creole rescued her, but she immediately wished he hadn't.

"Why did she need protection? What went wrong?"

Dread flashed through her and settled as a tight fist around her heart. "Wrong?"

Oh, God, if something had happened to Muse she'd never forgive herself. As if reading her mind, Creole reached over and grasped her hand.

Morris shook his head. "No, nothing like that. Agent Beaulieux is probably just being cautious. He may have suspected she was in danger of being exposed and took her into hiding."

"Isn't that something you should know?"

Morris looked down into the dregs of his coffee. "Normally."

Grace didn't like the sound of that, and when Creole narrowed his eyes, she guessed he didn't either. But he didn't comment. Instead he gave her hand a squeeze and asked Morris, "What is it you want us to do for you?"

Looking visibly relieved that he hadn't been further interrogated, Morris answered, "For now just what you've been doing. Continue to be Muse and her new man. One of our informants called to let us know your charade last night caused some comment and speculation around town. He thinks there's a good chance Fox will break cover to check you out. His manly reputation is at stake."

Creole smiled menacingly. "Good."

"There's one more thing."

"What's that?"

"Someone made you as a cop."

Creole swore and his grip tightened on her hand as a look passed between him and Morris, an unspoken cop-to-cop exchange that left Grace more than a bit rattled.

"What does that mean?" she asked worriedly.

Creole shifted his gaze to her, then withdrew his hand and drilled it through his hair. "It means I'm going to put you on the first plane back to Charleston. It's too dangerous for you to stay here."

She and Morris fell over each other to protest.

"I have to stay! Muse needs me!"

"If she disappears now, it'll drive them even further underground! It could be months before they surface again!"

"No."

"She'll be protected. I'll have two men watching her at all times."

"It's too dangerous," Creole repeated, glaring at the agent. "If they know I'm a cop, then they know who I am. They'll know I'm out for revenge over the death of my brother and figure I'm using her to get to them."

He left unspoken the implications of that scenario, but they didn't escape her. Her life would truly be in danger.

She didn't know when it had become just as important for her to help Creole put his brother's soul to rest as it was to be sure her sister was safe, but suddenly she knew she couldn't leave, no matter how much danger it put her in.

"Then I guess we'll have to be careful. But I'm not running away," she said quietly.

C'est fou, sa! It was crazy!

Creole didn't like it. Not one bit. They'd argued for a while, Grace and Morris against him, but in the end he'd given up and caved. Grace was adamant. With or without him, she was staying. *Mais, quelle espèce de tête dure, elle!* Damn, obstinate woman!

He'd never felt so torn before in his life, between wanting her out of New Orleans, out of danger, and wanting her to stay. Wanting her in his bed.

He prayed it was their logical arguments and not his libido that had finally convinced him.

With both the Feds and himself protecting Grace, it should be okay for a few days. If Fox hadn't shown by then, he'd ship her off, regardless of how much she—or his hormones—protested. There were other ways to catch a fox than by staking out a defenseless chick.

Even though the thought of her leaving left him short of breath.

"You are a stubborn little thing, you know that?"

Grace wrinkled her nose at him. "This morning you praised my stubbornness."

Creole glowered at her from above the screwdriver he was using to install the dead bolt he'd insisted they pick up on the way back to her apartment. "Don't remind me."

"I thought you wanted me to stay."

He paused in midscrew. "You know I do. But I'd rather see you stay alive."

She knelt beside him and bent to sweep up the chunks of wood he'd chipped out of the door to accommodate the new lock. "What could go wrong, with you and your faithful gun right across the courtyard to protect me?"

"Ah, non." He dropped the screwdriver and grasped her arms, dustpan and all. "I'm going to be right here with you, in the same apartment, in the same room. You won't even be able to blink without me watching."

She bit her lip and glanced up at him with an expression that hit somewhere between hope and terror. Which just about fit his own state of mind.

"You more afraid of me than of Gary Fox, *jolie?*"

"No. It's just that…" She bit her lip again.

"Chère, I held you naked in my arms all night and managed to keep the rest of me to myself. Nothin's gonna happen that you don' want to happen."

She gazed up at him with such longing that he had to physically restrain himself from pulling her to him, under him, and show her that her fears were unfounded.

But what about his own?

Women didn't stick around. Not around him, anyway. Starting with his own mother, every woman in his life had abused and abandoned him, each time leaving his body and his heart more shredded and his soul more desperate. The early ones had hurt the most. Women who were supposed to love him, nurture him, care for him, had all turned a blind eye, or worse, and in the end had simply dumped him to fend for himself in the bowels of another hellhole.

Later, he'd become inured. By then he and Luke had banded together to form a tight little knot of asylum from the cruelties of the outside world. Women hadn't been a factor for a good, long time after that. But when, years later, he'd finally opened himself up enough to be able to get close to a woman physically, and to test out the precarious emotional waters surrounding such intimacy, he'd found not one was willing to stick around long enough to get past the obvious difficulties.

Would Grace be any different?

He wanted to think so. But he'd been devastated too often to be able to trust. He'd seen it happen too many times before. The first time he slept with a woman, she was intrigued. The second time, eager for the fantasy. But after that, she'd grow tired of the complications, and waltz out of his life for good, taking a piece of his heart, and his hope, with her.

Grace would be no different, despite her apparent understanding of his background. She'd said herself she was attracted to men like him but would never get serious about one. Even if he managed to convince her to make love, she'd still take off when their FBI ruse was over. And probably be glad for the excuse.

Non. Better by far to stick to his usual modus operandi— no strings, no involvement, just a night or two of mutual pleasure and then splitsville. But with Grace, even that much would no doubt prove more painful than just letting the whole thing be. He was already too invested emotionally. If she slept with him and then left, as she was bound to do, his heart might never recover.

For as foolish and impossible as it seemed—and much to his own bewilderment—because of Grace, he'd discovered a craving deep within him. A craving for love and a normal life. For the kind of life and love he'd only thought existed for other people, or in fairy tales.

He was too bruised as it was. To have to endure another betrayal would leave him a soulless shell, unable to continue nurturing that tiny seed of hope and faith that somewhere one special woman would be able to heal his pain.

He looked down at her—at the woman whose arms he was gripping like a lifeline, not able to let her go, not daring to pull her close—and steeled his emotions, locking them deep inside as he'd learned to do, long, long ago.

"Nothing will happen, *chère.* I give you my word."

With that he let his hands fall away from her and reached for the screwdriver, determinedly returning his attention to installing the lock.

For a moment she seemed confused, but she quickly bent once again to sweep up the remaining curls of wood from the floor.

"Good," she said. "I just didn't want you to think—"

"I don't."

"Because last night I said some things—"

"It was the daiquiris talkin', I know."

"Well. Okay. We understand each other then."

"Yeah."

"Okay. Good."

She went to the kitchen, emptied and put away the broom and dustpan, then bustled around straightening things that didn't need straightening, chattering about innocuous stuff like the weather and what they would have for dinner in six hours.

"I'll take you to Ralph and Kakoo's," he interrupted as he put the finishing touches on the lock and tested it. He couldn't stand listening to her avoidance one minute longer.

That stopped her for about five seconds as she looked at him, blinked, then said, "You don't have to do that."

"I want to." He gathered up his tools and stowed them in the toolbox. "Just wear somethin' short and tight," he added with a wink and a grin to distract her.

The tension in her shoulders dissolved and she made a long-suffering face, rimmed with reluctant amusement. "You are impossible."

"Naw. Just like lookin' at your legs."

She rolled her eyes and walked to the living area.

Just then the doorbell buzzed loudly.

They both jumped, her in the air, him for his gun and to shove her behind his back. She slapped her hands over her mouth, and he went automatically into cop mode.

He braced his legs apart, aimed the Glock at the door and called, "Who's there?"

Chapter 11

"I said, *who's there?*"

"You have to use the intercom," Grace's quavering voice whispered over his shoulder.

"Huh?"

It was then Creole realized that whoever it was must be at the outside door downstairs. Hardly Fox being considerate by ringing the front doorbell. He let out his backed-up breath and relaxed his weapon arm, then strode to the intercom. "Yes?" he demanded gruffly.

"Wood's Photo," came the scratchy reply. "I have Miss Summerville's pictures. Where would you like the package?"

He shot her a confused look. "Pictures?"

Grace's eyes lit up, and immediately she was all smiles. "Oh, it must be the final photos for her book! Tell him to come up." She danced to the door as he gave the messenger instructions. "She mentioned last time we talked she'd made the final selections, but I'd completely forgotten."

Cautiously, in case it was a trick, he opened the door. It

wasn't. A few minutes and five bucks later, he was carrying a large flat carton into the kitchen.

"What's this about photos and a book?"

"Muse's pet project. A photographic book on Louisiana wrought iron fences."

"Excuse me?"

Grace grinned. "I know. Sounds a little out of character, doesn't it?"

After the week he'd had, nothing should surprise him any longer, but that sure did. He glanced around the room and for the first time took real note of several framed black-and-white photographs on the wall, placed between the Mardi Gras masks and draped strands of beads. "Muse is a photographer?"

Grace nodded, and her smile widened. "Amateur, but she's a darn good. Pretty aren't they? It's going to be a beautiful book."

"Sure is, if these are any indication."

"You should hear some of the stories that go along with the pictures. Really amazing."

"Like what?"

"Oh, stories of sex, romance and adventure."

He waggled his eyebrows. "Yeah? *Dis moi.* Tell."

Her mouth snapped shut. She turned and headed for the bedroom, flicking her hand in the air. "Now if I told, that would spoil the book for you, wouldn't it?"

He chuckled. "I guess. What are you doing?"

"I thought I'd change clothes."

Huh? Now what? "What you're wearing is fine for Ralph and Kakoo's."

"Short and tight, you mean?" She shook her head as she sailed through the door. "No. All week I've had to wear Muse's things."

Eyeing her sassy, thigh-length, buttercup-yellow sundress, he ventured, "So?"

"So it's been awful."

"It has?"

"Are you kidding? They're all so—" Abruptly she stopped and turned. Lifting her chin mutinously, she said, "I suppose you like her taste in clothes."

He pursed his lips to prevent a grin, knowing he was treading in dangerous waters. He sauntered to the bedroom door. "Now, honey, I like anything at all, as long as you're in it."

Her mouth wrinkled up like a prune. "Lord, you're smooth. Help me with this, would you?"

He frowned at her suitcase as he took it from her and hefted it onto the bed, dreading what he'd see inside when she opened it.

"You think I *like* looking like this?" She gestured at her cute outfit with open disdain.

He shrugged casually. "Don' know, but *I* sure like it."

He caught a sneaker just before it smacked him in the chest.

"Out!"

He retreated to the safety of the living area, resigning himself to a much more prim and proper Grace from now on. *Damn.* Though it would no doubt help his situation tonight if she didn't look quite so…delectable. Ah, well. With difficulty he shored up his earlier resolve to try to keep his distance from her. Prim and proper. A good start.

Then a ray of hope emerged from the bedroom in the form of a series of distressed mutterings and exclamations, and his resolve came tumbling right back down again.

"Somethin' wrong, *chère?*" he called.

"I can't wear these!" she exclaimed, coming to the door carrying a handful of extremely wrinkled garments. "It'll look like I slept in them!"

"*Sa c'est malheureux*…such a shame." Naturally, he was delighted. He wasn't a sexist or anything, but he surely enjoyed the sight of a *joli femme* in a sexy dress. Why hide it if it's worth looking at? Even if it was hell on a man trying to keep his hands off her.

She disappeared again. "Why didn't I hang these up when I first got here?"

He took a guess, "No room in the closet?"

He heard a distinctly disgusted snort. "And Muse doesn't even own an iron! I can't find one anywhere."

"Probably takes everything to the cleaners," he said noncommittally, remembering the dry cleaning ticket he'd run across in her briefcase when he'd searched it.

She huffed. "Bother." He heard her toss the wrinkled heap at the suitcase. "*Double* bother. I'll just have to go shopping. I've been meaning to pick up some things since I got here, but—" she darted him an accusatory glance through the bedroom door "—somehow I kept getting distracted."

"You find me distractin'?" he asked optimistically.

She scowled at him, crossed her arms and pretended to study something very interesting out the window. Her scowl deepened and she said, "And there's another thing I've been meaning to buy. Curtains!"

Now, that he could agree to. Even though he knew nobody could see into the apartment from anywhere but his own, and possibly the roof above it, he didn't like the feeling of the two of them being so fully exposed to the world. Especially with Morris' men lurking down in the courtyard through all hours.

"Good idea." He pleated his brow, a thought scampering around the outside edges of his brain. Then he had it. "But why buy new curtains when you can just pick up Muse's from the dry cleaners?"

She glanced at him, eyebrow hiked. "And how would you propose we do that? Go to every dry cleaning establishment in the Quarter and ask if I dropped off some laundry lately?"

Smug, he leaned back on his heels. "Naw. Just use the dry cleaning ticket in Muse's briefcase."

Her mouth parted and then reluctantly curled up at the corner. "I guess that's why they pay you the big bucks."

He winked, and with a flourish produced the ticket from the briefcase stowed under the bed. *"Voilà."*

She swiped it from his hand with a sheepish grin and headed for the door, apparently forgetting all about the awkwardness between them.

"Okay, Mr. Ace Detective. Let's go see if you're right." And with any luck, she'd forget all that nonsense about changing clothes, too.

"A hundred and ten yards?" Grace gaped first at the huge plastic-wrapped bundle on the counter and then at the bill. "You've got to be kidding," she mumbled, and reached for her checkbook.

"I'll get it," Creole said, handing the clerk his credit card.

"I'm so glad you came in," said the clerk. "I meant to call and remind you about them this morning, like you asked me to do."

"I did?"

"You said you'd probably forget about them." The petite foreign woman smiled broadly at Grace. "I guess I can see why."

Creole winked and signed the receipt, then hefted the bundle like a sack of flour over his shoulder. "Come on, let's hang these things up."

Luckily the dry cleaner was just around the corner from the apartment, so she didn't feel too guilty about Creole lugging the unwieldy package. She waved to their two FBI tails as she trailed him up the stairs, leaving them to melt into the courtyard greenery. The agents seemed like nice enough guys, but she was just as glad to be covering the windows properly. One man watching her every move was plenty, thankyouverymuch.

She opened the dry cleaner's package to find two separately wrapped bundles of curtains. "One must be for the living room and one for the bedroom." They looked about equal, so she handed one to Creole and tackled the other herself, dragging it into the bedroom.

"Um, Grace," he called after a few moments. "I'm really no good at this kind of thing. Any chance we can do this together?"

"I thought you'd never ask."

She dropped the mess she was making of her half, and went back to the living room. She was greeted by the sight of Creole, completely surrounded by a disorderly mound of white, diaphanous fabric dotted along one edge by a never-ending row of small white rings. He held up one end, looking very male by contrast, and completely overwhelmed.

"Oh, dear," she said, her lips twitching with amusement.

"*Je t'amuse?*—do I amuse you? If you laugh at me, I won't take you to dinner," he grumbled.

She stifled the grin that threatened. "Me? Never."

She grabbed the end from him and stood back to study the arrangement of the rod that stretched above the windows and French doors. "It should be easy enough to hang the curtains. Just slip the rings over the end of the rod."

He grunted and reached up to flick one end off the hook holding it up. "All right. You feed me the cloth." He plucked the first ring from her fingers and attempted to slide it onto the rod. After several stabs, he threw up his hands. "All right, smart aleck, I'll feed *you* the cloth."

After a good fifteen minutes she'd managed to thread about a third of the rings into place. "The curtains really are pretty," she remarked, glancing at the shimmering waves of transparent cloth, made of the finest white silk gauze she'd ever seen. "Like something from an old Southern mansion."

"I wouldn' know," Creole muttered, then glanced up from the tangle of yardage he was trying to straighten but only making worse. He gave her a penitent half smile. "But, yeah, they look nice."

"We're going to have to slide this lot all the way to the other end, so I can get the rest on," she said, peering at the far side of the rod, which still hung empty in place on the wall.

"No problem." He let go of his pile, went to the window and starting yanking the rings up the rod.

"Watch…" She looked on in horror as the rod bounced out of the hook and dumped twenty yards of foamy white silk. "…out!" Right onto his head.

Surrounded, he swore and thrashed about like a trapped alligator, nearly hitting her with his blindly flailing arms. She gasped at a near miss and dropped her end of the rod, which caused him to become even more firmly entrenched in the tangle. Somehow he lost his footing and landed with a muffled crash—and a few French swear words that, thankfully, she didn't understand—on his back on the floor.

"Oh, dear," she repeated, laughter bubbling up despite her best intentions. "Let me help you."

He went ominously quiet as she bent to tug at the disordered layers of curtain fabric that had buried him. Was that his teeth she heard grinding in the silence? It was impossible to tell, since his face was completely hidden in the jumble.

Honestly, she couldn't help it. Her laughter started against strict orders. At first only a few chuckles, then more and more until she was giggling furiously.

"I'm sorry. It's just—" she chortled wildly "—you look like a mummy gone terribly wrong."

His body shook once, whether in restrained anger or stifled amusement, she couldn't begin to guess. More laughter erupted before she could stop it. But there! That was definitely a masculine chuckle.

"Oof!"

Suddenly she found herself on her back. In a flash he was on top of her, and their positions reversed. Yards and yards of featherlight gauze ensnared her from head to toe like a wild, clinging petticoat. The distinctive, piquant smell of silk enveloped her, the glow of sunlight filtered through dozens of layers of shimmering gossamer.

"*Mais, toi,* you look like a beautiful bride."

The laughter on her lips evaporated.

"Just waitin' to be ravished."

And was instantly replaced by a breathless thrill at his rough-spoken invitation.

She tried to raise her arms, to reach for him, but found she could only lift them a few inches before being restrained by the cloth.

She was trapped! Caught beneath this electrifyingly sexy man, unable to do more than await his next move.

He froze. She heard a low curse, then he moved away.

"Wait!" Her heart pounded madly.

"What is it, darlin'? I'm about to break my promise here."

"If...if I were a bride," she whispered, "what would you do?"

The silence lengthened until she was certain he hadn't heard. Or wouldn't answer. But then slowly he lowered his tall frame back onto her. "If you were my bride, and I was your groom," his voice rumbled in a matching whisper, deep and rolling and filled with an emotion she hadn't ever heard from him before, "I'd peel away these layers, one by one. Kissin' your pale, smooth skin as each luscious bit was revealed, slowly strippin' you naked for the pleasure of my love."

A small moan of desperation escaped her throat.

Why, oh, why had she asked? She shouldn't be doing this! She'd never be able to resist his unrelentingly seductive nature. He was too great a temptation. But, oh, she wanted this dissolute, sensual man. A man who could make a woman forget all her plans, sacrificing all her caution to the overpowering siren call of being close to him. Under him.

As if reading her mind, his weight shifted off her, and he was gone.

She panicked, felt deserted in her burning need to touch him, be in contact with him, even through her silken net.

Suddenly she heard the whisper of feathery gauze and felt a layer of her cocoon lift from her legs and settle softly on her face and torso. He hadn't left!

A shiver rocketed down her spine. Would he do as he'd said?

"Creole…" she quietly pleaded, torn between needing to save herself and begging him to take her just as he'd described. What should she do?

"Hush, *ma douce amie*. Sweet darlin'. Let me love you."

She swallowed heavily and squeezed her eyes shut, wondering what he was really asking. Was it an afternoon of no-strings sex he sought? Or did she dare think he might be asking something much, much more?

He unearthed her ankle and grasped it. Strong fingers circled the narrow bone and smoothed slowly upward. She should protest, but her mouth refused to form words. All that came out was a weak, needy sound. His fingers stopped, withdrew, and she felt another tier of her make-shift petticoat lift. The skin of her calf tingled warmly, craving the return of his touch. She shifted, impatiently seeking his hands.

Sweet heavens. A moment ago she had meant to stop him. Now she couldn't stop *herself*. She wanted him. Wanted this. Wanted to experience the spangling ecstasy of being joined with this incredible man, regardless of the pain he would cause her when he walked away.

She swallowed again, knowing in her heart that this time it didn't matter what he asked of her.

Whatever he wanted, she would give.

"Yes," she answered softly. "Love me."

The layers of silk covering her lightened once again, and a few seconds later, again. This time both his hands found her, caressing her calves, lifting her knees gently from the floor. Her body thrummed with instinctive understanding of his positioning. She was ready.

His lips brushed over her feet, her ankles, and she heard

the sigh of the material as he languidly pushed it up her shins. The smooth scrape of a row of curtain rings trailed over her knees. Something tickled a spot on her thigh and her blood pulsed in dizzy anticipation. But he continued to tease with his lips. After an eternity, they moved from her calves to her knees, where they lingered maddeningly.

Achingly.

Frustratingly.

Surely she would scream if he didn't come to her soon!

"Mmm. You taste so good," he murmured, sliding his tongue up her inner thigh.

She shuddered in pleasure. "Oh, baby, I— Ow! What was that?" Something sharp and metallic pricked the top of her leg.

"I don'… Now, that's strange." He lifted his head and her mood wavered.

"What? What is it?"

"It looks like a…" He paused, and she felt the tangle of curtains being shifted from atop her thighs. "Well, I'll be damned."

"For crying out loud, what is it?" Sublime frustration sizzled through her. He would pick this moment to have his darn detective instincts surface!

"It's a key."

Creole stared at the thick, squat key dangling so enticingly between Grace's legs, then focused on the place behind it, and almost groaned out loud. What a choice!

Grace's arms lifted the pile of fabric from her upper body, and peered down at him through a tunnel of filmy white. There was a big frown on her face. "A key? What kind of a key?"

So much for their ambrosial afternoon and the passion it seemed she, for the first time, had truly, consciously, wanted to abandon herself to. Despite his earlier resolve to hold himself aloof, he hadn't been able to turn away when she'd reached for him with her seductive words.

He'd felt honored to share her gift, so very lucky to receive it. Unfortunately, it appeared his luck had just run out.

He sighed. "Looks like a safety deposit box key."

The frown deepened. She flailed a bit and sat up, perched in a cloud of silk. "Why would anyone keep a safety deposit box key attached to a curtain ring?"

"To conceal it?" he suggested, trying to fasten his brain on why Muse might have taken such elaborate pains to hide a key, and not on Grace's arousal-flushed face, still well within kissing distance.

"The deposit box must contain something very valuable."

He wrenched himself from thoughts of taking the damn key and hurling it out the window. "Valuable, or something she doesn't want anyone to know about." Then he added with sudden insight, "Except you."

She blinked. "Me?"

Slowly his mind fastened on the puzzle at hand. "Think about it. She left the dry cleaning ticket in plain sight in her briefcase. And even if you didn't find it, she'd asked the clerk to call and remind you about the curtains. She knew you'd put them up and find that key."

"But she's safe with the FBI. Why would she...?" Grace gazed at him, her sparkling blue eyes dimming with worry, her luscious rosy lips turning down at the corners. "We need to find out what's in that box."

Frustration flared for what might have been. But she was right. "Yeah. I guess we do. What time is it?"

They both turned to the clock. "Two-thirty."

"It's Saturday. Only half an hour before the bank closes."

"But which one?"

He looked at her anxious face, trying to think. He couldn't remember. "Have you seen a checkbook? Statements? Anything? Here, or at the office?"

She shook her head. "No, nothing like that. Wait! On

the computer! She had the Web site address for Louisiana Merchant Bank in her favorite sites folder. Isn't there a branch down on Decatur?''

"Bingo.'' He was already unfastening the ring the key was attached to. He grabbed her arm and pulled them both to their feet. "We better hurry if we're going to make it on time.''

Creole stood by as Grace extracted the contents of Muse's safety deposit box and spread them out on a polished wood table in the small room provided by the bank. They'd made it there in ten harrowing minutes, running the whole way, and spent another five talking the manager into breaking the no-Saturday-access rule and also letting him in with her—he'd had to show his badge—so they had just fifteen minutes left to examine the things Muse kept safe there. It was a piece of luck that Muse knew the manager and he recognized her. Or thought he did.

In the short stack of items, Creole spotted a birth certificate, a college diploma, which Grace gaped at in open surprise, a stack of savings bonds, a few pieces of jewelry which appeared old and valuable and which earned a misty smile from Grace as she laid them carefully aside. At the bottom lay a sealed envelope with "For Grace Summerville" written on the front of it in a slanting scrawl.

And a video cassette tape.

"Louisa, June 23,'' Grace murmured as she gingerly picked it up and read the hand-printed label.

Louisa?

He slipped the cassette from her trembling fingers. Both excitement and alarm zipped through his body as questions assailed his mind a mile a minute. Louisa was a hamlet on the Intracoastal Waterway, the one where they'd found Luke's body. If this tape had anything to do with James Davies or Gary Fox, it could be the break he was looking for. He sent up a desperate prayer on behalf of his brother's fate.

She reached for the envelope on the table. "Feels like a letter. What can it be?"

"Only one way to find out," he said as calmly as he could, to ease the obvious fright in her eyes. Dealing with his own was bad enough. "Let's go back to Muse's. You can read it there." He picked up the cassette and slid it into her purse. "Then we can see what's on the video."

The phone was ringing when they got back to the apartment. Grace ran to answer it while he slid the new lock home on the door behind them. He grabbed her purse from her and pulled the video out with two fingers. Until it proved different, he was treating the tape as evidence.

"Hello?" he heard Grace say, pause for a few seconds, then, "Um..." He glanced over and she silently mouthed *"It's Morris. What should I say?"* and shrugged uncertainly.

He pointed at the tape and shook his head in warning. If Muse had chosen not to share its existence with the FBI, Creole wasn't about to tip them off until he'd heard her reasons. Besides, it could turn out to be just an embarrassing home movie that had nothing at all to do with the case.

"I just needed some money," Grace said into the phone. "I lost my ATM card." She looked at him and made a what-was-I-supposed-to-say face. Then a frown creased her brow. "Of course," she said, glancing up at him in surprise. "Well, I, uh... Okay." She hung up, looking perplexed. "That was very odd."

"What did he say?"

"That he wanted to meet me. Alone. He said to watch for him and make some excuse to you so we could talk privately."

Creole stared at her, a thousand possibilities going through his mind, none of them good. "Don' even think about it."

"Of course not. But what do you think he's up to?"

"That, I would truly like to know." He extended his

hand for the phone, and when she gave it to him he punched in the three digits for Information. "I'd like the number for the FBI field office in New Orleans, please." He let the operator dial it, and when it was answered he asked for Agent Morris. He wasn't sure if he felt relief or trepidation when the man himself answered.

"Morris."

"This is Detective Levalois. Just wanted you to know I'll be taking Grace to Ralph and Kakoo's for dinner tonight at nine."

The agent sounded surprised to hear from him, but not particularly guilty. "Okay, thanks. Anyone show up yet?" Morris asked.

"No, nobody," he answered, and after a few more exchanges hung up.

Something was not quite right, but he couldn't put his finger on it.

"What was that all about?"

"Something I should have done right away. Make sure he's really with the FBI. He is. Are you certain it was him on the phone?"

She bit her lip. "He didn't exactly say, but it sounded like him. And who else could it have been? He asked about our run to the bank. His men must have reported we made them stay and watch the apartment."

It made sense, so he shook off the suspicious feeling and led her into the bedroom, where the VCR was situated, along with the TV. He carefully placed the tape in the machine but didn't start it just yet.

"Why don't you read the letter first?"

"Okay." She sat on the bed and broke the seal, extracting the letter.

"'Dear Grace, If you're reading this letter, I'm either dead—'" Her eyes widened, she gave a little mewling sound, and looked up in utter panic.

He sat down next to her on the bed and put his arm

tightly around her. "She's not dead, Grace. She's with the FBI." He hoped to God.

She gazed up at him with such trust in her eyes that it almost shocked him into retreat. He remembered that look. On Luke's face, the last time he saw him, bailing him out of jail for the dozenth time. When he'd told his brother he'd always be there for him, whenever he needed him, no matter what Luke had done. In the end Creole's reassurances had meant nothing. He hadn't been there when his brother needed him most. And he'd died because of it.

"I trust you," she whispered, and his heart wrenched. That's just what Luke had said. "Go on," he choked out, pointing at the letter, before she noticed his agony.

She nodded and read, "'…either dead, or I've disappeared, and you've come to rescue me, as always, dear sister.'" Her voice wobbled as she went on:

"Try not to worry. Unless something has gone wrong, I'm with the FBI—check with an Agent Morris. He was the blond man who was following me, by the way. But I don't quite trust them, so I am hiding this tape and the key, and trusting you, dearest Grace, to make sure it, and me, stays safe. I stole the tape from my ex-boyfriend Gary Fox, who stole it from his boss, James Davies, as insurance. Davies is a devil of a man, worse than anything you can possibly imagine. He must be stopped.

"Do *not* watch the tape, and keep away from them both, sugar, or they will surely hurt you to get to me and the tape. The FBI doesn't know about it. I fear there is someone inside who has been bought off by Davies. If the tape is discovered, I'm afraid for my safety, as I will no longer be useful to either side. Reveal its existence only if there is no other choice.

"Take care of yourself, sweet Grace, and give my love to Mama.

"Love, your devoted sister, Muse."

A tear plopped onto his forearm as he held Grace close, and he dragged in a ragged breath, silently vowing to keep her safe from these monsters. He only hoped the FBI agent taking care of Muse was doing the same for her.

"Don't cry, sweetheart, she's safe, I promise you."

Grace wiped her eyes and let out a shuddering sigh. "God, I pray it's true."

"Muse seems like a smart lady. She'll be fine."

He rocked her in his arms for a few minutes, feeling inadequate. Not knowing what he could do to ease her mind. He was so bad at this sort of thing. Comfort and solace. He had no experience at it.

Finally she looked up and said, "She didn't want us to watch the tape. I wonder why."

Instinct had him answering, "She didn't want *you* to watch it. She said nothing about me. It's probably not very pleasant. You should—"

"No. If you're going to watch, so will I."

He debated the wisdom of arguing with her. "All right, but if you close your eyes even once, I'm sending you into the next room and shutting the door."

She sat up straight and pushed out a breath, visibly gathering herself for the coming ordeal. "Agreed."

He walked to the VCR, pushed in the tape with a fingernail and pressed the start button.

But even he wasn't prepared for what he saw when the picture came on the screen.

His body froze in horror. Pain razored through his soul, slicing it to red, screaming ribbons.

There, beaten and bloody, sat a man, bound hand and foot to a chair and staring defiantly into the camera.

It was Luke, his brother.

Chapter 12

Grace's mouth dropped open in shock at the sight of the poor man on the TV screen. He was thin and rangy, his face clearly pinched with pain. His light-brown skin was covered with sickeningly large patches of black and blue, especially around his neck and shoulders, as well as with varying shades of crusted crimson. But his eyes were filled with a haughty disdain, directed at whomever was controlling the camera—and no doubt his suffering as well.

Grace gasped when a fist came out of nowhere and slammed into the man's jaw.

Suddenly Creole leaped to his feet and lunged to turn off the tape.

The screen went blank, and she turned to his stalled form, hovering over the VCR. She saw he was trying to punch the eject button, but his hands were shaking too much and missed at every stab. Dismay sang through her. What was wrong with him? He should be used to witnessing violence in his line of work.

"What is it? Creole?"

He didn't answer. With an anguished oath that sent chills down her spine, he gave up on the eject button. Hunching his shoulders up to his ears, he ducked his head between them and folded his arms up over his head, as if protecting himself from the blow that had struck the man on the video.

She slid to her knees and crawled to his side, wanting more than anything to throw her arms around him and hold him close, as he'd held her moments ago. She laid her forehead against the tense, bunched-up muscles of his biceps and just sat with him. And realized who the man in the video must have been.

After a long while, his fingers uncurled from the fists he'd made, and raked through his hair. His shoulders lowered a couple of notches and he dragged in a deep breath.

"It was your brother, wasn't it?" she said. "It was Luke."

He flinched, taking that imaginary blow to the face.

"Yes," he confirmed, his voice stronger than she could credit. "It was Luke." He turned to her, his handsome face stony and expressionless. "And no way are you watching that tape."

She only nodded. She had no desire to see what she knew the video contained. "You shouldn't, either."

His jaw set, and once again he amazed her with his unholy ability to shed all appearance of the emotions she knew for certain raged through him.

"I have to," he stated, and reached out with a steady hand to eject the tape. It wasn't rock steady, but close enough. "Get me a plastic bag, would you?"

Reluctantly she did as he bade, and he slipped it over the cassette as he extracted it, zipping it in safely. "I'm going to my place. I'll tell the men downstairs. Will you be okay alone for a while?"

No, she wouldn't be okay. Not knowing what he'd be going through. "You shouldn't do this," she quietly urged. "Call your captain or someone else. Don't put yourself through this, Auri."

"I made a promise," he simply said, and walked out the door, leaving her alone and in misery.

She watched him.

From her bedroom as he perched himself on the edge of a chair and started the tape. From her balcony as he sat for the first hour like a vulture ready to pounce on the man who was torturing his brother. From the living room and back to the bedroom while she hung Muse's curtains to stay busy for the second hour, and to keep herself from running to him the thousand times his body jerked up as if being struck. And as he sank farther and farther back in the chair, defeat and hollowness claiming his posture by the end of the ordeal.

She wanted to yell and scream and throw things in a tantrum that rivaled her worst-behaving student. It was so unfair. He'd been through so much already. Why must he go through something like this, too? It would surely break him.

He was so damned stubborn. Taking this need for revenge on himself, instead of leaving it to the officers in charge of the case. Making himself view something so heinous and vile that it would live with him, like a serpent eating at his insides, for the rest of his days.

What would it do to him?

To them?

Would it drive him back to hide deep inside himself, alone and guilt ridden, shutting her out forever? With a blinding clarity, she knew she couldn't let that happen. If he shut her out, he'd surely shut out everyone else, too. His difficulty with letting people close had been obvious from the first. If she let him retreat now, he might never find his way out of the pain again.

But there was more to it than that, she reluctantly conceded. Another reason she didn't want him to withdraw from her.

She was in love with him.

Completely and seriously in love with the man.

Even though she knew so well that he was wrong for her. Totally wrong. She didn't need another project—like her kids—another wounded soul to try to heal and bring back to the world of trust and love. A man who had told her outright he would never be the kind to fall in love and settle down, raise a family. He was a traveling man. No, not one like her father who literally packed his bags and left when things got too involved for comfort, but a man who did his traveling with his body, in physical reserve, and in his heart, with emotional distance.

When she fell in love, she'd always wanted it to be with someone warm and loving, supportive and giving. Someone she could come home to from her emotionally draining job and relax with. Someone she could share an ordinary, comfortable life with. A family with. Her heart with.

Someone who valued all those things, and wanted them as much as she did.

Not a half-crazy Cajun bad-boy cop who was bound to shred her heart to pieces and walk away without looking back.

But he was so needy, so vulnerable in his fortress-like strength and isolation, so very good deep inside, that she had not been able to keep herself from caring in a way she'd never felt before.

More than anything she wanted to break through that formidable reserve and close the endless distance between them. To show him that physical and emotional closeness were not something to be feared. Not if you were careful and picked the right person.

But to do that she had to believe it herself.

Was she willing to put her own heart on the line to teach him that powerful truth?

She gazed over at him, startled to see he'd finished viewing the tape, and was now out on his balcony, rolling a cigarette. It took him a long time and five tries to light it.

As he stood at the rail, smoking, staring down at the riot

of green in the courtyard, she was seized with a tenderness, a protectiveness, that threatened to overwhelm her.

She had tried to convince herself that her desire to make love with him this afternoon had just been physical, a result of her irrational sexual attraction to a dark, dangerous man. Nothing to do with her growing feelings for him. She'd been so sure she had those feelings, and herself, under control.

But now she realized her desire went way beyond superficial fascination. Oh, yes, she was still attracted to him physically. More than ever. Her insides nearly melted at the sight of him. But now she knew, despite the impossibility of their situation, and the inappropriateness of her love for him, that she wanted to make love to him with all her heart. *Really* make love to him. To show him loving emotion was good and right, and didn't have to be hurtful or lead to betrayal. So someday, when he met the right woman, he'd be able to commit to her totally and without reservation.

The thought of that illusive "someday" stabbed at her heart like a dagger, knowing it would never, could never, be her he committed to. But she saw it as her personal quest, her sacred duty to her unfulfilled, unrequited love for this man, to show him the way out of his unearned suffering. If she ended up suffering a little herself, she knew it would be just a fraction of what he'd been through in his life. He deserved every bit of light and joy she could give him, and more.

And she deserved a chance to know the touch of the man she loved with all her heart, if just one time, before she left.

She smoothed her yellow dress down her thighs and walked onto the balcony, going to the rail.

"How are you?" she quietly asked across the chasm that separated them.

Wordlessly he looked up. The hardest face she'd ever seen gazed back at her, bleak and bitter. Anger permeated every inch of his expression. She wanted to take a step backward, stunned by the seething intensity of his fury.

She leaned forward and whispered, "Come back to me, Auri. Come home."

He winced and shook his head, still saying nothing. She wondered if he was unable to speak.

"Please, baby. Let me help you."

Maybe it was the "baby" that got through to him, or the sincerity in her eyes. Or just plain desperation on his part. But he swallowed, dropped his cigarette to the balcony and ground it out with his shoe, and nodded once.

When she heard his footsteps on the stairs, she opened her door before he could knock—or change his mind. She considered it nothing short of a miracle that he'd come this far.

Opening the door wide, she backed away, giving him some space. Even so, he hung in the doorway, holding the bagged video in front of him like a shield.

"Come in," she urged. "Please?"

He did, with reluctance, closing the door behind him and backing up against it, regarding her closely, not unlike a cornered animal.

"How are you doing?" she asked softly.

"Bad," he said. "I'm angry. Real angry. I shouldn't be here." Still, he didn't make a move to leave. She took that as a good sign. "I definitely shouldn't be here."

She dared a step toward him. "What can I do to help?"

His eyes were fierce, almost savage, as he narrowed them on her. A muscle ticked wildly in his cheek. He didn't answer.

She took another step. "Tell me what you need."

He slashed up with a hand. "I need too much," he said, his voice raw and gritty. "Too much for you to give."

"I'll be the judge of that," she said, and closed the distance, easing the bag with the tape from his death grip on it.

His burden gone, he grabbed her arms, his fingers circling her flesh like tourniquets. She didn't quail, didn't show a sign of the blood that rocketed through her veins at his touch, the joy that he would trust her even this far. She looked up at him calmly, doing her best to focus his attention, his anger, on her, away from the ugliness he'd just witnessed, and channel it into something else. Something positive.

"I'll tell you what I need," he growled, and pulled her close.

Her senses filled with him and her pulse went crazy, an electrifying tumult charging places she didn't know she had. This was exactly what she wanted to happen. Making love would help him so much. *And her.*

"Tell me," she murmured, and felt the full impact of his hard, virile body against hers.

His hands slid up her arms to her neck and jaw, then his fingers bracketed her cheeks. Not painfully, but firmly, so she couldn't move her head.

He leaned in so they were nose to nose, lip to lip, sucking in the same hot, fevered air. "I'll tell you what I need," he repeated, and she was glad he was holding her, or she'd surely sink to the floor. "I need to forget."

Could she do this? "I'll try my best," she whispered, her knees shaking furiously. The emotional explosion she sensed they were on the brink of eclipsed anything she could have imagined. Her whole body shook with terror. And stunning anticipation. "How?"

He looked deep into her eyes for a very long moment, then moved his mouth to her ear and in a hungry murmur, he told her. Told her erotic, wicked things. Tantalizing things she'd never dreamed of. Passionate things that took her breath away. Carnal things she knew were meant to shock her into headlong retreat.

But she wasn't going to make it that easy for him. Not before and not now. Because she trusted him. And he needed her.

"I can do that," she managed, when his stream of earthy suggestions trickled to a stop.

His arousal grew hard and thick against her abdomen, and she exalted, knowing she'd turned the tide. Now all she had to do was relax and enjoy the resulting tsunami.

Relax?

The tidal wave came as his lips crashed down on hers. He pried open her mouth and plunged into her with his tongue, sweeping aside all thoughts of staying aware and focused on his needs. "Are you sure?" he gasped as they came up for air, long moments later.

"Oh, yes," she murmured, lost down the dizzy whirlwind of being in his arms. "Very sure."

He swept her up and strode into the bedroom, took the cassette from her and set it on the TV stand.

"I want you naked," he said, letting her feet tumble to the floor as he wrenched down the back zipper of her dress and yanked it off her. Excitement zinged through her entire body at the possessive look he raked her with. He reached for the clasp of her bra. "Completely naked."

He tore it and her panties off. As he quickly unbuckled his pants and unleashed his arousal, she ripped open the buttons of his outer shirt, stripping it from him before he could protest. She reached for the straps of his shoulder holster, but he grabbed her arms, whipped her around and pushed her onto the bed, front first. Tearing his handcuffs from his back pocket, he placed one ring around her wrist.

Before he snapped it shut, they both froze, each staring at the metal cuff with a sudden vivid awareness.

"Let's skip those," she suggested breathlessly, not wanting the reminder of restraints to lead to thoughts of his brother. Aside from any other reasons she might have.

He turned his eyes to her, keen but uncertain. "Won't it be too hard for you? I mean, not to touch—"

"I'll grab the bed if I feel the urge."

He was clearly torn. Had he ever made love without them?

"All right, we can try it." He tossed them aside.

Banding an arm around her abdomen, he slid between her legs, lifted her hips...and swore. Bracing herself for his entry, she peered around and saw him tear into a packet and sheath himself.

His eyes met hers. A shiver coursed down her spine and straight to her woman's center at the blatant hunger she saw glittering in their inky depths. A primitive, unhewn lust.

And something much more.

Need pulsed there, too, primal and basic. A need so centered in its intensity, she could not fail to recognize it for what it was—a need for *her*. Only her.

Holding her captive from behind, he thrust into her, deep, sure, arousingly forceful. The feeling was overwhelming; her body convulsed in pleasure. This was what she wanted, needed, had searched a lifetime for.

She closed her eyes and surrendered to the sensation of his body's possession.

She was his. Totally. Irreversibly. Agonizingly.

The denim of his jeans rasped against her thighs, and the weight of his gun in its holster pressed into the flesh of her ribs. His huge frame covered her completely, from her feet held down by his powerful ankles, to her back and bottom where he crushed into her with each commanding stroke of his hips, to her arms and hands which he held in place with muscled forearms and strong fingers woven with hers.

But instead of feeling trapped by his massive male body, she felt embraced. Desired. Needed.

Safe.

As if nothing ever again would or could hurt her.

Safe.

And also, incredibly pleasured.

He moved against her, thrusting deeper and deeper into her, filling her to the hilt over and over.

The combination of the emotional and the physical was incredible. An explosive, provocative, bone-deep feeling

that brought her right to the sharp, sparkling brink of ecstasy.

He groaned. "Ah, *chère,* I can't— I can't—"

Her name tore from his lips, catapulting her over the
edge of oblivion to the untamed roar of his release.

Creole lay sprawled on top of Grace for several breath-
gasping minutes before shame began trickling through his
consciousness, culminating in a low moan.

What had he done?

Her answering, "Mmm," sounded surprisingly agreeable
for someone being squashed by the brute who'd just taken
her like a half-feral junkyard dog. Make that fully feral.

Her fingers slipped from the black iron of the bedstead
she'd grabbed in the height of passion, taking his own with
them, as they were twined together like the tangled canes
of a rambling rose. Without letting go, she dragged his hand
to her lips and softly kissed his knuckles.

His heart squeezed. He guided his other hand to scrape
the damp strands of hair from her face.

"Ah, *chérie,* I'm so damned sorry," he whispered.

The corner of her mouth lifted faintly. "I'm not."

She shifted under him, making his body acutely aware
of her again. Her warm, smooth skin, her hot, wet velvet
glove. Still lodged deep inside her, he stirred, and just like
that he wanted her again. Painfully.

He pulled out. "It shouldn' have been like this. I should
have taken time—"

"You needed it like this."

It was true, but that didn't make him feel any better about
what he'd done. "I took my anger out on you, made it into
something—"

"Wonderful," she murmured, with a soft, radiant sigh,
filled with contentment. "Just wonderful."

Wonderful?

He'd thought he had no more emotions left inside to feel.
That they'd all drained out of him like rivulets of blood,

watching his brother die on that tape. But this was something new. Something he'd never, ever expected…or experienced…before.

Acceptance.

Inexplicably, the backs of his eyes stung. She'd taken him at his very worst, at the absolute lowest point in his whole wretched life, and with one word had turned it into something good.

He pressed his eyelids shut and sucked in a deep, cleansing breath.

He didn't deserve her.

But somehow, some way, he prayed he'd be allowed to keep her.

"Stay right here." He squeezed the words hoarsely past the huge lump in his throat and strode to the bathroom before he lost it in front of her. He disposed of the condom, then splashed his face with cold water, gripping the edge of the sink with white-knuckled fingers.

Wrong. It was too late. He'd already lost it, long ago. Probably the first minute he'd laid eyes on her. Certainly the first time he'd spoken to her. Now that he'd made love to her for the first time, he didn't stand a chance in hell of ever getting it back again.

His heart.

What there was left of it was hers forever.

"Auri?"

He looked up to the mirror and saw her worried reflection gaze back at him, concern filling her beautiful blue eyes. She leaned into him, laying her cheek against his shoulder.

"Are you okay?"

Again, his heart went out to this incredible woman whom he'd just used so selfishly. "Doin' better, *jolie,* thanks to you." He turned and put his arms around her. "Thank you for bein' here. I don' know what I would have done…"

He let the thought drift off, not even wanting to imagine what might have happened if she hadn't been there.

She circled his waist with her arms, resting her hands on the sink behind him, and hugged him close. "You shouldn't be alone. I know you're hurting." She put her honeyed lips to the curve of his neck and kissed him. "I wanted to make love."

"Me, too. Like crazy I did." He raised her chin with a finger and gazed into her eyes. "I just wish—"

"Hush, there's still time to do all that," she whispered, and lifted her lips to his.

He met them with a groan, "*Ma douce amie.* My sweet love." He filled his arms with her sweet body, his mouth with her sweet taste. "I love holding you like this," he murmured, sweeping his hands over her silky bare skin, her luscious nude curves. "*Si belle,* so fine."

She answered in kind, surrendering to his kiss, twining her arms around him but never touching with her fingers. He felt the old wariness and apprehensions start to slip. He knew he could trust her to take care of him, of his special dread. It was a profound relief.

So much so that when she reached for the straps of his shoulder holster, he pulled away in a sudden sweat, but didn't stop her from sliding them down his arms and placing the holster and weapon on the bathroom counter. He swallowed heavily, reading the understanding and encouragement in her expression as she saw his reaction to being stripped of his steady companion.

It wasn't the weapon itself that served to soothe his nerves so much as the tight cinch of the leather straps on his shoulders and the solid weight of the gun against his ribs, telling him he was in complete control of every situation.

But he wasn't in control anymore.

Without his unfailing security blanket, he stood before her feeling very naked and terribly vulnerable.

He saw the longing in her eyes to reach out to him, touch him, comfort him. He wished like hell his sickness would just go away, and he could let her touch her fill. For a moment the temptation to let her try swamped over him, nearly overcoming the knowledge that doing so would only lead to disaster and rejection.

Tentatively she toyed with the hem of his sweat-dampened T-shirt, glancing up for permission.

With an anguished shake of his head, he ground out, *"Non,"* crushed her to him, lifted her and carried her back to bed.

He darted a glance at the handcuffs lying on the nightstand, then rejected the impulse to reach for them. Just once he wanted to experience intimacy without that crutch. True intimacy.

"I'm sorry. *Dieu,* I'm so sorry," he murmured, coming down on top of her, pulling her into his arms. "How I want to be whole for you."

"It doesn't matter, baby. I like you fine just as you are. More than fine."

"You're too good for me," he whispered, aching because he knew it was true. A woman like her would never be content with a man as flawed as he was. *Should* never be. She deserved a man who was like her—perfect in every way.

"Not true," she sighed as he kissed a path down her throat. "You are so-o-o-o good. So very— Oh, Auri," her voice broke off when he nuzzled her breast and took the pebbled tip into his mouth.

Her breath gasped in, and he smiled as her nipple ruched against his tongue. This he could do. This was the one thing he knew he was better at than most other men. He had to be, since it was the only thing he could offer a woman in exchange for her time with him—enough blinding pleasure to make up for all the rest. At least for a short while.

With his tongue, he lathed first one breast, then suckled the other, nipping with his teeth, rolling the peaked crown between his lips. She writhed, and her hands came up, hovered over him, then plunged back and grabbed the iron headboard. Another great coil of tension left his body with a perceptible shudder. He was so incredibly lucky to have this phenomenal woman beneath him, gifting him with the treasures of her body.

Making love to her, he felt almost…normal.

She was a banquet, a feast to his starving soul. To the crushing need in him for simple human contact. He touched her everywhere, with every possible surface of his body. Wishing there were some way for her to do the same for him, but still thrilled to the core for all he was able to experience of her, with her.

He slowly, thoroughly, kissed every single inch of her front, turned her, and worked down her back from head to toe. Then he started over. Licking her, caressing her, running his cheek and nose over her, nipping at her, everywhere, everywhere. Learning her whole body, committing it to memory, until he knew it as well as he knew his own, or better.

Then he went back and did it again.

And again.

He couldn't get enough of her. The feel of her, the scent and taste of her. The sound of her needy whimpers and heated sighs. The sensation of her limbs trembling with desire under his hands and lips.

"Auri, please, I can't take much more of this," she pleaded, inflaming him further with her passioned entreaty. "I want you, I need you inside me."

"Soon," he murmured, loath to end his blissful exploration. He was so hard, so ready, he knew that when he entered her his time would be limited. He wanted this to last all night. All night and all day. Hell, a lifetime of nights and days.

"Soon," he whispered again, and moved down her body to part her legs, and settled his shoulders between them. He put his fingers to her feminine folds, so swollen and wet for him. "But first…"

A needy moan floated over the bed, and he couldn't have said if it was hers or his own.

He put his mouth to her, his tongue and his lips, and he loved her. Showed her in actions what he couldn't say in words, for fear of scaring her off sooner than she was bound to be otherwise. How he loved her!

Her legs came up and around his neck and shoulders, gripping him tightly. *Si bon.* So good. He heard her arms whoosh down and, amazingly, didn't flinch. Arching under him, she clutched at the sheets next to her hips, affirming his trust in her. The last steel band that encased his heart loosened and fell away, along with the cloak of caution he'd always worn in bed before. That, and the absence of his holster and Glock under his arm, made him feel strangely...weightless.

An incredible lightness settled over him.

An incredible rightness.

All because of this woman.

He tasted her, licked her, drank of her essence until he could feel the first tremors of her release. With a growl, he spread her wide and coaxed the impending explosion with his tongue on the pearl of her need.

She cried out his name.

His name.

Then her whole body shuddered sweetly.

And came apart beneath him.

Creole kissed her thigh, lovingly, lingeringly, drawing out a moment of anticipation as his woman floated back to him from her cloud of spent passion.

Now it was his turn.

He ached to throw himself into position and plunge into her. To thrust and scythe until he reached that burning pinnacle of need, and spill himself into her welcoming heat, over and over, on and on, until he had nothing left to give. No seed, no love, no heart, no soul. He wanted to give it all into her keeping. Everything. For, what use did he have of those things once she had left him?

She made a low hum of satisfaction, urging him up with

her sultry tone, and with the pressure of her legs on his backside.

"That was...unbelievable," she said on a moan as he glided up her body and lowered himself onto her. "I've never..." She swiped a tongue across her lips and smiled. "Never."

He smiled back at her lack of words, well pleased that he had given her an experience she'd remember, he devoutly hoped, for the rest of her days.

"I want you to hold me," he said quietly, and lifted her arms to circle his neck.

Her smile deepened. "I'd like that." She curled her fingers into her palms and rested her arms across his shoulders, pulling him close. She kissed him sweetly, lovingly. "Know what else I'd like?"

"What?" he gently asked, determined to make this time perfect. Whatever she wanted, he would give her. *Tout quoi e' veut.* Anything at all.

"I'd like to feel your skin against mine." She gazed up into his eyes beseechingly. "I'd like you to be naked, too."

Chapter 13

Grace watched Creole's face drain of color, leaving his rich, olive complexion nearly as pale as hers.

"Darlin'..." His eyes lowered and his jaw worked. "You don' know what you're askin'."

"No, I'm sure that's true," she murmured, feeling the tension bunch in the muscles of his shoulders. "Would you rather not?" she softly asked, not wanting to spoil the special place they'd already found together.

His breath jetted out, and he looked into her eyes. "Is it very important to you?"

She didn't know how to answer. Yes, it was important to her. To know he trusted her with his body enough to risk total intimacy. More important than she could say. But she wouldn't demand it, not unless he felt ready to take that step.

"I just thought— Well, we've been...good...together so far. I was hoping you might feel comfortable enough...."

He stared at her intently, unreadably. Finally he said, "What if you don' like what you see?"

That was the one objection she hadn't anticipated. She'd assumed his reluctance was due to his hypersensitivity over being touched. But the possibilities contained in his somber question were legion. And a bit unnerving.

"Of course I will."

He continued to study her, and she could almost hear the war roiling behind those brooding eyes.

"Why? Is your tattoo a dirty word?"

That earned a quirk of his lips. "No, nothin' like that."

"Well, then."

He let out a little sigh. "All right. *Tout quoi ti veux.* Whatever you wish."

His weak smile reached only about halfway to his eyes, but before that could register, he rolled off her and onto his feet beside the bed. In a few swift, efficient movements, his jeans and BVDs were lying on the floor. To her relief, other than a somewhat diminished arousal, everything looked normal.

Well, *normal* wasn't really the right word. More like magnificent.

Muscular athlete's thighs were covered with a light dusting of curly black hair, a lean washboard stomach peeked out from beneath the bunched-up hem of his T-shirt. And in between stood a stunningly large—

She felt herself blush furiously. She wasn't in the habit of ogling naked male—naked men. Regardless of how stunning they were. But to save her life she couldn't tear her eyes away from his—from him.

"Don't see a problem so far," she managed to choke out.

With just a fraction of a second's hesitation, he tugged off his T-shirt.

Sitting up, she gasped. "Oh, Auri! He's beautiful!"

Creole's tattoo wasn't a dirty word, or a word at all. It was an alligator—and beautiful didn't come close. He was almost as magnificent as the man carrying him.

Sprawled across Creole's broad shoulders like a scaly

fox stole, the ornate blue beast stretched from one corded biceps to the other. Its mouth gaped wide at the ball of Creole's right shoulder, showing an impressive array of teeth. Like a protecting dragon, it was poised to strike at whomever dared threaten his flesh-and-blood master. Its clawed feet were planted firmly by his clavicles. The monster's tail curled around his other biceps like a Celtic bracelet, ending in the pointed tip she'd seen under his sleeve at the café the other morning.

Grace rose on her knees and moved closer, admiring the intricate, artistic lines that made up the tattoo.

"I've never seen anything like it," she marveled. "It's so primitive, yet…"

"It's Maori. At least the artist was. Is. Friend of mine from way back. He designed them specially for me and—"

His words cut off, and he looked suddenly pale.

"For you and Luke," she completed, realizing now why Luke's shoulders had seemed especially bruised on the video. It must have been the blue of his matching tattoo showing through.

"Yeah."

"Come here," she whispered, holding out her arms to him.

Joy coursed through her when he put his knee on the bed and came to her, enveloping her in his embrace, pulling her tight to his chest. She was careful, so careful, not to run her hands up and down his back as she so wanted to do. She kissed him tenderly, loving the soft firmness of his lips, the spicy taste of him, even the bitter tang of smoke that clung to his tongue.

"Turn around," she whispered, wanting to see all of him, using the tattoo as a good excuse. "Let me see the rest of it."

His mouth opened, then closed. He nodded. Taking a step back from her, he turned.

"Ohhh, baby, it's so realistic! I can almost—"

Suddenly the breath halted dead in her lungs, ambushed

by a strangling sensation in her throat, so painful she wanted to cry out. But she couldn't find the air or voice.

The top of his back was covered with horrible scars.

The tattooed scales of the alligator's body did a creditable job of disguising them, but there was no hiding the pits and ridges of the dozen and more round scars branded into Creole's skin.

Cigarette burns. Old ones, by the look of them.

Tears sprang to her eyes and squeezed past her lashes before she could stop them. An anguished cry sobbed out from her constricted throat. "Oh, my God, Auri."

She twined her arms about his waist and pulled him back to her. Standing on her knees, she held him tight, and laid her damp cheek to the worst of them. Salty tears trickled down her face, spreading over the puckered scars as she tried to kiss away the evidence of the very worst of humanity.

A long sigh shuddered through his body. "*Chère,* don't. It's okay."

"No, it's not okay."

"It was a long time ago."

"And you're still suffering."

He turned in her arms and gazed down at her, taking her wet cheeks between his hands. "No."

"But not with me. Not tonight," she said in a quavering whisper, ignoring the denial they both knew was a lie. Praying she could make it true, if only for a little while.

Some of the darkness in his eyes disappeared. The beginnings of a genuine smile softened his mouth. "No, not with you, *ma coeur.*"

He lowered her down onto the bed. But before he could get comfortable, she rolled him onto his back beneath her.

"Grace—"

"Do you trust me?"

After a short pause he whispered, "I trust you."

At the quiet confession, his face swam before her, surrounded by an unfocused kaleidoscope of shiny pink.

"Let me love you," she murmured, echoing his words from the night before. "Let me touch you, in ways I know you like."

His tongue swiped over his lips. Reaching up, he skimmed the tears from her lashes with his thumbs. *"Jolie...* I really don' think—"

"You can tell me to stop anytime."

The longing that shimmered just below the surface of his eyes burst into a flare of hope, but he still looked as though he wanted to bolt.

Easing herself from his hold, she raised up to straddle his hips. She bent over, and slowly let her long hair trail across his chest. Down, then up again. He held his breath, following her movements in almost terrified fascination.

Nothing was going to stop her from touching him. Just as he had done to her. In as many ways as she could think of, without actually using her hands.

"Have you ever been on the bottom before?"

His eyes darted to her face, shocked. She smiled. She couldn't believe she'd asked it, either. Totally unlike the prim and proper Grace Summerville she'd been, up until just a few short days ago.

"No? Just relax," she whispered. "I promise you'll enjoy this."

Before either of them could change their mind, she leaned over and kissed him, pouring her whole heart and soul into it.

With her tongue and lips she caressed his mouth, starting shallow, slowly going deeper and deeper. The taste of him spread through her body like a scented breeze in a meadow of wildflowers. Warming. All-encompassing. Filling every nook and cranny of her soul, swirling around her insides like a living, pulsing heat.

She thrust her tongue far into his mouth, claiming every dark, wet recess for her own. Marking him as hers. Battling with his tongue for possession of their kiss.

He wrapped his arms around her, enveloping her, and

she felt his surrender. He opened himself to her questing, to her thrusts and parries, to her rapt, fluid penetration, allowing her complete liberty. Until they were joined almost as closely as the act they sought to imitate.

They moaned together, his deep bass hum blending with her higher one in perfect harmony.

His hands skated down her body. "Ah, *chère,* you melt me with your kisses."

She dragged her tongue over his chin and down his throat, lapping at the little hollow below his Adam's apple. He swallowed, and it bobbed against her cheek. But he didn't protest as her mouth continued on its journey over his chest.

His hands found her breasts, and for a moment she forgot to breathe. His long, strong fingers enveloped them, testing, teasing, plucking at the tips.

"No fair," she gasped, and touched his flat brown nipple with her tongue.

With a groan he grabbed her head with both hands. And held her there. His nipple swirled tight as a nut as she licked and sucked. His heart pounded fast and furious under it. She switched to the other side and another groan erupted from deep in his lungs.

Lifting, she brushed her breasts over his chest, his stomach, his abdomen, and lower, drawing out the pleasure for both of them. Her body was on fire, aching to be joined with his. But she wouldn't, not until she had proven to him how incredibly sensual a man he really was. That his body held untold delights to be basked in, not avoided. She moved lower still, eager to taste all of him. Again, his hands shot out and held her fast. This time preventing her from coming any closer.

"Don' even think about it, *chère,*" he rasped out.

Inches from her lips, his arousal throbbed to the hammer of his heartbeat.

"Not that I wouldn'—" He cleared his throat. And again. "Let's save this for another time, *non?*"

Understanding, feeling as much on the brink as he, she nodded. His fingers loosened, just enough to allow her to place a kiss on the silken tip.

Half of her wanted to defy him, to immerse herself in the unexperienced pleasures of knowing a man—this man—so intimately. But the other half knew she'd regret not being with him, holding him deep inside her, when he came apart in her arms.

"I won't forget, you know."

"I'm countin' on it."

She sat up, taking in the sight of him. Reclining on the soft pink satin sheets, backdropped by the ornate iron lace of the headboard and the frilly, feathery Mardi Gras masks on the wall behind it, he should have looked ridiculous. At the very least, out of place. Instead, the feminine trappings only enhanced his formidable masculinity. He looked like a dark, nefarious demigod, come to earth to corrupt the flesh of an innocent maiden. Ironically, it was the maiden herself who was trying her best to seduce the flesh of her corrupter.

She reached for an elaborate mask, just above the bed. And plucked a feather from it.

A long, supple, responsive feather.

His eyes widened. "What do you plan on doin' with that, *jolie?*"

She smiled enticingly. "Exactly what you think I'm going to do."

"Now, honey, no need to go overboard. You've made your point."

"And what point would that be, baby?" She drew the edge of the feather along his jaw.

"That I like—" his words choked off as she trailed it down his throat and chest. "—bein' touched," he wheezed out.

"Hmm," she said, continuing to torment him. Pausing in her ministrations, holding the feather just above his taut nipple, she innocently queried, "You want me to stop?"

For an explosive second they studied each other. Then in a strangled voice he whispered, "No."

"Close your eyes," she urged, jubilant. She had won the first hurdle. Now together they could fight to get him over the rest. Given enough time. She pushed aside the bleak knowledge that time was the one thing they did not have. For now she would rejoice in their successes.

She lowered the feather, and the bead of his nipple twisted to a flint-hard point. Hissing out a gasp, he squeezed his eyes shut in an almost tortured expression of pleasure. She touched the other brown nub, running the serrated edge of the feather over it. A zing of arousal sang through her own breasts at his agonized moan.

"Do you like that?"

"Ahhh, yeah."

So did she. His reaction to her teasing was turning her on incredibly. Notched between her legs where she straddled him, his arousal pulsed hotly, sending waves of desire spiraling low through her belly. The urge to tip forward and take him into her was nearly irresistible. But no, it was too soon. She slid from his thighs and knelt next to him, continuing her delicious torment, avoiding any contact that threatened to put him over the edge.

"Turn over," she murmured, when he looked ready to jump from his skin with blinding need.

"No," he groaned. "*Pitié.* Have mercy, woman. I'm about to explode!"

"Me, too," she whispered in his ear. "Turn."

He did, and she instinctively knew he'd forgotten about everything except her and the feather. She touched it to the small of his back and dragged it up, up, his spine, to the cluster of scars that covered his upper back. His whole body shuddered, and he grabbed at the iron curlicues of the headboard. A muffled groan slid out from the pillow where he'd buried his face.

"*Chère—*"

She zigzagged the feather over his whole back, over his

buttocks and down his thighs. A cascade of goose bumps followed in its wake, like the notes of a beautiful symphony rising to the beck of the conductor's baton. Then, she touched between his legs.

Suddenly she was on her back beneath him.

"*Assez!* Enough!"

The feather fluttered slowly to the floor. Just as slowly, quiveringly, he spread her legs and entered her.

"*Je suis en feu,*" he whispered. "I'm on fire. For you."

He was long and thick and scaldingly hot. He filled her, languidly, deliberately, seizing every inch she offered, and still he kept pressing in. Farther and farther in he came, until he was so deep inside her she was certain she could feel him touch her very heart.

He watched her blissful acceptance of his body into her. His eyes never left hers, even when she had to close them for the dazzling pleasure that burst through her. She whimpered, and twined her legs around his waist, seeking more, seeking...more.

His face was intense, covered in a thin film of sweat, jaw clenched in a furious tension of restraint.

"Look at me, *chère,*" he commanded, low, rough.

She opened her eyes, and for several fervent moments they just gazed at each other. Their bodies pulsed to the same heartbeat, breathed the same air, shared the same space. They were one.

Looking into Creole's black, fathomless eyes, she felt the first tight coil of sensation ripple through her womb. Never had she felt so heavy, so filled, so intoxicated with desire. So ready to splinter at a single word or sign from the man who completed her.

His hand found hers, and he brought it to his mouth. He kissed the back of it, kissed each of her knuckles in turn, caressed the hollow of her palm with the firm pressure of his lips and tongue.

Then with fingers trembling against hers, he slid the flat of her hand to his cheek, and held it there.

Tears pooled in her eyes.

"Oh, my love," she whispered on a quiet sob.

He moved inside her, out then in, filling her whole body with his overwhelming, potent presence. With the raw pleasure of his love. Her muscles tightened unbearably around him. She moaned his name.

Still, he held her hand to his cheek. "*Rest avec moi, mon amour.* Stay with me, my love," he groaned. "Stay." He thrust into her again.

"Yes," she cried out, throwing her other arm around his neck. "Yes!"

His mouth crashed down on hers, capturing, plundering. Her fingers rested on his cheek, holding, touching, claiming. He was hers! *All hers.*

She convulsed around him, unable to keep from shattering. A thousand, million searing sensations ripped through her in a tumult of emotion. With a guttural shout, he joined the tempest, swelling to unbearable proportions, stiffening, erupting in a deluge of molten heat against the very mouth of her womb.

She held him tight, riding the storm, gathering to her every miracle and texture of their tumultuous fulfillment.

He was hers, and she would not give him up.

Creole awoke in an instant.

He wasn't alone.

Warm curves, pale hair and the scent of sweat-slick female skin engulfed him in a sensual tangle. *Grace.*

For a minute he was completely distracted by the lithe limbs and plump breasts that pressed into him as he lay over her, clutching her possessively to his chest in slumber even as he had held her in the throes of passion.

Then he heard it again. A soft click from the other side of the bedroom door.

They weren't alone.

He grabbed for the weapon under his arm. It wasn't there.

He froze. *What the hell!* He always carried his weapon, no matter what. The Glock was the one thing in his life he could always count on being there for him.

Until last night.

With dawning horror, he remembered. Last night with Grace, he had traded one comfort for another of a very different sort. In a moment of weakness he'd left his only security on the bathroom counter along with his shirt, where they still lay in a useless heap.

And now he'd pay the price. *Merde!*

Before he could react, or even think what to do, the bedroom door flung open, ricocheting off the wall behind it.

"Move and I'll blow you away," a male voice scratched from the darkness.

"Auri, who is it?" Grace mumbled, coming awake under him, attempting to raise her head.

"Well, hello, sweetheart," the man replied, with way too much familiarity for Creole's taste.

"Morris?" Grace asked, rubbing the sleep from her eyes. "How'd you get in?"

Creole glanced at her with a frown. What had given her the idea the intruder was the FBI agent? Clearly it wasn't.

"I'm hurt, sweet thing," the intruder said. "Guess again."

"But...the voice from the phone. I thought—"

Creole silently cursed and eased himself off her, rolling onto his back and sitting up. Well, that explained a few things about the mysterious phone call.

The lamp on the dresser clicked on, backlighting a figure in the dim glow—along with the automatic pointed right at Creole's head. Instinctively, he reached for the sheet and drew it over Grace.

"I said, don't move."

He raised his hands. "Just coverin' the lady."

The man snorted. "Now, that's funny." He moved to the foot of the bed, and the hair stood up on Creole's neck.

The face staring back at him was eerily familiar from a rap sheet as long as Florida.

Gary Fox!

Fox's eyes traveled between them, then narrowed on Grace. "I must say, I'm surprised, sugar. Your tastes change since I saw you last?"

"What do you want, Fox?" Creole interrupted.

He heard Grace's strangled gasp, and felt her slide behind him, nestling into his back. Inwardly he swore long and ugly. He'd never forgive himself for not having his weapon at his side. Or at the very least under the pillow. It was inexcusable.

Again Fox scrutinized Grace, then him, with a penetrating stare. "The question is, what do *you* want?" His gaze flicked to the rumpled bed around them, then back to Grace. "'Cause, I don't know who the hell you are, but one thing's for damn certain. You are *not* Muse Summerville."

After a stunned moment Creole muttered another curse. So much for their little charade. How had the creep guessed so quickly?

"What's the matter, cop? Your plan backfire?"

He had a fleeting thought for the two FBI agents stationed below in the courtyard. How had Fox managed to slip past them?

As if reading his mind, Fox sneered. "Don't hold your breath waiting for those two clowns to come to the rescue. That coffee I delivered should keep 'em out for hours."

Grace had probably been shocked speechless by the revelations up to this point, but suddenly she scooted around him and blurted, "What we want is my sister. What have you done with Muse?"

"Your sister, eh?"

Creole tensed his muscles to jump the guy while he was distracted. Too late. Fox sensed his move and trained the gun on Grace's temple.

"I wouldn't."

"Easy." Creole lifted his hands, palms out.

"Enough of this crap. Just hand it over, and I'm outta here."

A whip of alarm bolted through him. "Hand over what?"

"Don't play games with me. I know you got it out of the safety deposit box today. Just give me the damned tape. *Now.*"

Blind panic paralyzed him. He couldn't lose the video! It was his only evidence against Davies. Without it his brother's murderer would walk. Over his dead body would that happen.

"We don't know what you're talking about," Grace chimed in with far more conviction than he could have summoned at the moment.

But Fox wasn't buying. Keeping the automatic leveled at them, he glanced around the bedroom. A sinister smile slithered onto his lips when he spotted the cassette sitting in full sight on top of the TV. He reached for it.

"Non!" Creole lunged.

In slow motion, he saw Fox raise his weapon and sweep it toward him as he sailed through the air, determined to bring the bastard down. Grace screamed.

It was the last thing he heard before the world exploded and everything went black.

Chapter 14

"Creole!"

On her hands and knees, Grace dipped a cloth in a bowl of ice water and applied it to her lover's bleeding forehead. "Please, baby, wake up."

She weighed the consequences of slapping his cheeks, and decided a light smack was worth the risk, if it revived him.

"Come on, honey. Auri? Open your eyes," she urged his inert form as she gave him a few gentle slaps. He had a nasty gash on his temple, and had been out for almost a full minute. She was getting desperate.

Relief flooded through her when he cracked open his eyelids and peered groggily at her. "Where am I?"

"On the bedroom floor. I didn't dare move you after Fox whacked you over the head with his gun. Are you all right?"

His miserable groan spoke volumes. "He got away?"

"I'm sorry," she said, her voice wavering with contrition. "You were hurt, and I didn't know what to do. I've never shot a gun—"

"Hush. It's my fault. Not yours." Creole's eyes squeezed shut, and a look of such anguish swept over his face her heart twisted. "All my fault."

"But how could you have known?"

"I'm a cop! It's my job to know!" he barked out, and jerked upright to a sitting position. He immediately grabbed his head. "Damn, that hurts!"

"I have some ice here," she said soothingly, and handed him a bag with cubes in it. Already, his angry, bleeding wound had grown a bump the size of an egg. "It'll help bring down the swelling."

"I don' want any damn ice! I'm goin' after Fox and getting that tape back!" He stumbled to his feet and promptly collapsed into her arms.

"You're not going anywhere right now. Sit down," she firmly ordered, leading him to the bed. "Better yet, lie down while I call a doctor."

"Grace—" He grabbed the sleeve of the robe she'd thrown on. "No doctor. Please. I'm fine." He put the improvised ice pack to his temple, as if to show her he'd behave. "See?"

She blew out a breath. He was a big boy. Old enough not to need a mommy. "Okay. No doctor. But I'm going on record that I don't like it."

He may not need mothering, but as she helped him onto the bed, she barely resisted the urge to smother him with kisses. Somehow she didn't think he'd appreciate the gesture at the moment. His scowling face was positively fierce. The intimate mood they'd created together last night was but a distant, shattered memory.

Probably just as well. After they'd made love, she'd deluded herself into thinking what they had could be more than was really possible. That she might be able keep him. Make him happy. But in the bright light of morning, she knew better. Creole didn't want that kind of relationship. Best not to kid herself.

"I should check on the men downstairs. And call Morris," she added, tucking a pillow behind Creole's head.

He grunted in response, then groped for her hand. "Grace…thanks."

She smiled sadly at his closed eyes. It was obvious he was torturing himself over the loss of the tape. Blaming himself, where there was no guilt. "You're welcome," she murmured, and rose, tightening the belt on her robe.

On her way through the kitchen, the phone rang.

"Maybe that's Morris," she said, lifting the receiver. "Hello?"

"Miz Summerville?"

Her thoughts scrambled. "Frank?"

"Yeah, I'm—"

"Listen, Frank, this isn't really a good time. Can I phone you later—"

"No, Miz Summerville. I won't be here. I've called to say goodbye."

"What?" She sat down abruptly on a kitchen chair, her brain spinning. "Goodbye? What's going on?"

"I, um…"

She could hear his breathing on the other end, heavy and nervous. "Tell me," she urged.

"I gotta get outta town," he finally clipped out. His tone had become cold and belligerent, much more like the tough guy she'd dealt with three years ago than the sensitive boy she'd slowly been able to excavate from that mass of adolescent cockiness.

"What happened?" She prayed he hadn't done something really stupid. Something that would land him in jail.

"Nikki's pregnant," he said in a rush, "and no way am I gettin' stuck with the kid. Not my thing. She's better off without me, anyway. Not dad material. Don't want to be tied down. Ya know?"

Shock and dismay had her rooted to the spot. Her mouth worked, but no sound came out.

Yeah, she knew. Better than anyone, she knew. Knew what it was like to have a dad who felt that very same way. Knew what it was like to live every day of your life without a father's love. Without even a postcard at Christmas.

"Yes, I know," she replied, anger surging through her veins. "And I think it stinks. I think everything about it stinks. I think you stink. But if that's how you feel, nothing I can say will make any difference."

"Miz Summerville, please, you gotta understand," he pleaded, his macho front temporarily crumbling. "I can't do this. I don't know nothin' about being a father. I can't. I just can't."

"There are other options."

"Nikki won't even talk about 'em. Her mind's made up, she's keeping this baby. And I'm leaving town."

"You're a coward, Francis Vincent Morina! You're always saying how you don't want to be like your father. So prove it to me. Prove it to yourself! Do the right thing."

"And what would that be? Marry her? Have a wife and a kid when I haven't even graduated from high school? What kind of a life would that be for me? For any of us? What do you think I should do, Miz Fancy Counselor, with your fancy degrees and fancy cash in the bank and no problems in your fancy life?"

Grace couldn't even begin to react to the unjust accusations being hurled at her by the boy. She choked back the tears that clogged her throat from his verbal betrayal and replied, "I don't know, Frank. But I do know that running away isn't it."

"Sorry, no can do. See ya 'round, Miz Summerville."

There was a sharp click, and she knew she'd lost him.

She carefully put down the phone and covered her mouth with trembling fingers. The collective sound of a hundred colleagues' I-told-you-so's echoed through her mind.

Grace Summerville's failed again. Chalk up one more

kid to the dark side. Don't know why you even try, Grace. These boys never change.

Never change.

Never.

"Who was that?" Creole's voice echoed from the bedroom.

It was you, her mind answered before she could stop the thought.

Oh, God. A single tear squeezed past her defenses and slowly trickled down her cheek. It was so horribly, pathetically true.

"It was Frank," she replied mechanically.

Men like Frank and Creole didn't change.

"What'd he want?"

Want? They took what they wanted and moved on. As her father had. As Frank was doing. As Creole would surely do if confronted by the same situation. She'd be a fool to think otherwise.

"He wanted to say goodbye."

"Eh?"

"I should, too." She mercilessly pulled back a lock of hair, still disheveled from their night of passion. How long would it take for Creole to say goodbye? To decide he'd had his fill and needed to move on?

At the first sign of trouble, she'd guess.

"I should've known," she murmured. "I should have kept myself from caring. But I'm just not like that. I should resign myself to the inevitable. But I can't do it from here. I have to leave."

"*Chère?*" Creole's battered form filled the bedroom doorway, leaning against the frame for support, ice held to his temple. "What the hell are you talkin' about?"

She looked up, aghast. Had she been speaking aloud? "I—"

She gave herself a mental shake and quickly swiped the tear from her cheek. "I have to go. That was Frank. He's in a terrible jam."

Even if it did no good, she couldn't give up on the boy. She had to talk to him face-to-face before he bailed out. Try to knock some sense into the frightened kid she knew had, deep down, been asking for help. And if that didn't work, at least she could offer Nikki her support.

As an added bonus, her own problem with Creole would be solved by default.

"Go?" Creole was staring at her, disbelief filling his dark-smudged eyes, making them swirl black as midnight. "As in leave? Town? For good?"

Her bottom lip quivered. "Yes. Frank needs me."

"And what if *I* need you?"

She blinked. Their situation came rushing back, filling her with even more guilt. Fox. The tape. Creole's possible concussion. Sweet mercy, she couldn't desert him, either! "I—"

A scowl swept over his features. "You said you would stay with me. Change your mind so soon?"

What? In the heat of lovemaking, he'd asked her to stay with him, but that was— Her cheeks flamed. "Oh! I thought— That is, I thought you meant…" Could it be he'd really intended—

Suddenly he turned his back, retreated into the bedroom. "Of course I did. By all means, don' stay on my account."

"But the case. I promised to help."

"Don' worry about it." He walked toward the bathroom. "Our charade worked for a while, but ended up bein' a disaster. I'm better off on my own."

As he swiped his T-shirt from the floor and yanked it over his head, she couldn't help thinking he wasn't talking about Fox or the case. But he seemed calm enough. Obviously, her leaving didn't unduly upset him.

"Creole, I—"

He spun, eyes pinioning her where she stood. "So it's back to Creole, eh?" He grabbed his holster and strode over to pluck his pants from the floor. "Suits me."

"No! I mean— Please, Auri, we had a wonderful night together, but we both knew it wouldn't last."

"Yeah. I knew you'd leave."

He didn't tack on *me* to that statement, but she had the most inconceivable feeling that he'd wanted to. Which, of course, was ridiculous. He couldn't possibly want her to stay. Not forever. He wasn't that kind of man. He must have meant for a few days or a week. Just until he got bored.

Men like Creole didn't change.

She approached and tried to put her arms around him, but his body stiffened and he eased out of her reach. He turned away, cinching himself into his shoulder harness. She wanted to weep over the loss of closeness, the complete reversal of all the good they'd found together last night.

"I'll check on the two men in the courtyard," he said, all cool, strictly business. "Can you track down Morris and get him here?"

"Of course. But you should be resting."

"Lock up behind me."

Before she could stop him, he was out the door and gone.

She gave a deep, cheerless sigh. Yes, for her own sake she must go. Get herself away from a man who would only hurt her, who was already breaking her heart. But she hadn't wanted to leave like this. Not anything like this.

He might at least have kept up the pretense for a few hours longer. Instead, he'd shown her how little the night had meant to him. How little *she* meant to him. Slam-bam, thank you, ma'am. Leaving? Okay, have a good life. *Bonne nuit, chérie.*

Pain sliced through her like broken glass. She had made the right decision. If she stayed, even for one more day— or worse, one more night—she didn't know if she'd survive the anguish of leaving him. His cold indifference would surely kill her.

With leaden hands she picked up the phone once more and dialed the number for Agent Morris.

* * *

When Creole reached the bottom of the stairs, he grabbed the wall in agony and leaned against it for several minutes, unable to move. He didn't think a body could bear such pain and live. And it wasn't his head that felt crushed by the killing blow. It was his heart.

She was leaving. Leaving him.

Betrayed again. Just like with all the others. Empty words. Sweet promises. Then comes the morning and with it, bitter reality. After last night he'd truly thought Grace was different. That she cared about him. Really cared.

Obviously, he'd been wrong. Some kid she had no personal relationship with was more important to her than he was, more important than her words and promises.

As usual.

At least he'd found out before it was too late. Before he'd made a complete idiot of himself and proposed, or something equally insane. *Dieu,* she'd probably have laughed in his face.

Slowly he felt the comforting numbness descend upon his body, enveloping him in its solace of blessed indifference. A lifetime of bitter disillusion had taught him what to expect. And this was what came of losing sight of the path he'd long ago carved for himself. For a brief, shining moment he'd actually thought he could break out of his destined fate and be happy.

Hope had been the culprit. Hope—that cruelest of all conditions, far worse than physical abuse. But this time he'd learned his lesson well. Never again would he make the mistake of hoping.

Pushing himself off the wall, he lurched through the front door, suddenly strangely unable to focus. The courtyard swam before him in a pond of green foliage and red brick. He almost stumbled over the first FBI agent, sprawled across the cobbles of the entryway as if struggling in the last moments of consciousness to reach the door.

Creole blinked away his visual affliction and forced him-

self to concentrate. Enough of this maudlin feeling sorry
for himself. He had to get back to what was important. He
had a job to do. A brother to avenge. And a man to kill.

An hour later Morris had come and gone, along with an
ambulance summoned to cart off the two drugged agents.
The EMTs had insisted on checking out Creole, as well,
and he'd endured their poking and prodding, light shining
and bandaging with surprising equanimity. It still bothered
him when they'd put their hands on him, but he'd been
able to grit his teeth and get through it.

He and Morris had had a brief argument over leaving
Grace unguarded. Morris felt that since the tape was gone
and Fox had left her unharmed, her life was no longer in
danger. Creole disagreed, but he'd been outranked and out-
voted. Morris had assumed he'd still be there to watch over
her until she departed for the airport later today. He hadn't
had the guts to set the man straight, so it looked as though
he'd be stuck doing just that.

But he'd be damned if he'd do it from the same apartment where she'd been hiding out avoiding him for the past
hour and packing her bags to leave. He'd take up his old
spot on the balcony, or better yet, watch her from bed. His
head had started some serious pounding. The two pills the
EMTs had given him hadn't even made a dent.

Dragging himself up to his apartment, he opened his curtains wide, poured a glass of ice water, and fell onto the
bed he hadn't slept in for two nights. Two nights he was
not going to think about.

As he lay there, he rubbed the icy glass back and forth
across his forehead, trying to tame the throbbing that ham-
mered through his skull. He glanced over to Grace's apartment. He could see her where the curtains were drawn and
fluttering in a light breeze from the French doors. She was
in the bedroom getting dressed, facing away from the windows. The thin strap of a bra bisected her bare, graceful
back; a long, slim skirt clung unzipped to the lush curve

of her hips. He groaned, banging his eyelids shut against the sight. An all-too-familiar sight. The sight that had started this whole damned, miserable affair a few short days ago. Back when the last vestiges of a heart and a soul still resided inside him, where now just a hollow shell remained. The only thing he couldn't figure out was how an empty husk could hurt so damned much.

He made another pass with the chilly glass across his sweat-damp forehead. Unable to resist, he followed her every move as she finished dressing. Apparently, she'd decided wrinkles didn't matter, because the outfit she'd chosen to wear for the journey home was obviously not one of Muse's slinky ensembles. Her elegant brown skirt reached to midcalf, and the white blouse she'd paired it with had a round, high collar and short, puffy sleeves. Back to the prim and proper Grace, to whom the sensual woman he'd come to know bore little resemblance.

Unbidden thoughts crept through his mind. Could he love this Grace? The real Grace? Or had he simply fooled himself into thinking she was someone bolder, more daring, passionate and accepting than she really was? A vacation persona, someone she would never, ever consider being in everyday life?

He shoved the glass impatiently onto the nightstand. *Que diable*—none of it mattered. He'd never get the chance to find out which was the real Grace. She was leaving, and that was that.

Sighing, he gingerly kneaded the unbruised area of his temple. *"M'fous pas mal."* Who the hell cared. After today he'd never see the woman again.

Creole snapped back to consciousness with a start. He must have drifted off for a minute. Forcing himself to turn on his side, he perused Grace's place. She'd drawn the filmy white curtains in the bedroom. The curtains they'd almost made love on top of.

With an angry curse he shook off the unwanted memory

and peered into her living room. He didn't see her, but two small suitcases stood ready and waiting by the door. And there was a man sitting on the couch.

Creole bolted upright. *What the hell…*

His blood curdled in his veins when he looked closer at the man's face. *He recognized that face.* He'd never forget it as long as he lived, etched as it was into his darkest memory—*from the video of his brother's murder.*

For a brief moment he was paralyzed with horror. Where was Grace? What had they done to her? He scoured what he could see of the apartment for any sign. There! Something moved behind the opaque curtains in the bedroom! He could just make out two silhouettes—those of Grace and another man, facing each other.

Almost blind with terror, Creole launched into action. Groping for his weapon—*right where it was supposed to be.* Stumbling to the phone—*C'mon, c'mon Morris, answer!*

"Morris! Davies is in Grace's apartment. I'm going over there."

Suddenly the man grabbed Grace's arms, savagely twisted them behind her and pushed her to the bed.

Non!

Creole threw down the phone and raced to the balcony. *Le bon Dieu—*

Before he could complete the thought, he hurled himself over the rail like a madman and jumped. Praying he'd make it across the four feet of thin air to her balcony. In time.

Chapter 15

Grace struggled with all her might against the disgusting man who held her fast. She knew it was useless. Even if she got loose from this one, there were two others in the living room to catch her.

He only laughed. "Give it up. Nothing you do's gonna save your cop lover boy." He sniggered, then pushed her onto the bed and leered into her face. "Or you, neither, sister."

The perverse irony of his "endearment" hit her hard. Muse had risked her life to put this detestable scum and his boss in jail. Tears of pride stung Grace's eyes as she sank her teeth into the creep's arm. She could do nothing less.

He backhanded her. "You little bit—" The crash of something heavy tumbling onto the balcony floor cut off his insult. "Just in time," the man sneered, looking up. "Wouldn't want to start the fun without your boyfriend here to watch."

"Creole, no!" she screamed. "It's a trap!" Her captor

drew a huge, ugly gun and dragged her to the French door. "Watch out!" she sobbed.

He wrenched open the door, and for one horrible moment her heart stopped beating. Creole lay on his back on the balcony, frozen in a Mexican standoff with the two men from the living room—all guns drawn and pointing at each other. Nobody moved.

The man holding her broke the impasse by pulling her forward and pressing the barrel of his weapon into her temple. "Drop it, Levalois, or I'll kill her now."

"Let him!" she cried, and stomped the heel of her sensible loafer onto the man's instep, devoutly wishing she hadn't been so quick to discard Muse's lethal stilettos. "Run!"

The three bad guys spared her amused glances before turning back to Creole, who gave her a look of such profound regret that her hovering tears threatened to spring free. He lowered his gun.

"Let her go, Davies," he demanded quietly, as the other goon took it and yanked him to his feet. "It's me you want, not her."

"Oh, but you're wrong," said the third man, a man whose eyes looked so evil it sent a chill down her spine. He slid his sleek weapon into the back of his waistband and straightened his stylish trousers. "I want both of you."

It was then she knew with horrifying certainty, Davies was going to kill them.

Somehow she found the strength to go on breathing. She could not give in to the pure dread that gripped her whole body in a suffocating vise. It would be too easy to succumb to it, to let her fate be decided by these corrupt, immoral demons who thought life was so cheap and meaningless. She must fight for what she believed in, fight for the lives of Davies's future victims if he succeeded in killing them and eluding justice once again. And fight for her own love, the man who sat across from her in the black limousine they'd been forced into, but who might as well be a million miles away.

As they drove through the Quarter toward the Mississippi, Creole's expression was shuttered and unreadable in the bright afternoon light slanting through the limo's tinted windows. She wanted to reach out to him. Hold him. Reassure him that she didn't blame him for their awful predicament. Let him know she'd gladly die if it meant he'd go free.

But they'd bound her wrists with duct tape and used Creole's own handcuffs to shackle his hands behind his back. He stared straight ahead at the air between them, refusing to meet her gaze. He was doing it again, exercising that uncanny ability of his to go into cop mode, to shut off all emotion, all sign of personal feeling. The only flicker she saw was when they cruised through an old, run-down section of the riverfront and pulled up to an ancient building labeled Louisa Street Warehouse. Why was that name so familiar?

Letting out a deep sigh, she wondered what was going through his mind. And hoped like hell it was a plan to get them out of this mess.

The fetid decay of wharfside refuse wafted from tumbledown structures as they were herded through a partially boarded-up door into the cavernous, deserted warehouse. The scuttle of small creatures and creepy-crawlies greeted her ears in the gray dimness, and she pressed closer to Creole.

The whole place was horrifyingly familiar. From the brief glimpse she'd gotten on the tape. One look at Creole's face confirmed her darkest fears.

Okay, now she was really scared.

Up until this minute she'd been sure they would somehow escape. That Creole would find a way to overpower their captors. Or that Morris would come to their rescue. Something. Anything. But as she was pushed unceremoniously into a robust wooden chair similar to the one that had held Luke, and had her wrists taped to the heavy, splintery arms, she felt her confidence slither away like a rat abandoning ship.

Omigod. She was going to die here. Just like Luke.

"Please," she said hoarsely, speaking for the first time since being shanghaied into the limo, "What do you want from us? I don't have the tape anymore. Fox took it."

"Fox will be dealt with," Davies said, his tone brittle and cold as flint. "As for you two...let's just say your interference in my business is starting to annoy me. I don't like being annoyed."

Despite the ovenlike heat that suffused the warehouse, Grace shivered. She didn't know how to respond. To deny their involvement would be folly on many levels. To apologize, unthinkable.

"You'll be a hell of a lot more annoyed when you fry for killing a cop," Creole said as if unaffected by the threat they were under. "Even you haven't been that stupid up till now."

Grace licked her lips. Obviously Creole had also decided they were going to die, and meant to go down in flames. There was a certain dignity in self-destruction under these circumstances, she supposed. Still, she didn't like the look that came over Davies's face at Creole's commentary. Maybe if they didn't antagonize him, he'd make their deaths quick and painless.

A light snapped on, circling her in a yellowish glow. Her stomach clenched when one of the two goons entered the warehouse carrying a video camera on a tripod. The unbidden image of Luke's bound and battered body snaked through her mind.

Sweet mercy. Would she be forced to endure a similar fate? And Creole, too? Suddenly death seemed a much more appealing alternative.

She glanced at Creole where he'd been bound to a matching chair. His face was white as a ghost, his eyes glued to the camera. His throat worked, and for a second she thought he might be sick. They had discarded the handcuffs and taped both his wrists and ankles to the sturdy arms and legs of his chair, which had been placed a few yards away and facing her. He yanked at his bonds, trying in vain to free himself.

"Let her go, Davies," he repeated in a ragged shout, and she suddenly realized the terror that blazed in his eyes was for her—not himself. "I'll die real good for you. You don't need her." Again he jerked at the tape.

The devil laughed. "Sure you will, if I decide to kill you. Maybe I'll just burn out your eyes and let you live. After seeing what I do to your lady, living might be worse torture than anything I could come up with." Again demonic laughter. Then he stuck his face close to Creole's. "And teach you cops to leave me and my business alone!"

She watched in horror as Creole spat in Davies's face. And felt her blood curdle. It was going to go badly for her. Very badly. And in the worst possible way—impersonal, cold-blooded, unmerciful cruelty, with no rhyme or purpose other than to hurt Creole.

Davies calmly walked over to her, accepting a thin, cloth-covered bundle from one of his henchmen. Eyeing the long package nervously, she took a deep, steadying breath. There was no way she would play along with this macabre script. No matter what was done to her, she must not show her suffering. She would spare the man she loved that much. He had enough agony to live with. She would not add her own to his burden.

She closed her eyes and prayed for strength as she listened to the tink of metal implements being unwrapped, the click and whir of the camera being set up, and Davies's voice giving the order to shoot Creole's legs with his own gun if he tried anything.

She kept them shut tight when her blouse was ripped open and torn from her shoulders. And when she heard Davies light a cigarette in front of her, and smelled the nasty, acrid scent of the smoke as it curled over her face.

But when she heard Creole's strangled, *"Non!"* and burst of Cajun invective, she wrenched them opened and looked past her tormentor, latching steadfastly onto her lover's desperate eyes.

Despite shaking like a leaf, she straightened her spine and tried to appear strong and calm, as though she weren't about to faint from sheer terror. To reassure him she could take whatever was dished out. But she hadn't seen the tape, and the panic in his eyes told her he knew better than to believe her naive assurances.

"I love you," she mouthed, knowing it might be the last time she'd be able to say the words. Regret, sharp and poignant, stabbed through her. Why hadn't she told him last night, as she lay in his arms?

She noted almost absently that the lens of the video camera was pointed at Creole's tortured face, and not at her as she'd expected. A bead of sweat trickled down his cheek and over his clenched jaw, dropping onto his stark white T-shirt.

Davies stepped closer to her, lowering the cigarette in his hand to the level of her chest. A deathly calm wrapped itself around her soul, and she braced herself for the impact of its red glowing tip onto the flesh above her breast.

She clamped her teeth against it, against the scream fighting to erupt, and bit into her tongue until she tasted blood. Waiting...

Suddenly Creole roared, and with a sharp crack and a crash was on his feet, the heavy chair fractured to kindling. Splintered wood sailed everywhere.

At the same time a loud bang cracked through the warehouse. From her fog of panic, she saw Creole swing his fists wildly, aided by the chair arms still taped to them. His two guards flew to the floor.

Dimly, she realized that Davies hadn't even reacted.

He stood over her, paralyzed, not moving a muscle. The cigarette dropped from his fingers, landing in her lap. An odd expression seeped over his face, and the strangest thing happened. A delicate spray of scarlet rain sprinkled over her, and a bright red coin-size hole appeared in the middle of his forehead. Everything went deathly quiet. Fascinated, she watched a stream of crimson spurt from the coin and spread over his face. Then he collapsed at her feet.

All at once the warehouse was full of people. Agent Morris shouted at the center of the hubbub. She didn't understand what all the fuss was about. Creole suddenly yelled and dove at her, brushing at her legs with frantic fingers. Vaguely she was conscious of a hot biting sensation in her thigh, and the smell of burnt fabric. The cigarette, she thought impassively, as he ripped the duct tape from her wrists.

He uttered her name in an anguished voice, pulled her to her feet, and then she was surrounded by his strong, wonderful arms. Everything else melted away but the scent and feel of his powerful body cradling hers. He muttered something in Cajun, then held her out and asked, "Are you all right? Talk to me, woman."

"I'm good," she murmured. "Now." Sighing, she pressed back into his warm embrace. Not for anything would she let him go. Not ever.

He kissed her hair. "*Dieu,* I thought I'd go crazy."

Over his shoulder she saw something that made her mouth part in surprise. It was a woman—a woman who looked remarkably like her. A gun was cradled in her unsteady grip, pointing shakily at Davies, as though she was afraid if she lowered it the monster would rise up from his pool of blood on the floor and sneak away.

A tall, dark-haired man stood at the woman's side, gently rubbing her arms, speaking earnestly, trying to coax the gun from her fingers. She appeared numb with shock, and resisted his efforts. Morris hovered behind them, teetering in a comical vignette of indecision. She looked at the woman again.

Grace gripped Creole's shoulders, unable to believe her eyes.

Muse? Could it really be? Her look-alike suddenly glanced up, meeting Grace's stunned gaze, and the gun tumbled into the man's waiting hands.

It was!

"Muse! Oh, my God, it's Muse!"

Creole took several steps backward and observed the sisters embrace, hugging and crying, hugging and crying some more. He wanted to be happy for Grace. After all, it was for this touching reunion with her twin that Grace had come to New Orleans.

And he *was* happy for her. Honestly, he was. But he wanted it to be *him* she clung to like she'd never let go.

He sighed, brushing off the EMT who was attempting to examine his arms for splinters. And no, he didn't need to be smeared with any damn antiseptic ointment, either. What he needed was a good, hefty dose of anesthetic. Something that would dull the craven fear that had lodged in his heart the second Davies lit that cigarette, knowing what he planned to do with it—and on whom. Something strong, that would take away the nightmare of not being able to prevent it from happening. Something numbing, that would deaden the pain of Grace turning to another for comfort and support after the ordeal was finally over.

She'd left him. Even after she'd said she loved him.

His chest tightened unbearably, remembering the tender look in her eyes as she'd silently formed those three precious words across the no-man's-land of hopelessness that had separated them. As if she'd truly meant it.

Dieu, he couldn't recall the last time he'd shed a tear. Not as a child. Certainly not in the last three decades of his life. But at that quiet declaration of love, a lifetime of pain and unfairness had become too much to bear.

Even before those words he would have done anything, anything at all, to save her. But tasting the salt of his own desolation had ignited something deep within him. Fury over their destined fate had exploded into a burst of rage so overwhelming it had fueled him with the strength of ten men.

He'd wanted to kill Davies with his bare hands. And he would have, too, given another five seconds. Instead of the gratitude he should feel toward Muse for sparing him the evil and doing the job for him, he only felt an immense frustration that he'd been denied the opportunity.

Seeing Morris was about to cart off Davies's two cohorts, he strode over to rescue his Glock from them—and a mountain of federal paperwork and red tape. Angrily he thrust the weapon into his empty shoulder holster and adjusted the straps. This time the familiar weight didn't help a damned bit. He still wanted to stalk across the room and snatch Grace from the shelter of her sister's arms and back into his own. He fisted his hands against the urge, telling himself to get a grip.

He was being a selfish jerk and he knew it. *Grace* was the innocent victim here, not him. *She* was the one who'd nearly had her flesh burned, not him. And it had been Grace's sister who'd rescued her, not him.

He had no right to feel abandoned or betrayed. No right to feel bitter that someone else was holding her and soothing her. He had no claim on her, and she didn't need him. She'd made that clear enough this morning. Her pretty, impulsive words had changed nothing. She'd only said them because she thought they were about to die. He knew that.

But he also knew he had to get out of there. Quick. Before his hurt and jealousy became painfully apparent to everyone on the planet. Schooling his expression, he spun on a toe, heading for the warehouse exit. And ran smack into the dark, rangy man who'd talked Muse down after the shooting.

"Sorry, didn' see you," he clipped out, trying to step around the man he figured for FBI.

"No problem." The man casually blocked the path and jerked his chin at Davies's body, which was being examined by the combined FBI and NOPD Crime Scene Units. "A nasty piece of work, eh?"

Creole backed off, putting some space between them. "Yeah." He crossed his arms and peered over at the remains of the man who had been his obsession for the past three months, and very nearly the death of him. "Yeah, *bien mauvais,*" he muttered. Very nasty.

He should be relieved that it was all over. His brother's killer was dead, his own vow fulfilled. But mainly what he felt was…hollow.

The FBI man held out his hand, sympathy flowing from his discerning gaze. "You're Detective Levalois, *non?* I'm Special Agent Beaulieux. Remi to my friends."

Another Cajun? "Creole," he replied, making an effort to lift the corner of his mouth as he shook the man's hand. He eyed the door, wanting nothing more than to disappear through it. He got the uncomfortable feeling this Beaulieux guy could see right through him, past the facade of professional indifference he'd adopted during his internal battle over Grace, straight into his churning insides.

"You the agent who's guarding Muse Summerville?" he asked noncommittally, pretty sure the FBI man must want something, he was being so chummy.

"Yeah." Remi darted a glance toward the sisters, and his mouth thinned. "I need to ask you a favor."

Big surprise. "Oh?"

"I'm not sure how much you know about our situation…"

Creole recalled Muse's letter with its statement of trust for this man, and her warning about a possible corrupt agent. "Muse left Grace a note," he said.

"*Bien.*" The other man nodded, cautious relief in his expression. "The deal is, I need to get her away from here for a few days while we tie up some things."

The reference was vague, but his aggravated tone was enough to catch Creole's attention. Definitely something going on there—besides a possible dirty FBI agent. Interesting.

"Things?"

"After she gives her statements about the shooting, of course," Remi said, totally avoiding his question.

For the first time Creole gave Beaulieux a thorough going-over.

Undercover was written all over the guy. He was tall—even had a few inches on him—lean and broad-shouldered. His hair was a midnight black, not unlike his own, but Remi's was long—long enough to give Creole a shudder of bad childhood memories—and pulled back in a ponytail. A diamond stud glinted in one ear, and he wore clothes more suited to a gambler than an FBI agent. Black. All black. With silver-tipped lizard-skin boots. *Bad boy,* Grace would instantly label him.

Bon Dieu. Remi Beaulieux reminded Creole just a little too much of himself for comfort. Did the sisters have similar tastes in men? Hell, no wonder ol' Remi was having problems with "things."

"So, what can I do for you?" he asked, feeling almost sorry for the man.

A curving scar glinted above Beaulieux's lip as he shot Creole a glance. The thin white slash should have given him a sinister air, but somehow missed the mark because of the kindred man-to-man appeal for help shining in his black eyes.

"I, uh… Well, dammit to hell, the woman just shot Louisiana's most-wanted bad guy. Both the Bureau and NOPD are going to want to debrief her." Remi exhaled.

"But?" he prompted.

"I think she's still in danger. The sooner I get her out of town the better. As far as I'm concerned, tonight isn't soon enough."

Creole turned and lifted a brow. The light wasn't all that great in the warehouse, but he could swear the man's face turned red as the fresh patch of blood on the floor. Danger? Uh-huh.

"Look at them." Beaulieux indicated the sisters across the room.

Creole obliged, casting his reluctant gaze on Grace and Muse. They stood, talking softly, wiping tears, arms around each other as the EMTs saw to Grace. Her tattered blouse was gone, replaced by a policewoman's uniform shirt, and someone had wiped the sprinkles of blood from her face.

His heart howled with loss, and he had to look away. "What about them?"

"Muse will never leave Grace as long as she thinks her sister needs her."

"So?" He had a bad feeling about what was coming.

"So I want you to make it clear she doesn't. Need her." Remi paused meaningfully. Creole arrowed him a narrow look, but the agent cut him off before he could say a word. "Don't even try to deny you're in love with Grace. I've seen the way you look at her."

"You're imagin—"

Remi raised a hand against the automatic denial that had sprung to his lips. "Don't worry, it's not obvious to anyone who isn't in the middle of it himself."

At the plainly uncomfortable confession, Creole bit back a retort, and muttered a particularly potent Cajun oath. Remi gave him a smile of wry understanding, and just like that a tentative friendship was born.

"Thanks, *mon ami*. I owe you big-time."

No damn kidding.

He'd been *that close* to walking away from Grace. To accepting the inevitable, swallowing his pride and burying his out-of-control feelings for her. Now, for the sake of a few stupid French phrases and some no-doubt-misguided male bonding thing, he felt obligated to go back and face another indefinite period of time with her. Endure the sweet torture of her company until she, once again, left him in misery.

Remi owed him? Oh, yeah, that was for damned sure.

"You have no idea, *mon ami*. No idea at all."

Chapter 16

If Grace sensed he was torn as he slid an arm around her waist and allowed himself to be introduced to her twin, Creole couldn't detect it.

He could, however, detect Muse's astonishment. Her eyes grew wide at the sight of his proprietary hold on her sister, and even wider at his appearance. He figured Grace's avoidance of "men like him" had been both adamant, resolute and successful up till now. Ah, well, that would be solved soon enough. But first he had to clear the path for Remi to hustle Muse away for whatever purposes he deemed so urgent.

Grace didn't elaborate on her minimalist "This is Creole," so he pulled her even closer and acted like he had every right to do so. With a quick kiss, he fastened the top button of her borrowed uniform shirt, which gaped open. Her sister clearly expected Grace to balk at the intimacy, but when she didn't, a strange smile came over Muse's face, and she searched his closely. He gave a slight nod, and her smile expanded to a grin, her shoulders literally relaxing before his eyes.

He felt like a complete fraud. But he wouldn't go back on his unspoken promise. He'd take care of Grace until she no longer needed, or wanted, his help.

Grace herself seemed oblivious to the undercurrents that swirled so profusely around her as the four of them were taken to the Eighth District station and dragged through a bevy of police and FBI procedures—statements, identifications, evidence—accepting his nearness and support as both natural and welcome. He always kept a casual arm around her, placing chaste kisses on her temple when the occasion warranted. She didn't seem to notice that mentally and emotionally he kept himself apart, never getting overly personal. He was only doing this for Remi, he reminded himself, when tempted to give in to his true feelings.

Her own touch was jerky. As if she would suddenly remember his difficulty with it or become aware of the setting and circumstances. Or maybe it was her own uncertainty over their relationship that caused her hesitations. After all, despite what they'd subsequently gone through, their parting that morning had not been a good one.

Or maybe she was just reacting to the natural stress of being kidnapped and nearly tortured, and he was reading far too much into it.

God knew, he was feeling a bit jittery himself. Especially after his captain had called and ordered him to report straight to his office first thing in the morning. This was one psych evaluation that might actually do him some good. Or maybe he wouldn't have to worry about an evaluation. Chances were only about fifty-fifty he'd still have a job after that interview with the cap.

"I'm so glad you're with Grace," Muse whispered as she gave him a hug goodbye. They were all standing outside the restaurant where they'd indulged in a fortifying late meal after finishing up at the station. "She's needed someone for so long. And, well, I just couldn't leave her here by herself.''

Again he felt a twinge of guilt. Remi had made it clear over supper that he was taking Muse away from New Orleans regardless of both women's protests. Creole knew it was only his presence that had prevented Grace's sister from digging in her heels. As it was, she was spearing Remi with dagger looks. He didn't envy the poor bastard their upcoming skirmish.

''Don' worry, I'll see she gets back home safely,'' he replied, deliberately ambiguous.

That much, at least, was the truth. He didn't know if he could bear sleeping in the same apartment as her, much less the same bed, as Muse obviously believed. Maybe the balcony wouldn't be so bad. But either way, he'd make sure she got on a plane to South Carolina, safe and sound.

''Then I'll see you soon,'' Muse said, throwing a glower towards Remi. ''Just as soon as my bossy, overbearing, so-called bodyguard stops jumping at shadows.''

''Agent Beaulieux has your best interests at heart,'' he assured her, sidestepping the other statement. ''You do what he says.''

''Harrumph.''

Remi had snagged a taxi, so, after a final hug and whispers for Grace, the two of them drove off.

It was late, and the sky hung thick and sultry, heralding rain. On the black pavement around them, light spilled from the restaurant windows in muted pools of neon.

''Feel like a drink?'' he said into the sudden silence, wanting to delay the coming awkwardness as long as possible.

Grace shook her head and pulled the blue uniform shirt tight around her midriff. ''No, thanks. I'm feeling a little tired.''

''Of course.'' She did look a bit pale.

He stuck his hands in his pockets and walked alongside her for the several blocks to Burgundy Street, aiming scowls at the chattering tourists who dared to stare at her disheveled uniform and his T-shirt and holstered weapon.

He opened the iron courtyard gate for her, and as they approached the stairs to her apartment, he took a deep breath. "Would you rather I—"

"No!" she practically shouted, then bit her lip. "Please, I don't want to be alone just yet."

"All right."

Following her into Muse's place, he briefly wondered how Grace was really holding up. She seemed fine. Cogent and calm, she'd been articulate for her police statements, unperturbed during the photo ID of her assailant and had smiled and laughed at all the appropriate places during their meal with Remi and Muse. If she'd seemed distant at times, he'd chalked it up to her wanting to redraw the line in their relationship, but being too polite to do it in front of witnesses. After all, her hasty declaration of love might have given him the wrong idea and could prove embarrassing if he questioned her about it.

After locking the door, he hung back at the kitchen table.

Walking toward the bedroom, she suddenly stopped and turned. "I, um, I'm going to take a shower, okay?"

"Sure," he said softly, running his fingers along the top of a kitchen chair. "I'll just…" He shrugged, unable to come up with anything.

But she didn't seem to notice. She nodded and continued into the bedroom, then disappeared into the bathroom, leaving the door open a crack. He stared at the crack a moment, scrubbed his hands over his face and told himself it wasn't an invitation.

He spun, searching determinedly through the kitchen for something liquid and potent, sending up a prayer of thanks when he found his own bottle of bourbon and tobacco pouch tucked into a corner on the counter.

Snatching them up, he headed out onto the balcony for a large drink, a long smoke and some much-needed breathing space. But he had to settle for the drink and the

space, because the minute he lit up his hastily rolled cigarette, his stomach roiled at the smell and he had to stomp
it out.

With a curse he hurled the pouch and its contents over
the balcony rail.

Hell, he'd wanted to quit anyway. Hands shaking, he
tipped the bottle to his lips and took a lengthy pull. Fire
burned its way down his throat and into his stomach, searing away the nausea, replacing it with an uneasy smolder-
ing.

Fifteen minutes later he was pleasantly numb. Not drunk,
just…numb. Which was purely fine with him. It was taking
all the numbness he could get to listen to the shower going
in Grace's bathroom and not think about that crack in the
door.

But after another couple of minutes of listening to the
rush of water, he started getting worried. The EMTs at the
warehouse had pronounced her fit, but he'd seen enough
delayed reactions to this kind of situation to be nervous.

Five minutes later he sat up in his chair and tried to think
logically. He couldn't. In three strides he was there.

"Grace?" he called, rapping on the bathroom door. "Are
you all right?"

No answer.

"*Chère?*"

Just the sound of water running. No other movement.

To hell with this. He cautiously pushed the door open.
A wave of jessamine-scented steam thick as pea soup rolled
over him. He peered in.

"*Le bon Dieu!*"

She was curled up in a ball, water streaming over her in
torrents, pressed into the corner of the shower. Still fully
clothed.

What an idiot he was! The woman was in shock. He
should have realized, should have done something sooner.

"Grace, darlin', speak to me," he called, whipping open
the glass shower door. Thank God the water was still warm,

but not too hot. He spun the faucets to Off and threw himself to the floor next to her.

"Honey, look at me."

"No!" she screamed, and flattened herself against the tiles. "No! Don't touch me!"

For a second he froze in panic. Then the memories crashed over him, memories of lashing out with similar words and actions as a child. Nobody had dared touch him when he'd screamed to be left alone. Nobody'd wanted to. But he'd needed it. Needed the touch and the sympathy of someone who cared. Needed it desperately.

"It's me, Grace. It's Creole. Let me hold you, darlin'."

"No!"

Her muffled sobs were breaking his heart. He grasped her arms, holding tight when she tried to shake him off.

"Don't touch me! Don't touch me!"

"Come on, *chère.* Look at me."

He turned her, firmly holding her wrists when she would strike out at him. He cursed softly, and gathered her into his arms, holding her tight to his chest. He sat on the wet shower floor and cradled her in his lap, rocking back and forth, back and forth, until her struggles ceased and she lay limp in his arms, sobbing.

"Hush, don' cry. It's all over. Shhh, I'm here, darlin'."

The sound of her heart-wrenching tears touched something deep inside him, something dark and hard that had lingered there in his soul, festering for untold years. The clean purity of her goodness, the unselfish ache of his love for this woman, wrapped themselves around the blackness within him, and slowly, slowly, washed by her tears, it dissolved. In its place was a delicate, tender void, waiting to be filled with something light and good.

In his heart he knew he could finally leave the past behind.

After long minutes her tears slowed to a stop. One last tremor racked her body, and she looked up. Slowly her red-rimmed eyes focused on him.

"Auri?"

He let out a long sigh. If only he had a future worth leaving it for.

"*Mais,* yeah, *mon coeur.* It's me."

"What happened?" she whispered.

He brushed a wet strand of hair from her forehead and buried thoughts of himself. "A little delayed reaction," he said, sitting up straighter. "Maybe some mild shock. I found you lyin' on the floor. You okay?"

She appeared to take inventory, then nodded. "I think so. It's so strange…I remember sitting down. Feeling faint. I was just so tired and thirsty. And then, nothing. What did I do?"

He wiped the tears from her cheeks and smiled tenderly. "It's over now. Luckily the water kept you warm, and lyin' down put your blood back in circulation."

Reaching out to the rack on the wall, he pulled off a towel and dabbed at her face and hair. "Probably would have been a good idea to get undressed before you got in the shower, though." He winked.

Surprised, she glanced down at herself. "Sweet heavens." An embarrassed laugh escaped her, and her eyes strayed to his T-shirt and holster. "You're soaked. Did I—"

"I'll dry."

"But your gun—"

"It's fine."

Her gaze returned to him, and the embarrassment died. She looked deep into his eyes. Into the fragile soul she had unknowingly cleansed.

"Thank you for being here," she whispered. "For being *there.* I don't know what I would have done without you. Not when—" She took a long, shaky breath and laid her hand on his chest. "You're a good man, Auri Levalois. A very good man."

He wanted to look away, to say, no, he wasn't a good

man, but he was *her* man, and would do anything in the world for her.

But he couldn't move. His throat tightened and he couldn't speak, either. Her fingers curled into his T-shirt, and she laid her cheek against his shoulder. He kissed her hair and breathed in a faint, lingering scent of jessamine, the mysterious, spicy sweetness that would never fail to remind him of her. Of the all-too-few moments they had spent together. Of the unbearable pleasure she had given him in her arms. Of the incredible feeling of his body joined with hers as they made love.

She shifted, and suddenly he was aware of her position, warm and intimately nestled in his lap. Painfully aware.

The walls of the tiny cubicle zoomed in, making him dizzy with her nearness. Her fingers stretched over the ribs of his collar, touching skin, igniting a burning need to touch her back.

"You should get out of those wet clothes," he said, desperate to direct her attention back to the practical, away from his inappropriate arousal. That was the last thing she needed to deal with right now, and in about three seconds it would be impossible to miss. "You'll catch your death."

The statement was ridiculous. Steam still swirled around them, and the temperature in the small bathroom matched that of the blood pumping through his body. Hot. Very hot. Obviously, he wasn't thinking straight.

Her arms crept around his neck. "You think?"

"No," he croaked, unable to recall just what exactly he was answering. "That is—what?"

She raised her lips to his and kissed him. Vaguely he wondered if this was some weird side effect of delayed stress. Or maybe *he* was the one in shock and that's why none of this made any sense. It was certain, *one* of them needed to rest. Or something.

"Chère—"

"Mmm," she hummed in approval when he started responding to the caress of her mouth.

He shouldn't. Definitely shouldn't. Doing this would only complicate their parting immeasurably. And they had to part. He knew that.

But he couldn't help himself. She was so sweet, so right, and he was so hungry for one last taste of her. Rest and reason could come later…after.

He pulled her close. He could feel the hard tips of her breasts poke into his chest, the soft mounds around them pillowing against him erotically. Her mouth opened, and he sank his tongue into its waiting velvet. Wanting. Tasting. Savoring.

"Maybe you could help me take them off?" she murmured when they broke for air.

"Quoi?" What? He struggled for thought, his mind empty of all save the spice and the feel of her.

She licked her lips. "My clothes."

With a groan he stripped off her shirt and reached for her bra, then halted in uncertainty.

"Please." She unfastened the wisp of silk herself, took his hand and placed it on her breast. "Don't stop."

Her breasts were warm and wet, her nipples puckered to tight buds. He smoothed his hands over them, caressing her gently. "Sure?"

"Sure."

She reached up, her hand hovering next to his cheek. Without thinking, he leaned into it, craving the feel of her touch on his skin. How he would miss her!

"Take me to your bed, Grace. Let me make love to you."

Her answering smile was all he needed.

"Can you stand?"

He helped her up, and they stumbled to their feet, looking askance at their wet clothes. With a shake of her head she kicked off her shoes and grabbed her skirt waistband.

"Wait! Let me." Wrestling with the zipper, he went down on a knee and dragged her long, brown skirt over her hips, taking her panties and hose with it. And then she was gloriously naked. The sight of her smooth, welcoming flesh sent a surge of pure need winging through his veins. Need, and temptation.

She leaned back against the ceramic tile and regarded him through half-lidded eyes. "Now you."

Excitement purled through his loins, swelling him, electrifying him. And he obeyed.

Grace waited eagerly as Creole made short work of his clothes. Her heart sang that he was giving her this one last chance to experience the rapture of his body. She didn't think she'd ever be able to make love again, not after being with this extraordinary man, and she wanted a lifetime of memories to remember him by.

She reached for him, but he lifted her in his arms. "Bed."

His legs ate up the short distance to the iron bed. Her brain registered the dull thunk of his holster landing on the nightstand, and then he was over her, inside her.

She sucked in her breath at the feeling as he hilted, stretching her, filling her with his sumptuous male presence.

"Damn!" he cursed. "Don' move. Don' move!"

"Why?" she asked breathlessly.

"I don' want to get you pregnant."

The hasty, graphic words hung between them, thick and burning. Their eyes collided. Her heart hitched. "No. Of course not. That would be…"

That would be…what?

What would it be like to have his baby? To carry a part of him back to Charleston with her, to nurture and cherish forever? A poignant wanting lanced through the core of her innermost being, sharp, almost painful.

"A disaster," he said, completing her dangling sentence.

Her want turned into a barren ache. Clearly, it was not what *he* wanted. She shouldn't, either. God knew it would change her life irrevocably. And he'd want no part of it.

"Yes, a disaster," she agreed.

She shifted slightly, pulling him in deeper, cradling him more fully within her body, the action unconscious, not deliberate. Or was it?

"Chère—"

She was playing with fire. She knew that. But she couldn't help herself. "You feel so good," she whispered, and looped her arms around his neck, barely resisting the urge to run her fingers up his neck and through his hair. "So very good."

His heart thudded powerfully against her breast. "You do, too." He didn't move. Not a millimeter.

She brushed her lips over his, and his breath grew harsh. She could feel the strain of his corded forearm muscles along her back, the dig of his fingers into her shoulders. His stubbled jaw scraped over her cheek, sending shivers of delight straight to the tips of her breasts. She didn't dare so much as breathe, for fear he would withdraw and end the sizzling contact.

She closed her eyes and heard him swallow heavily, his rasping breath hot in her ear. The tension climbed, along with her arousal. Her body cried out to receive the thrust of his maleness deep into her, over and over until she exploded.

With a potent oath he rolled off her. The instant chill of missing him swept through her body, cold and empty.

"A pure disaster," he repeated in a voice sharded with emotion. Could it be regret?

No. It had to be simple lust. The word *disaster* said it all. He had no interest in a family. None. She knew that. Had known from the first moment she'd met him.

She took a deep breath, fighting her own regrets, shoving them back to the realm of true madness, where they belonged. He sheathed and returned to her, and all was right again when he slid home.

"Touch me," he said.

Startled, she looked up.

"You're leaving tomorrow, aren't you."

It was more of a statement than a question, said on a sigh. She wasn't sure what it had to do with touching him, but she briefly considered tomorrow's options and realized there were none. She had to go, away from him. Staying on, delaying, even for another day, would be too painful. And there were also Frank and Nikki to consider.

Filled with heartache, she nodded. "Yes."

He nodded, too, avoiding her gaze. "Then I'd like you to touch me."

"I don't understand."

He chewed the inside of his cheek, the first sign of uncertainty she'd ever seen him display.

"Just once," he said, and cleared his throat. "Just once I'd like to make love like an ordinary man. This might be the last time—" he closed his eyes and exhaled "—the last time I trust someone enough to try."

Tears sprang to her eyes, and her mouth opened on a soundless cry. "No," she whispered. "Don't say that. Someday the right woman will come along and make you wonder why touching ever bothered you. You'll be ready, and it will be wonderful."

He looked at her a long time before he murmured, "Yeah, it will." He gathered her in his arms, sinking deeper into her. "Touch me now, Grace. Make it wonderful."

So she did. Gently. Cautiously. Mindful of his intense reactions the whole while. Awed by his faith and his trust.

Hesitantly at first, she ran her hands over his broad shoulders, fingering each intricate line of his beautiful tattoo, following its graceful blue curves, tracing her fingers over its mouth and tail and its dangling claws.

Gaining confidence, she trailed down to browse Creole's black-furred chest, circling the dark knots of his male nipples, all the while watching, watching his tight-squeezed eyes and jaw-clenched pleasure for a sign of protest.

None came. Instead, he started moving, just a little at

first, nudging in and out of her. She wrapped her legs around his flanks, urging him to increase his slow, sensual glide. His ride grew harder as she became bolder in her explorations, certain now he wouldn't balk or restrain her because it was too much to take. She caressed his lips, his cheeks, his sweat-damp brow, receiving kisses and urgent little licks to the pads of her fingers and powerful thrusts between her thighs.

When she slipped her hands around to his back, she feared he'd grab her wrists and put a stop to her trespass. But after sucking in an initial gasping breath, he just held it. And gazed at her with stormy, impassioned eyes. She brushed first one, then another of his angry scars, until she'd paused over each and every one. Until his jaw trembled, and he let his breath out slowly.

"You okay?" she whispered. She slid her hands lower, to the small of his back, and then his waist.

"Wonderful," he said, his voice ragged with a potent mixture of strain and elation.

"Shall I stop?"

In answer, he scythed into her. She sucked in a gasp of her own.

His eyes twinkled mercilessly, turning the tables. Joy permeated his whole expression. "You okay?"

"Wonderful," she echoed, and moved her hands lower still.

"Shall I stop?"

Under her hands, hard muscles clenched tightly. "Not in a million years."

"Good," he whispered. He plunged into her, making her squirm and writhe with unsated need. Need to be close to him, to be a part of him. Need to hold him to her heart and let him fill her body, her life.

He thrust in and out, in and out, building up speed and urgency in both of them. She moaned, her head tossing to and fro, unable to do more than hang on. He was killing her. Killing her with desire. And with the knowledge that he would never be hers.

His lips crashed onto hers, halting her feverish movements, drowning her in the succulence of his taste. His savory muskiness swirled through her senses clear to her toes, filling her with the longing to belong to this man and no other. She moaned again.

His answering groan vibrated through her very soul. The rumbling started there, physical, earthy, deep inside her, triggered by the urgency in his voice, in her heart. It swelled bigger and bigger with each silken thrust, peaking with an unendurable yearning, until she shook with the need to shatter in his embrace. Only his.

The blazing need overtook her and she tumbled over the edge. She screamed. She heard her name called out in a ragged, guttural, male cry. And she came apart in the arms of her love.

Chapter 17

For a long time Grace just lay there, soaking in the feel of Creole's weight on her, testing the sensation of his body resting in and around hers. She held him tight, rejoicing in his trust, in the fact that she could reduce this hard, intense man to the state of complete dissolution he was so obviously enjoying at the moment.

After his labored breathing slowed, he even slept. And she must have, too, because the next thing she knew, she woke wrapped in his arms, back to front, as she had from her dream two days ago.

Again she lay for a long time, unable to go back to sleep, her mind pulling her inexorably toward their parting in the morning.

She had known it would be bad, the heartache she was destined to endure if she became involved with Creole Levalois. But this was far, far worse than anything she'd ever imagined. Almost unbearable. She went over every detail of their short time together, searching for a logical reason for her feelings for him, why this man—of all the men on earth—pulled at her heart in a way no other ever had or ever would.

She wanted to blame it on raging hormones or the lure of the forbidden or his sexy Cajun accent—on anything but the truth. A truth so vivid and clear it shone through her dismal excuses like a blinding beam of light.

Under the abused, devil-may-care, bad-boy exterior, Auri Levalois carried a goodness, a sensitivity, a loyalty to those he cared about, and an ability to convey love, deeper and stronger than any other person she'd ever met. It put her own meager attempts to shame. And she loved him for those worthy traits, those and a hundred more, good and bad, which she'd discovered in their brief hours together.

A crack of thunder jolted through the room, and she was sure it was the sound of her own heart breaking in two. How would she ever be able to leave him?

For the hundredth time she reminded herself of the type of man he was. Despite his loyalty and sensitivity, he was not interested in bestowing those qualities upon her alone. He didn't want a wife or kids or a settled life.

Frank Morina was loyal and sensitive, too, in his way, and just look at how he'd reacted to the first sign of threatened familial responsibility.

She sighed, letting the memory of her own father's desertion sift through her heartache, adding another layer of hurt. She'd need all the bad examples she could get to bolster her courage to leave Creole in the morning.

Unable to bear the comfort of his arms around her, she eased from his embrace, and from the bed, making her way to the French door.

The weather seemed to amplify her melancholy mood. A soft summer rain pitter-pattered onto the balcony floor and dropped from the silhouetted hanging plants. The dark, sultry smell of wet soil and cobblestones drifted up from the courtyard below. Above, a dim yellow outline of a crescent moon barely glowed through the thick, close blanket of gray clouds enveloping the Quarter.

Still naked, she stepped outside into the warm rain and stood, lifting her face to its cleansing caress. If only the rain could wash away her memories. Rinse away her hurt. Let her simply enjoy this amazing man, and then be able to walk away with no regrets in the morning. As he would.

"Grace?"

She squeezed her eyes shut for a moment, then turned to face him with a smile. "Hi."

His gaze roamed over her, saturating her from head to foot as thoroughly as the rain had already done. Her body reacted instantly, attuned by two nights of passion to his every mood and nuance. Her mind may be looking to tomorrow's sad parting, but her body was still in the here and now, eager to please and be pleased.

"What are you doing out there?"

He was still naked, too. Rumpled and bedroom-eyed, he was a dark, powerful statement of masculinity at its most virile. Her knees grew weak just looking at him.

"Couldn't sleep."

"There are better ways to cure insomnia than standing in the rain." His lips curved.

The erotic invitation in his sleepy smile took her breath away. "Oh?"

He took a step toward her, onto the balcony, into the rain. "*Mais,* yeah."

Rivulets trickled down his face and shoulders, dripping onto his broad chest, jeweling in the crisp, black hair. Her gaze snagged there, as the raindrops gathered together, cascading into the hollow of his belly button. Fascinated, she watched the pool of moisture spill over, flowing down the arrow of dark hair toward— She caught her breath, once again awed by his thickening arousal. What a magnificent man he was!

"See anythin' you like?"

She let her eyes adore him, all of him, and she answered truthfully, "Everything. I like everything I see."

Her hushed statement seemed to catch him by surprise

for a moment, and she remembered how recently he'd been unable to take off his clothes in front of her. Then he came to her and pulled her into his arms. His kiss was sweet and tender.

"You're too good for me," he whispered, and her heart broke all over again, for it wasn't the first time he'd said it, and it was so very untrue.

"No," she refuted, but could say no more because he kissed her again, long and thoroughly, holding her naked there in the rolling thunder and the steamy rain. How she wished it could go on forever just like this.

"What were you thinking about?" he asked when she sighed.

"Nothing," she murmured, marshaling her wits so she wouldn't break down.

"Earlier. When I first came out."

She compelled a smile to her lips, nestling deeper into his arms. "What do you think?"

He smiled back, a bit wistfully. "*Non.* Before that."

She pushed out a breath, and lied. "Muse. Just wondering what's going on. Why they had to leave so soon." She shrugged. "If she'll be okay."

"She'll be fine," he assured her. "Remi'll see to that."

"I know. I just…" She looked up into his serious eyes and saw that he knew she'd lied. That he knew she'd been thinking about them all along, not Muse. Because he was, too.

"Come with me," she said. The words were out of her mouth before the thought had even formed.

His eyes softened. "Bed?"

"Charleston."

His brow lifted. "Charleston?"

She nodded, pulling him closer. "Come back with me. So we can always be together."

Wariness flitted through his eyes, then he chuckled in skeptical amusement. "You asking me to marry you, Grace Summerville?"

She swallowed, and again her tongue just took over before her brain got involved. "I guess I am. Will you?" No one was more surprised than she at those words.

Well, except for Creole. His face completely drained of color as it filled with undisguised shock. His mouth dropped open, and he stared at her in stark disbelief, streams of rain running down his cheeks and off his wobbling chin.

The moment dragged out interminably, and still he said nothing, until she realized he was probably silent because he couldn't think of a polite way to tell her she was out of her ever-lovin' mind.

And he was absolutely right. What on earth had possessed her?

She forced a laugh past the huge lump that suddenly blocked her throat. "Had you worried, didn't I?" She laughed again for good measure. "Just kidding."

His mouth closed, then opened. "Grace—"

"Bed. Of course I meant bed."

She pulled his ghost-white face to hers and kissed him. Squeezed her eyes shut and kissed him as if there'd be no tomorrow.

Because there wouldn't be. Not for her. Not without him.

But she'd never let him guess how serious she'd been. She wouldn't let it show how much she hurt. How it was killing her to let him go.

"*Jolie*—"

"Shut up and kiss me."

She'd had her heart broken before. She'd gotten over it. And she would this time, too. One day at a time. Then one week at a time. Eventually, she'd forget him.

"Darlin'—"

"Shhh, I said I was kidding."

Creole Levalois was not the right man for her. She'd known it all along. She needed someone stable, someone she could build a family and a secure future with, knowing he'd never walk away from her or their children. Someone safe, that's what she needed.

Safe.

Not dark and dangerous and sexy and volatile.

Thankfully, Creole must have decided she really was kidding, because after a last searching look, he relented and let her pull him into a searing kiss. As his mouth covered hers, she sank into it, into his heated embrace, determined to take advantage of every last solitary second with him that she possibly could....

Before she left him and her world crumbled.

Hands jammed in his pockets, Creole stood at the huge plate-glass window at New Orleans International Airport and watched Grace's plane roll down the runway and lift off, taking her away from him.

He couldn't believe she was actually gone. For good.

His world tilted and started to crash around him. But before it could get too far, anger swept through his veins and rescued him from breaking down in front of a hundred witnesses and bawling like a baby.

How could she have left him after all they'd shared?

And for what? Some pip-squeak, good-for-nothing delinquent kid who didn't even give a damn that she cared enough to come home to drag his sorry behind out of trouble. He spun away from the window and stalked outside, catching a cab downtown.

At ten o'clock, it was hardly "first thing in the morning" but he figured he'd better go in and get his little interview with the captain over with. He jetted out a breath, glaring through the cab window at the heavy traffic on Interstate 10. If he was really lucky, he'd get fired. *That* would be the perfect end to a really perfect day. Then he could just put a bullet through his head and finish the job Grace had started by walking out on him.

Sure, sure, he'd been through it all before. But this time...this time he just didn't have the will to fight it any longer. The feeling of betrayal and abandonment was so total, so overwhelming, that this time he knew he wouldn't recover. Grace's cruelty had slashed him like a razor to the heart.

For a short time, for one breathless, suspended moment, he had actually thought she loved him and wanted him. When she had proposed marriage, he'd been stunned speechless, unable to utter a sound for stupefaction, but he'd believed she was serious. The look on her face had been so incredibly hopeful and sincere. Or so he'd thought....

Hell, it didn't matter what he'd thought. It had all been a cruel joke. She hadn't meant it. She'd laughed in glee at the very idea. Thank God he hadn't had the time to respond and make a total fool of himself by saying yes. Thank God she'd wrapped her siren's body around him and slowly seduced his senses to oblivion, reduced his mind to nil, so he couldn't think, could just feel her satin heat slowly drive him mad with want.

Walking through the door of the downtown police headquarters where he worked, he snorted at his incredible gullibility.

Just kidding... Had you worried, didn't I?

Yeah, he'd been worried all right. Was still worried. Worried for his blessed sanity.

The captain's secretary gave him a furtive glance as she motioned him into the corner office. *Bon.* So, he was history. Hell, it was almost a relief. Not having a job would be one less thing to worry about.

The cap lit into him the second he entered. "What have you got to say for yourself, Detective Levalois?"

Creole ground his jaw and was tempted to keep his mouth shut. Instead he stood straight and looked him in the eye and said, "Man who killed my brother's dead. Sir."

The cap's eyes narrowed. "So I hear." Then he frowned. "Gary Fox was brought in this morning by the FBI. He'd handed over a video tape to them."

Creole sucked down a wave of nausea but didn't comment.

The older man took a deep breath and let it out slowly, and regarded him as though deciding his fate at that very moment. In reality Creole was sure the cap knew exactly what he was going to say and do with him.

"You're a loose cannon, Levalois."

"Yessir."

"You disobeyed my orders. I don't like my officers disobeying direct orders."

"No sir."

"What do you think I should do with officers who disobey my orders, Levalois?"

"Fire 'em, sir."

The cap leaned back in his chair and steepled his fingers. "How about this instead. You're confined to desk duty for two months, pending investigation of the Davies incident at the Louisa Street Warehouse last night. You're to undergo a psych evaluation, and whatever counseling the psychologist recommends, you do every damn hour of it. You better walk the straight and narrow from now on, Levalois, or you're out on your loose-cannon butt. You got that?"

Suddenly it was all too much for Creole. The whole damn thing. He was so damn tired of working himself to death to bring order to the chaos, only to be slapped down at every turn.

He couldn't fight it all. Not the bad guys, the cap and the system, too. This morning he'd lost the only thing in the world that might have made it worthwhile to keep fighting the uphill battle. But now that he'd lost Grace, what was the point? He didn't have the will to do it. Not for a minute more.

All he wanted was to lie down for about a year and not move. Better yet, drink himself into a stupor for several years and not move. No investigation. No psych eval. And no damn counseling.

"*Non,*" he answered.

The cap snapped his head up and glared. "Excuse me, Detective?"

"I said no." With that, he dug his badge out of his wallet, yanked the Glock from his holster, and slapped them both onto the polished oak desk in front of the cap.

"I quit."

Grace stared in astonishment at the man standing on the other side of her cluttered desk, and a huge grin broke out all over her face. "You did *what?*"

"I married her."

"You married her. Just like that."

"Yep. I couldn't do it—leave town, that is. I couldn't leave her. I love her. And our baby. Did I do the right thing?" Frank Morina's earnest young expression pleaded with Grace.

"Oh, Frank." She jumped up and ran to give him a hug. "You did the right thing. You have no idea how right a thing you've done. I'm so proud of you!"

It had been over a week since she'd gotten home, and the whole time she hadn't been able to find the boy. He was no longer living at home, and she had truly feared the worst. But this morning Frank had walked into her high school office with Nikki on his arm, fresh from a civil wedding ceremony in Alabama.

"We're converting the garage studio to a place where we can live until we both graduate and I can find a job."

"At her parents'?" That explained why she hadn't been able to find him.

He nodded and glanced out to the hall, to where Nikki waited, and looked at his young wife with soft, melty eyes. "They are being really nice about the whole thing. I can't believe it. I think they actually like me. Despite..." He shrugged, looking about as guilty as a handsome, seventeen-year-old scoundrel could manage to look.

"Of course they like you," she reassured him with a

proud smile. "You're a good person, and you'll make a wonderful father."

"You think so?" His eyes sparkled with a joy she'd never seen in them before.

Her heart squeezed. "I know so."

"It's all because of you, Miz Summerville. Thanks for believing in me when nobody else did. If it weren't for you…"

Hushing him before they both started weeping, she gave him another hug and pushed him out the door toward his new wife.

Fighting back her tears, she scolded, "You've only got two weeks before school starts. You better get working on converting that studio, young man."

After congratulating Nikki with more hugs, she gave them a watery-eyed wave on their way into a life of complications and hardships, but with any luck, also love, companionship and devotion. And most of all, family.

She closed her office door and leaned her back against it. And burst into tears.

With a sob she stumbled to her chair and fell into it, burying her face in her hands, and cried her heart out.

She'd been a hopeless jumble of raw emotion since leaving New Orleans. She missed Creole so much there were moments she thought she would simply wither up and die.

She'd been so certain she had done the right thing by leaving him. He was no good for her. There had been plenty of reasons to believe that. Her father's example, and the other reckless boys who had broken hearts right and left in high school. Frank and the dozens of similar high-risk kids she counseled as an adult had all followed the same pattern. And hadn't Creole's own reaction to her ridiculous marriage proposal shown her how he felt about making a commitment?

Men like her father, Frank and Creole, they didn't settle down, and they didn't change.

And yet, here was Frank, just seventeen and cocky as

hell, showing her it really *was* possible for a man like him to change. To her amazement he'd done a hundred-eighty-degree about-face, all on his own. And she knew his interest in graduating and getting a good job wasn't because he had suddenly been bitten by the responsibility bug.

No, it was all for love. Frank loved Nikki and their unborn child and was willing to grow up and face his private fears and demons to make a life with them.

Did she dare hope Creole could do the same?

Grace wiped a tissue over her eyes and drew in a shuddering breath. Unconsciously she lowered her hand to the curve of her belly. She'd been on a physical and emotional roller coaster for days, feeling ill and faint and heartsick all at once. She'd attributed it to lingering aftereffects of the trauma of being kidnapped, almost tortured and losing the man she loved, all within twenty-four hours.

At her mother's urging, yesterday she'd gone to the doctor, to have herself checked out, to have blood tests and to get a prescription for something that would take the edge off her terrible depression. Today he'd called back. And told her she was pregnant.

Gathering all her courage, she took her shaking hand from her stomach and lifted the phone receiver. She'd looked up the number just before Frank and Nikki stopped by, so she had no excuse to delay any longer. She punched in the eleven digits for the New Orleans Police Department and asked for Detective Levalois.

"I'm sorry, ma'am, he's no longer with the department."

"What?"

"I can connect you with another detect—"

"No! There must be some mistake. Detective Levalois worked there just last week. He can't be gone!"

"Sorry, ma'am. He quit after that warehouse shooting."

"He *quit?*"

"Yes, ma'am."

She hung up feeling even more disoriented than she had before. Why would he quit the NOPD? She dialed Muse's apartment, in case he was there, and he wasn't. Then she called information for his apartment's phone number and tried there, but the phone had been disconnected.

She stared at the instrument beeping in her hand. She couldn't believe this. A minute ago she had been spinning wild fantasies about the man. About how maybe he would change if she told him about the baby. She knew he cared about her. Was more than attracted to her. And he hadn't really said no to her unorthodox proposal—she hadn't given him a chance. Once she'd made up her mind he was looking for a way out, she hadn't let him get a word in edgewise. Later, in bed, he'd tried to bring it up again, but she'd cut him off with passionate kisses, afraid to hear the rejection she'd been so certain was coming.

But listening to Frank talk about Nikki and the baby, a tiny hope had blossomed in her heart. Could she have been wrong? Had Creole been trying to tell her that, yes, he loved her and wanted to marry her?

She had been so blind about him, seeing only what she'd wanted to see—his rough-edged, confirmed-bachelor, bad-boy image that held her in such fear because of her father. But the truth was he'd been a cop for years and had climbed out from his terrible beginnings to become a respected detective—a steady model citizen if ever there was one. You really couldn't get much more committed than that.

Admittedly, his personal life had been troubled and superficial up until now, but he'd had ample reason for that. Maybe he wanted to change that aspect of his life, too, and she just hadn't given him a chance to say so. But now he was gone, and she'd never know.

Where in the sweet name of heaven was he?

She put her knuckles to her mouth, stifling a whimper. What if she never found him, was never able to tell him about his baby?

The office door swung open. She looked up, tears trembling on her lashes. And in answer to her silent prayer, there stood Creole.

* * *

Creole was more nervous than he'd ever been in his life. All at once this whole idea seemed purely crazy. *Le bon Dieu mait la main.* God help him. What had he been thinking of?

Grace stared up from behind her desk with an expression lodged somewhere between dazed and dumbfounded.

He flexed his shoulders, adjusting the uneven weight of his shoulder holster, and then remembered it wasn't there. He'd taken it off after turning in the Glock and hadn't worn it since. No wonder he felt off balance.

Suddenly Grace burst into tears.

"What's wrong?" he demanded.

At his unintentionally harsh tone, she covered her eyes with the phone receiver she was holding in her hand and cried even harder.

Damn. This wasn't going well. Not at all how he'd planned it out.

He took a step backward. "Look, this was a mistake. I'll just leave—"

"No!" Those big, expressive blue eyes were plastered on him in an instant. "Don't go! Please, Auri."

He hesitated. She'd called him Auri. That had to be some kind of a good sign. "Why are you crying?"

The phone receiver in her hand beeped loudly. She glanced at it as though startled to see it there, then hastily returned it to the cradle.

"I was just—" She wiped her eyes. "I tried to call you, and I couldn't find you anywhere. Your phone was disconnected and they told me you quit your job, and you weren't at Muse's place and—" Her words rushed to a halt.

A whip of alarm sliced into his gut. "You tried to call me?"

"Why did you quit your job?"

He took a step toward her. "Is something wrong? Why did you call?"

She wrung her hands in her lap, avoiding his gaze. "I'm…I m-missed you," she stammered.

A sweet flutter of hope touched him deep inside. He took another step. "Yeah?"

"And when they said you'd left, I was just so worried."

She looked up at him through still-wet eyes, and for a second his heart forgot how to beat. He couldn't believe what she was saying. "You were?"

"I thought I'd never see you again." Her breath hitched and ended on a hiccup. "Oh, Auri, what happened with your job? I know how much it meant to you."

He gave himself a silent kick. The last thing he wanted to be talking with her about was his job. Not when she'd just told him so sweetly how she'd missed him and had worried about him to the point of tears.

He gave an impatient wave of his hand. "My heart wasn't in it anymore." No, it was fully engaged elsewhere. Too engaged to care about anything else until he had her by his side forever. "Grace, I—"

"But you loved being a detective!"

"No." He sighed, and shot a hand through his hair, making it stand on end. Just like she'd done to his world. "I loved putting away scumbags. I just thought being a detective was the most effective way of doing that. But because of you, I realized I was wrong."

Her jaw dropped. "Me? What did I do?" Guilt and confusion swam in her pooled eyes.

He rounded the desk and perched on the corner next to her, pushing aside the stacks of papers and files. "You showed me a better way. You showed me a better way to do a lot of things, Grace."

She looked up at him, her lush, rosy lips parted slightly. "I did?"

He wanted to sweep her into his arms and kiss her senseless for bringing her own poignant brand of goodness and light into his life. And not let her go until she promised to keep it there for the rest of it. "Yeah. You did."

A little frown appeared. "And that's why you quit your job?"

He pushed out an impatient breath. Why did she keep harping on that damn job when he wanted to talk about more important things?

"Yeah," he said, determined to settle this stupid topic once and for all. "I was so damned angry when you left me. So incredibly jealous of that kid Frank for takin' you away from me. But after a week in the bottom of a bottle, I finally realized you'd had no choice. You'd never sell your students short by leaving them behind—even at the cost of your own happiness. You believe too much in them, in what you're doin', to betray their trust. With my background, I have nothing but respect for that."

He reached for her hand and continued, "It also made me realize I was at the wrong end of things. I shouldn't be catching criminals. I should be working with kids, tryin' to keep them from turning to crime in the first place. Like you."

Her eyes had rounded to the size of saucers. "Really?"

"Really. Now—"

"There's a job here at the high school they've been trying to fill all summer," she interrupted breathlessly. "For a police liaison. Working with kids."

"Not anymore, there isn't."

Her face fell. "It's filled?"

"Yeah. By me."

Her eyes captured his. "Oh, Auri. That's wonderful!" Then a smile crept over her face, radiating like the sun, so beautiful it almost hurt to look at. "But that means…it means…"

"We can be together. If you want."

Emotions bounced through her wide eyes like bullets ricocheting off clouds in a blue sky—emotions he couldn't begin to recognize. Fear seized him by the throat, fear worse than anything he'd ever felt facing down bad guys on the streets.

"You did this for me? To be with me?" she said in an uneven whisper. "You left New Orleans…left your home…to…to…"

He slid from his perch and hit his knees beside her chair, swiveling it around to face him. "No, *chère*." He shook his head and her chin trembled. "I've never had a home. Never even wanted one. Not until I met you."

"Oh, Auri," she whispered, and her eyes filled up again, making him want to kick himself up one side and down the other for making her sad, when he wanted only to make her happy.

"Grace, I— Aw, hell." He plucked her hands from her lap. "God knows, I'm no prize. I've got more problems than a two-legged dog, no place to live, and a brand-new job I probably suck eggs at. But I love you, honey. And you once said you loved me. I figure you regretted askin' and that's why you wouldn' let me answer, but hell, baby, you asked me to marry you—sort of—and I couldn' live with myself if I let you go without giving you an answer. So that's what I'm here to do, whether you want to hear it or not. It's yes."

"You love me?"

"I love you. Like crazy I love you."

She blinked, causing a lone tear to track down her cheek. "Do you want kids?"

He blinked back, hating that he was the reason for her tears. "What?"

"Do you want to have children?"

He swallowed, focusing. Children? Hell, what kind of a question was that? "I…well…" *Dieu.* "I've never—I guess so. Yeah. Dozens."

Slowly her pretty mouth curved into another brilliant smile. His pulse started up again after flat-lining for the past few moments. She squeezed his hands. "Good. Because I'm having our baby."

Every molecule of air disappeared from his lungs, leaving him fighting for a breath.

Baby?

Suddenly something happened with his eyes and he couldn't see worth a damn.

Baby?

She reached out and cupped his cheek with a wet hand. Or was it his cheek that was wet?

"I want a real wedding."

Blindly he nodded.

"With a white dress and bridesmaids and a big party."

He was still paralyzed back at— "You're having a baby?"

"*We're* having a baby."

"But how?"

She let out a watery laugh. "The usual way. It must have been that time with the feather. I guess we both forgot—"

"*Merci, Dieu,*" he murmured, and pulled her down off the chair and into his arms. "Thank You, God."

He didn't know why he was shaking so hard. He could barely stay upright on his knees. She sighed and wound her arms around him and held him tightly, so tightly he could finally suck in an inadequate breath, secure that she would catch him if he fell.

"I swear I'll always be there for you and our baby," he managed to squeeze out past his heart, which had lodged in his throat—just behind the giant lump that had been there ever since she'd said she loved him that long, painful week ago. "Always. For as long as you want me, I swear I'll be there for you. Do you really love me?"

"Forever," she whispered back, and kissed him. A sweet, perfect kiss, filled with the promise of a future that held love and warmth and respect and everything he'd ever yearned for, and much, much more. "I love you, Auri Levalois, and I'll never, ever let you go. So you just may as well unpack your bags and plan on staying forever."

He was so happy he just couldn't understand why there were tears streaming down his face. He looked up to the ceiling and laughed. "*Mais, non.* Me, I don' have no bags. What you see's what you get, *chère.* Sure you want me?"

He lowered his gaze to hers, his heart aching in his chest at the look of love and adoration he saw there.

"Oh, yes. I want you. Every last, wonderful, gorgeous inch of you."

That fragile, tender place in his soul slowly filled with her, clear to the trembling brim, filled with this strong, loving, capable woman who had taken him so easily into her arms and into her heart.

And for the first time ever, he was complete and whole.

He smiled, knowing he was the luckiest man in the universe. He put his lips to hers and whispered, "That can be arranged."

Epilogue

Two Years Later...

Grace leaned back in the warm, white beach sand and luxuriated in the feel of the sun on her skin, the wind in her hair and the love in her heart. Just two short years ago she wouldn't have believed it was possible to be as happy as she was at this moment.

The air smelled of salt, summer breezes and suntan lotion. Folding her hands under her head, she squinted out at her husband, frolicking in the sparkling blue ocean with their son, Luke.

"Quite a sight, isn't it?"

On a blanket next to her, Muse watched her own husband charge through the surf at full tilt toward the pair, snatching a squealing Luke from his daddy's arms and skimming him over the water like a dive-bomber.

Grace chuckled. "I'll say. Who'da ever thought?" She glanced at her sister and grinned. "The two of us, married with families and living within spitting distance of each other.''

Muse grinned back. ''Mom's in hog heaven.''

Grace gazed fondly at her sister. ''Me, too. I was so glad you two decided to settle here in Charleston.'' She looked back toward the waves. ''And so's Creole. He loves having a big family around him. Especially his brother-in-law.''

She and Muse watched as the two handsomest men in the world played together in the warm ocean with Luke. It did Grace's heart good to see her husband so carefree, like the kid he had never been allowed to be. He'd come far from that first week in New Orleans when they'd fallen in love.

Luke shrieked with laughter, reaching for his dad. Creole scooped him out of the other man's hands, giving the little guy a bear hug. Just then, a huge wave swamped over them, plunging the three of them into one tumbling mass of arms and legs and flailing bodies. Luke surfaced above the water, suspended in Creole's steady hands, laughing and shaking the water from his eyes. The two grown men floated in the receding wave, giggling like toddlers. Then as one, they rose from the sea, slung their arms around each other's shoulders and charged to shore, carrying Luke in front of them like a squirmy figurehead.

Grace scrambled backward as they made a beeline for the blankets, mischief twinkling in three naughty pairs of eyes.

''No!'' She screeched with delight as several hundred pounds of streaming wet male flopped down, rolling on top of her and Muse. ''Careful of the baby!''

There was a short pause as the men assessed whether she meant Luke or the baby still nestled inside Muse's seven-month belly. But just then Luke launched himself onto Creole's back, throwing his tiny arms around his daddy's neck.

''Dadadadadadada!'' he shouted at the top of his considerable lungs, and the adults broke into laughter. Grasping handfuls of Creole's hair to hang on to, Grace's baby boy peeked around his dad's neck and grinned down at her, his innocent eyes brimming with trust and merriment.

Grace thought she would simply burst with love for father and son, whose faces were so alike it made her heart twist.

"Hey, T-Luke," Creole said, using the Cajun nickname meaning Little Luke, and turned his head to give him a big smooch. "Why don' you grab your bucket and finish our sand castle? I'll be along in a flash. Jus' gotta tell Mama somethin'," he added.

"'Kay. San-cass." Luke slid from Creole's back, already absorbed in the project as he toddled on plump legs for his shovel and pail.

Together they watched their son for a moment, then looked at each other and smiled. She slid her arms around Creole's neck and burrowed herself deeper into his embrace, loving the feel of being sandwiched between the wet softness of the sand and the warm, sensual hardness of her husband's body. She would never tire of feeling his skin against hers.

"I love you," she whispered, gazing up into his soulful eyes. Life just couldn't get better than this.

"I love you, too," he said, and put his lips to hers. "More and more each day."

She savored the taste of him as he kissed her, long and tender. Humming in contentment, she ran her fingers through his hair and over his shoulders. Well, maybe one other thing would make their lives together even more perfect.

"*Je suis en feu.* I feel like I'm burnin' up." He winked, leaned down and nipped at her ear. "How 'bout spreadin' some sunblock on me?"

That would be a good start. "Mmm. How 'bout waiting till tonight? Baby oil, a bucket of ice, a bottle of wine..."

His brow lifted, and he gazed at her, eyes filling with languid anticipation. "Feathers?"

She laughed throatily. He'd grown inordinately fond of

ice and feathers over the past two years. "And feathers," she promised. He was so easy.

"You tryin' to seduce me, wife?" He didn't look as though he objected one bit.

"Absolutely."

He grinned down at her. "What are you after this time?"

"A girl."

His mouth parted in surprise, then rebounded into a glowing smile. "Now, that's a fine idea, *chère*. Purely fine."

He gathered her in his arms and covered her mouth with his, surrounding her, filling her with his love. A precious love that had given her more happiness and fulfillment than she'd ever imagined.

She melted into him, rejoicing in the knowledge that this incredible man was hers, only hers, for all time. A man she was exhilarated to spend her days with, adoring him, keeping him safe and treasured. And thrilled to share her nights with, reveling in his cherished devotion and his sweet, loving touch.

* * * * *

CODE NAME: DANGER

The action continues with the men—and women—of the Omega Agency in Merline Lovelace's *Code Name: Danger* series.

This August, in TEXAS HERO (IM #1165) a renegade is assigned to guard his former love, a historian whose controversial theories are making her sorely in need of protection. But who's going to protect *him*—from her? A couple struggles with their past as they hope for a future....

And coming soon, more *Code Name: Danger* stories from Merline Lovelace....

Code Name: Danger **Because love is a risky business...**

Discover the secrets of

CODE NAME: DANGER

in

MERLINE LOVELACE'S

thrilling duo

DANGEROUS TO KNOW

When tricky situations need a cool head, quick wits and a touch of ruthlessness, Adam Ridgeway, director of the top secret OMEGA agency, sends in his team. Lately, though, his agents have had romantic troubles of their own....

UNDERCOVER MAN & PERFECT DOUBLE

And don't miss
TEXAS HERO
(IM #1165, 8/02)
which features the newest OMEGA adventure!

If you liked this set of stories, be sure to find
DANGEROUS TO HOLD.
*Available from your local retailer
or at our online bookstore.*

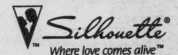

Where love comes alive™

Visit Silhouette at www.eHarlequin.com   PSDTK

I N T I M A T E   M O M E N T S™

presents:

Romancing the Crown

*With the help of their powerful allies,
the royal family of Montebello is
determined to find their missing heir.
But the search for the beloved prince
is not without danger—or passion!*

Available in August 2002:
SECRETS OF A PREGNANT PRINCESS
by Carla Cassidy (IM #1166)

When Princess Samira Kamal finds herself pregnant with a secret
child, she goes under the protection of her handsome bodyguard—
and finds herself in danger of falling in love with the rugged,
brooding commoner....

*This exciting series continues throughout
the year with these fabulous titles:*

*Available only from Silhouette Intimate Moments
at your favorite retail outlet.*

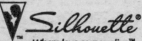

Silhouette®
Where love comes alive™

Visit Silhouette at www.eHarlequin.com

SIMRC8

magazine

♥———————————————— **quizzes**

Is he the one? What kind of lover are you? Visit the **Quizzes** area to find out!

♥———————— **recipes for romance**

Get scrumptious meal ideas with our **Recipes for Romance.**

♥———————————— **romantic movies**

Peek at the **Romantic Movies** area to find Top 10 Flicks about First Love, ten Supersexy Movies, and more.

♥———————————— **royal romance**

Get the latest scoop on your favorite royals in **Royal Romance.**

♥———————————————————— **games**

Check out the **Games** pages to find a ton of interactive romantic fun!

♥————————————— **romantic travel**

In need of a romantic rendezvous? Visit the **Romantic Travel** section for articles and guides.

♥———————————————— **lovescopes**

Are you two compatible? Click your way to the **Lovescopes** area to find out now!

Silhouette® —

where love comes alive—online...

SINTMAG

If you enjoyed what you just read,
then we've got an offer you can't resist!

Take 2 bestselling love stories FREE!

Plus get a FREE surprise gift!